NASHVILLE CHROME

Nashville Chrome

RICK BASS

HOUGHTON MIFFLIN HARCOURT

Boston | *New York*

2010

Copyright © 2010 by Rick Bass

For information about permission to reproduce selections
from this book, write to Permissions, Houghton Mifflin Harcourt
Publishing Company, 215 Park Avenue South, New York, New York 10003.

WWW.HMHBOOKS.COM

Library of Congress Cataloging-in-Publication Data
Bass, Rick, date.
Nashville chrome / Rick Bass.
p. cm.
ISBN 978-0-547-31726-7
1. Country musicians — Fiction. 2. Country music — Tennessee —
Nashville — Fiction. 3. Nashville (Tenn.) — Fiction. I. Title.
PS3552.A8213N37 2010
813'.54 — dc22   2010005732

Book design by Patrick Barry

Printed in the United States of America

DOC 1 2 3 4 5 6 7 8 9 10

 FOR NICOLE AND BOB

They said that it was no accident of circumstance that a man be born in a certain country and not some other and they said that the weathers and seasons that form a land form also the inner fortunes of men in their generations and are passed on to their children and are not so easily come by otherwise.

—CORMAC McCARTHY,
All the Pretty Horses

NASHVILLE CHROME

Prologue

For a little while, the children — Maxine, Jim Ed, Bonnie — were too young to know the weight of their gift, or even that their lives were hard. Their parents had always been poor, but never before had there been such desperation. Never before had there been a time when one's talents — whether hunter or farmer, salesman or tailor — had been insufficient to keep food in the mouths of their family. Now the country was saying the Depression had ended, but where they lived, in south-central Arkansas, not so far from Mississippi — back in the swamps, between the rolling ridges that looked down on Poplar Creek — nothing was different. Things had been bad before the Depression, then got much worse during it, and people were not yet recovering, even though what little news they heard back in the hills told them that everything was better now.

The children's parents, Floyd and Birdie, were still starving, still ravenous — still wondering why they had been put on earth, why they had been brought into the world.

But for a while, the children didn't know this despair. They would have breathed it like the fog vapors that rose some nights from the swamp, would have absorbed it night and day, until it became so wreathed within them that soon enough it would have begun to replace the spirits with which they had come into the world: but not yet, not then. Floyd was drinking hard and logging harder, felling the oaks and hickories with axes and crosscut saws and sledging them out of the swamp with mules and, when the mules were injured, with men too poor sometimes to afford even a cup of fuel for their bulldozers and tractors — and so their gnawings at the old forest seemed as infinitesimal as they were ceaseless. It seemed that the old forest might grow back in just as fast as the men could sledge the logs out.

The places where they worked opened the forest briefly to the sky, let in little patches of white light in which ferns and orchids grew, blossomed, and prospered briefly before the young canopy closed back in over such clearings.

The children, before they knew their calling, sat at the edge of the creek next to one such clearing and watched the slow muddy waters of Poplar Creek drift past. The nearest town, Sparkman, was eight miles away. To them the world was still beautiful, and only beautiful. They sat there quietly, in the last free days before they became aware that they had a gift — not a gift they had asked for or labored toward, but which had been impressed on them from birth — and they waited, one must assume, for the wisps of despair and misery to begin to soak into their skin like the smoke from the burning of the slash piles, blue smoke hanging in sunlit rafts all throughout the forest, as if a great war were being fought, one about which they knew nothing, one of which they were entirely unaware.

THE FIRE

HER FIRST MEMORY is of heroism and stardom, of great accomplishment and acclaim, even in the midst of ruin.

She was five years old, firmly in the nest of her family, at her aunt and uncle's cabin. The adults were in the front room, sitting in front of the drafty fireplace. Maxine was sleeping in the back room on a shuck mattress, Jim Ed was on a pallet, and Bonnie was in her cradle. Maxine awoke to the sight of orange and gold flickerings the shapes and sizes of the stars, and beyond those, real stars.

The view grew wider.

Stirred by the breezes of their own making, the sparks turned to flames, and burning segments of cedar-shake roofing began to curl and float upward like burning sheets of paper.

She lay there, waiting, watching.

It was not until the first sparks landed on her bed that she broke from her reverie and leapt up and lifted Bonnie from her cradle and Jim Ed from his pallet, a baby in each arm, and ran into the next room, a cinder smoking in her wild black hair, charging out into the lantern-light of the front room as if onto a stage, calling out the one word, *Fire,* with each of the adults paying full and utmost attention to her, each face limned with respect, waiting to hear more.

They all ran outside, women and children first, into the snowy woods, grabbing quilts as they left, while the men tried to battle the blaze, but to no avail; the cabin was on fire from the top down, had been burning for some time already while they played, and now was collapsing down upon them, timbers crackling and crumbling. In the end all the men were able to save was the Bible, their guns, and their guitars, fiddles, banjos, mandolins, and dulcimers.

There are a thousand different turns along the path where anyone could look back and say, *If things had not gone right here, if things had not turned out this certain way — if Maxine had not done this, if Jim Ed and Bonnie had not done that — none of all that came afterward would ever have happened.*

Only once, looking back, it would seem that from the very beginning there had been only one possible path, with the destination and outcome — the bondage of fame — as predetermined as were the branches in the path infinite.

That the greatest voices, the greatest harmony in country music, should come from such a hardscrabble swamp — Poplar Creek, Arkansas — and that fame should lavish itself upon the three of them, their voices braiding together to give the country the precise thing it most needed or desired — silky polish, after so much raggedness, and a sound that would be referred to as Nashville Chrome — makes an observer pause. Did their fabulous voices come from their own hungers within, or from thrice-in-a-lifetime coincidence? They were in the right place at the right time, and the wrong place at the right time.

There was never a day in their childhood when they did not know fire. They burned wood in their stove year round, not just to stay warm in winter but to cook with and to bathe. In the autumn the red and yellow and orange leaves fell onto the slow brown waters of the creek, where they floated and gathered in such numbers that it seemed the creek itself was burning. And as the men gnawed at the forest and piled the limbs and branches from the crooked trunks, they continued to burn the slash in great pyres. The smoke gave the children a husky, deeper voice right from the start. Everyone in the little backwoods villages sang and played music, but the children's voices were different, bewitching, especially when they sang harmony. No one could quite put a finger on it, but all were drawn to it. It was beguiling, soothing. It healed some wound deep within whoever heard it, whatever the wound.

The singers themselves, however, received no such rehabilitation. For Jim Ed and Bonnie, the sound passed through without seeming to touch them at all, neither injuring nor healing. They could take it or leave it; it was a lark, a party trick, a phenomenon.

Where had it come from, and when they are gone, where will it go?

THE BRIDGE

THE SUMMONS HAD to have emerged randomly, there on the banks of Poplar Creek, and merely passed through them. It had to be a freak of nature, a phenomenon, a mutation of history. As if some higher order had decided to use them as puppets—to hold them hostage to the powerful gift whose time it was to emerge; and as if that gift, that sound, had finally been elicited by some tipping point of misery, hunger, squalor, and yearning into a finer metamorphosis. No work is ever wasted, and all waiting is ultimately rewarded.

Their father, Floyd Brown, had a relationship with the bottle, there could be no denying that, and this, too, was surely one of the little pieces that built their sound, sharpening their ability to temper and moderate their voices, each in accordance with and adjusting to the others', even midnote, each of their three voices writhing and wrapping around the other two until a swirling, smoky sound was created. Each listening to the other keenly, with a sensitivity trained in part by trying to assess quickly—immediately—with but the faintest of clues the status of Floyd's moods. He had already lost one leg in a logging accident and was mortally afraid of losing the other, but that was not why he drank now; he had started long before that.

The Browns would not be the first to be shaped to greatness by living in the shadow of an alcoholic parent. But their sound did not come from Floyd, or from their mother, Birdie. The sound was so elemental that it could have chosen anybody.

Early on, in the days before they came to suspect that they had been burdened with something rare—that they had been chosen to carry it—the world nonetheless would have been preparing them for their journey, would have been teaching them, in the crudest of lessons, the paths their lives would take.

There was an old wooden bridge that spanned Poplar Creek, down where one hollow closed in on another. The Browns lived in one of those hollows, and the moonshiners from whom Floyd bought or bartered his whiskey lived in the other. Anyone approaching the moon-shiners' hollow had to go across that one bridge, so that there was no possibility of a surprise visitor, only the regular clientele.

Floyd usually drank his supply down to almost the last drop — some-times he took it all the way to empty — before gathering up enough coins, or eggs, or a load of prime lumber, and driving across the bridge to make his next purchase. When it was time to go, it didn't matter if they were coming home from church, or on their way to Saturday-night music over at his brother's, or en route to town for groceries: when he needed a drink, he needed a drink.

They were all seven in the car the time that the Browns learned about bridges — had the lesson of bridges blazed indelibly into their young minds, in the architecture of myth or destiny.

Floyd had finished his last drop and had made a run over to one of the local distillers, taking along the entire family for one reason or another. It was springtime and had been raining for a week without stopping. The woods were too muddy to log, and he didn't have any fuel to run the mill anyway. He'd been drinking for all of that rainy week, finishing the last of the last, and so when he came to the bridge, the fact that the bridge was now underwater did not deter him in the least. He could still see the trace of the bridge beneath the swollen current, the ripples indicating its approximate location; and with his family still loaded in the Model A, he eased forward, the rain com-ing down in sheets. Birdie fussing in the front seat, holding the baby Norma, with Maxine, Jim Ed, Bonnie, and Raymond crammed into the back.

It was dusk, and Floyd forged on, navigating by feel alone, the tires groping for the wood that lay invisible beneath a foot of shuddering current. The creek was twelve feet deep in the center. Floyd said that they had to cross now or never, that the water was only going to get higher, and if he didn't make it now it might be a week before he could cross.

He had not made it even halfway before he lost his way and the car tipped, spun halfway around, and angled downstream. The passen-gers were spilled from the car.

There were children everywhere, bobbing and floating and grab-bing for whatever parts of the car they could reach: a door handle, an open window frame, a headlight. Steam rose from the radiator as if from the blowhole of a whale. Rain lashed their faces. Birdie was screaming, grabbing Norma by the nape of the neck as if she were a kitten. Only Floyd stayed with the car, gripping the steering wheel as if temporarily befuddled, but still anticipating success.

The car continued to lie there, swamped sideways with but one tire gripping the raised center boards of the bridge, shuddering in the cur-rent. The current was spinning the free wheels, as if the car were labor-ing, like a wounded animal, to resume its travels.

Their first task was simply to hold on, but they could not hold on forever. Floyd had begun to realize the situation — the river was up to his chest — and he reached out and began pulling the children back into the flooded car one at a time. The children were creek-slick, and from time to time they would slip from his grasp, and in his grasp-ing for the slipping-away one, the others would come temporarily un-bound and he would have to sweep them all in again. Other times, the slip-away child would grab the outstretched hand of one of the other children, so that for a while, extended in the current like that, they would appear as a kite tail of children; and no one who might have looked down upon the scene would have given them any chance of coming to a good end.

In the dusk, however, and in the rain, on the high bluff above, an old man appeared. He was barefoot and stubble-faced, wearing a rain-beaten straw hat that was misshapen now into something that resem-bled a tuft of moldering hay. The old man was smoking a corncob pipe from which rose, heroically, a wandering blue thread of smoke, so lu-minous in the dusk that it seemed the smoldering might have come not from mere tobacco but from some oil-soaked concoction of bark and wood chips. The old man was sucking on the pipestem as if draw-ing from it with each deepened breath the sustenance required to keep him upright in such a storm.

He had heard the car laboring to cross the bridge, had heard Floyd's drunken gunning of the engine and the shouts and cries of the occupants as they lost their way and went over the edge. The old man held a frayed and muddy rope, at the other end of which was tethered a dirty white mule. The mule's head was pitched downward as if in defeat, beaten by the steady rain, or perhaps as if lamenting or grieving already the predicament it was witnessing below.

For what seemed a long time the old man and the mule just stood there, as spectators — while they stood there, the dusk slid farther into darkness — though finally, as if after the most strenuous of mental assessments, the old man started down the steep road that switchbacked its way toward the river, leading the mule behind him as if to sacrificial ritual.

At water's edge, the old man retrieved a rusty section of heavy logging cable that was coiled in a tree, used in older times as a crude ferry-assist for rowboats that had passed back and forth to the moonshiners' territory. After looping this to the mule's neck with no harness or trace, just a metal noose around the mule's muscular chest, the old man walked into the river, straight into the washboard rapids that roughly defined the bridge.

The effect it gave was that he was walking on water. He appeared unconcerned about either the car's or his own situation, never getting in a hurry, but simply walking as if on a stroll, or as if considering that a more hurried approach might somehow disrupt the fragile friction-hold the car and its occupants had negotiated with the bridge. As if believing that if he hurried, he himself — their miraculous rescuer — might frighten them all into spilling into the river, like startled sun-basking turtles tumbling from a log with all the slipperiness of a deck of new cards clumsily shuffled.

The old man reached the car and knelt before it tenderly, as if administering to a wounded animal — a horse or a cow in the throes of a difficult birthing — and looped the free end of the cable around the front bumper. There was barely enough cable to reach and tie off with a knot — had Floyd lost his way only a couple of feet earlier, the cable would not have reached — and the old man had to empty his pipe and submerge briefly to finish tying the knot, taking a deep breath before disappearing beneath the water's surface with the cable.

He reemerged, dripping, made a gesture toward Floyd, indicating he should stay put even when the car started moving, and then he trudged back toward the waiting mule, moving now in total darkness and holding on to the taut cable.

He became invisible to them long before he reached the shore. Birdie had stopped hollering, though the baby was still crying. The children were shivering, their teeth chattering, and they clutched the car and each other and waited for the car to move.

They wondered how strong the old mule was, and whether it would be able to find footing in the slippery clay. They could not help but imagine the mule slipping and the car falling back into the creek and going straight to the bottom, pulling the mule along behind it like a baited fishhook attached to a weighted sinker. The mule eventually bleaching to nothing but an underwater skeleton, still fastened to the wire cable, and the Brown family likewise becoming skeletal, entombed within the old Model A.

Up in the world above, the car began to slip forward ever so slightly. The Browns felt it immediately as an increased pressure by the river, and tightened their grips. The car began to rise, lifting free and clear from its side-tipped position, being hoisted back as if cantilevered. As the car regained its footing, water came roaring out of the windows and from beneath the engine's hood and from the seams of the trunk; and suddenly the Browns were slithering back into their car, and sitting in their seats, still up to their waists in water, but afforded once more the dignity of being vertical.

For each of them, it was even more of a second chance than had been their rescue from the fire. They felt both terror and relief, twin and oppositional currents within them as they were pulled by an unseen force through an unseen medium of shuddering resistance, advancing into the darkness.

They each knew that they were on the bridge once again, though they didn't know for how long; and each was stripped barer than they ever had been before of the thing they desired most, *control*. Never had any of them possessed less of it than on that rainy, creek-swollen night, and they sat quiet and shivering in the waterspouting car as they were pulled into the darkness, with the odor of whiskey still present in the car and on Floyd's body, despite the muddy flushing.

Finally they reached the other shore, with the current no longer vibrating against the car — a quietness around them now, as if they had been delivered into a new world, and dripping, as if from a second birth — and the old man called to the mule to cease his efforts and directed the animal to back up a step, so that the knot could be unhitched. He helped the Browns out of the car, a conveyance with which the old man was so unfamiliar that at first he could not determine how to open the door. And then, rolling up the cable as he walked back toward the mule, the old man ushered them up the bluff, toward his cabin on the hill.

As they drew even with the mule, which was just standing there, quivering slightly, as if in either the ending or perhaps beginning of ecstasy — the mule trembling and appearing somehow to radiate a state of grace, having accommodated the one thing in the world it was made and meant to do — they stopped and petted it briefly before leaving it to its isolate bliss. Then they continued on up the slippery hill, with the rain falling as hard as it had all night, and with the water that flowed over the bridge still surging, a few inches deeper now.

When they reached the cabin, Floyd went into the barn with the old man to have a drink — the man said not to worry about the mule, that he would come home on his own and would not even need drying off but would lie down in the straw if he got cold — and while the men drank and visited, Birdie took the children into the cabin, where she rekindled the ashes in the fireplace, beside which the children huddled, steaming.

They stayed the night there, Floyd drinking again. The next afternoon the old man led the mule back across with the same cable, and though the bridge was still submerged, Floyd navigated the bridge successfully this time. The old man came back and rowed Birdie and the children across in a rowboat — they refused to ride in the car — with each child clutching a length of driftwood to cling to and float should the current capsize them. The old man was a powerful and experienced rower, however, and they reached the other side without incident, while Floyd sat on the slick bank with his brown bottle in hand and called out advice and encouragement.

There were no borders that could not be crossed, then, and no crossings that would ever be easy. They had learned already everything they would need to know for their journey.

THE FOREST

THE LITTLE SAWMILL was perched at the edge of the dark woods, resting atop the rich soil, with the workers gnawing their way slowly into the old forest. Some years the workers would bring the logs in to the mill, and other years — depending on transportation logistics and contracts — the mill would pack up and move a little farther into the woods. There were still panthers in the swamps and bears in the mountains, or what passed for mountains in those old worn-down hills.

This was another of the paths of their childhood, the physical and sensual sounds and odors of the mill, with the blades whirring on and off throughout the day — the high whine of the spinning, waiting blade powering down to a deep groan as the blade accepted the timber, the blades sending out a different pitch for rough cut, planing, or finishing, and likewise a different tone based on size, density, even species of timber and time of year, and whether the tree grew on a north slope or a south slope.

Different smells, too, wafted through their lives in ribbons of scent — the green odor of the living wood and the drier one of dead wood, the latter a scent like that of a campfire; the smell of the diesel engines as well as those of the mules and horses that sometimes skidded the logs out of the swamp when gasoline was scarce or could not be squandered; the scent and creaking sound of the leather harnesses and other tack of the mules and horses; the stale alcohol-sweat and the tobacco of the laborers, all of them missing fingers, even hands and arms, sometimes from the blade but more often from the logs themselves, thousand-pound rolling pins cascading off the truck, crushing and pinching anything in their way.

And where the workers had not lost some of the various parts of themselves — where there was still a full complement of teeth and fingers and thumbs, hands, feet, arms, and legs — there were internal injuries: broken bones, alcoholism, rage, and the mute desperation of a poverty unknown by several previous generations.

There were outright deaths, too, accidents sometimes of fatigue — falling off a truck, walking under a falling tree, or any of a hundred other unspectacular possibilities. The mill lost a few workers each year in that manner, like the trees themselves, so that between the dying and the injured, there was always a setback, and always some sort of ongoing or attempted recovery.

Even to those who had never been in a war, it must have seemed that this was what it would be like: that the forest was the enemy and that the workers' task was to try to gain a little stronger foothold and advance into the enemy's territory a bit farther each day.

Only a hundred and fifty years separated these new workers and their families from the straight bloodlines of Oglethorpe's ruffians, the prisoners who had been turned loose into the lawless woods — a hundred and fifty years being an utterly insignificant amount of time for such bloodlines to be filtered out of those workers, washed clean by time and the influence of the forest and its ravines and ridges, the tempering that must always be negotiated between any landscape and any species, any newcomer to the world.

The children knew no other world. The forest — both the injured forest as well as the uninjured — combined with the children's spirits like the gold light that came down through the dense canopy of broad leaves in the morning: each pattern of leaf, each lobe and serration, already accommodated to the specificity of its time and place.

In that forest, the shady dapple of the leaves moderated the temperature of the soil and gave nutrition to the legions of meek insects, the lives of which also helped enrich and process the soil, and each morning in the spring and summer, the forest would begin to hiss with chlorophyllitic excess — a tremendous, thunderous, silent power, a silent energy shimmering above the leaves with such verve that it was almost audible.

The green light bathed the children, infiltrated their lungs, shimmered its golden way up into their minds. They could have stayed there forever — as had the generations before them — but the force that had come into them desired otherwise.

THE SINGERS

THEIR PARENTS' MILL could in no way afford a kiln. The trees were milled green, the lumber then stacked to dry. The green wood was still heavy and dense. Often it was wood that had been hauled out of the forest only a day or two earlier, and might still be coated with mud and grit from the sledge. Such timber wore down the blades quickly, and the knots where newly severed branches had once grown also chipped the blades. When the blade hit such nicks, it sent out a single squawl of protest. There was no rhythm to these outbursts, but the sound punctuated the days, as did the accompanying lull of the engines when the operator had to idle down, pull the log back, and make another, more cautious approach.

And in that quieter powering-down, that readjustment, the Browns felt a relief and release from the all-day roar and whine. When the mill was running, though, a tension permeated, and shook every atom in the air in the clearing around the sawmill, and in the bones of all who could hear. The vibrations traveled back into the forest itself.

Always, after such a setback, the engines ran harder and harder, powering up to make it all the way through the cut — slabs of lumber peeling away like long curls and shavings of butter — until some new resistance was struck yet again and the peace of near silence returned.

The workers, leaning in close to the saws and the engines, benumbed by years of their labor and going quickly deaf, had become inured to any such momentary releases. Many of them had become lithified to the world, with only the perspiration that sprang from them beneath the bright sun, and the occasional blood that leapt from them when injured, indicating they were still creatures of this world and not some strange half-machine beings themselves.

But the children, with their souls and spirits yet so soft-formed, were still deeply alert to the tension of the engines and sawblades. The loud *ching!* of the blade getting jammed, followed by the groan of the engines shutting down and the quiet cursing of the operator, would have been a part of not just their auditory lives from the beginning, but the pattern and pulse of their every breath, whether they knew it or not: the incessant low-level anxiety of waiting for the sound of disaster, or failure.

The children and some of the adults crept through the days finely tuned to sound; and when the pressure of the revving-up of the engines was released, the children would have been able to hear once again the shrilling of the seven-year locusts, a sound coming from the forest, as if the forest were healing itself.

Once daily the sawmill operators would shut down for lunch in the rising heat of the day. The engines would fall silent and songbirds back at the shadowy edge of the forest would resume their calls. The locusts would be sawing, but that was a lulling sound.

The workers' meals, while much of the rest of the country was starving, were fit for kings and princes: cold biscuits with blackberry jam and honey, thick sandwiches stuffed with salt-cured ham, fresh tomatoes, or fried chicken, or a sandwich made with leftover venison.

The men visited among themselves, talking quietly about weather or hunting, or about the wood they were milling, or about the machines to which they were hostage — the machines the men served and serviced; machines that, if they stopped running, took away the workers' pay and dictated, with their sputtering valve-worn unpredictability, whether the men's families would have money for the most basic of items: flour, salt, sugar, shoes.

Few of the workers owned any machines themselves, but rode horses or walked. Too many of them spent their money on whiskey, purchasing it from neighbors or buying the supplies and making it themselves. They were as dependent on it as they were on one another, and the machines, and they sat there at the edge of shade, in the clearing where they were gnawing deeper and deeper into the forest, and stopped and caught their breath, even as the rest of the country floundered in the Great Depression, threatening to sink back down into the gruesome poverty of a hand-to-mouth existence in which starvation was still an ever-present reality, as it had been ten thousand years before.

And resting there — stalled there — the men had no real idea that for the first time they had much in common with other lives beyond their small hollow: that people on the other side of the great forest, whom they would never see—urban people whose lives were surely more complicated than their own, and who also surely possessed and moved through the world with some sort of laminar grace unbeknownst to the hill people—were now in the kind of dire economic straits that the hill people had known all their lives.

As the meniscus of the forest separating the two grew thinner, and the desperations on either side of the forest more similar, it would have seemed that both sides might somehow have sensed they were becoming more similar, shaped and molded toward a sameness of circumstance if not spirit.

But that was not yet the case. The men sipped their cooling coffee from battered steel thermoses and waited for their sweat to cool. They talked either reverently or scornfully about their machines, and when they were ready for the second part of their day, they disassembled the sawblades from their axles, and while the engines cooled further, some of the men would set about sharpening the circular blades of their saws, rasping with a motion so practiced that it was possible to tell who the saw sharpeners were by their musculature alone: a certain slope of shoulder, a particular thickness of forearms gotten from days and then years of grinding steel against steel.

The saw sharpeners would place the blade flat on a spindle and file outward, honing the steel to address every point on the blade. They could tell roughly from their long experience when the critical edge was regained—the sharpness that would make their work go a little easier in the second half of the day.

They could feel the softening, the sudden slipperiness, as the last of the resistance was worn away and the edge was gained. They could hear it, too—anyone could notice it—and when this happened, the saw sharpeners would straighten up from their work as if rising from a trance. They would give the blade just a few more light touches, as if to be sure that the edge was real, and then they would brush and blow the steel filings from the blade and knock the magnetized crumbs of iron from their files, and press a thumb or finger lightly to the sawblade to confirm with touch that which their ears, as well as the sudden slackness and ease in the muscles of their arms and backs and shoulders, had already told them.

That was pretty much the spot where sharpeners at other mills stopped and put the blade back onto the planer and the men would start the engines back up. And for the next few hours, the newly sharpened blades would address the green wood with greater ease. It was good enough for most, and because most of the lumber being milled was rough-cut anyway, the extra edge did not much matter.

Floyd, however, had a special way of sharpening his blades. He insisted that each blade be fully tempered, or retempered, in the middle of each day. It was important, he said, that the blade be able to fully control the wood. It saved money, too. The edge of a tempered saw not only held longer but cut sharper, resulting in less engine wear, as well as a higher quality of lumber.

The secret to his lumber's quality lay in his children's ability to discern pitch. At the end of almost every lunch break, the Brown children would be summoned to the saw-sharpening table, where the newly honed blade would be placed on an axle with a motor and then spun rapidly, as if being made ready for a cut.

There was a certain sound, a ringing, that a fully tempered saw made when it had achieved that absolute perfect edge. It was a sound that the men could sometimes hear, but other times, for whatever reasons, was indiscernible to them. The sound they listened for — the perfect blade — held an eerie resonance, the faint sirenlike echo of a high harmonic that was little different from the tempered harmony the Browns were already learning to achieve with their voices.

Their individual voices were becoming ever more exceptional. Something inexplicable was happening to them. Anyone could see it, could hear it, and with them still just children. People talked about them when they sang in church choirs, or at weekly social gatherings on the weekends, and relatives' birthday parties. The Browns listened to the Grand Ole Opry on their family's radio, as did everyone they knew. If a family did not own a radio, that family would travel on Friday and Saturday nights to the home of a neighbor who did.

All throughout the dark woods at night, the scattered and far-flung impoverished hamlets would be stitched together in one fabric, the community of sound, as they sat and listened to the weekly radio shows.

Even as young children, the Browns could imitate with perfect pitch any of the performers they heard on the radio. They were eager to please; the oldest, Maxine, was particularly desperate to please. Floyd was hardest on her, the one most like himself. He tried to manage her like his mill, or any of the other things in his life he could not control. In his mind, anything she did could always be better. Day after day, he transferred his dissatisfactions with himself onto her.

The men would strive to hear what the children were hearing. They would watch the children to see if it could be discerned at what point the children heard what it was they were listening for.

There was no mistaking when the Browns heard it, even if the men, with their hearing battered by the years of saw-roar, could not. The children, though they would already have been listening intently, would become even more stilled. Whereas in the beginning each of them had been listening to the sawblade as an individual, there was some unnameable point where they were suddenly listening to it as one, the three of them focused on something no one could see, and which few, if any, could hear, though which many of the men could now sense.

They might as well have been striving to hear a deity. The way the deity seemed not to be there — in a room, in a building, in a grove of woods — and then the way it *was* there; not instantaneously, but completely.

There in the clearing, when they heard the higher harmony, the secret pitch and pulse of the round blade having achieved its perfect temper, the children's faces would soften; as if, even though they were children, they had nonetheless been carrying around burdens and tensions, had already absorbed them from the lives of those who surrounded them.

Some days it might be Jim Ed who first heard the sawblade's release, and other days, Bonnie or Maxine would hear it before the others. But always, once the ringing started, it would be only a second or two before they all three heard it, so that they each became entranced simultaneously.

Sometimes the children would not hear the sound. Despite the best and most practiced efforts of the saw sharpener, the tempered pitch would not yet be achieved, and the round table's motor would have to be shut off, and the files brought back out, and the blade addressed yet again. And here, too, the children were useful, for they could indicate to the saw sharpener an approximation of how far off-temper the sound had been.

The eyes of the men watching them, awaiting the verdict. The three children already standing in a line, as if on a stage.

After the children finally detected the harmony, the spinning blade on the round table would slow to a stop. The relaxation on the children's faces would fade, vanishing with the sound itself, and the children would rise and return to the shadier, cooler forest to resume their duties of being children, unseen by and unknown to the world. Playing their guitars. Singing a little. Pretending they were famous.

The men remained behind, attached to the machines. With the blades adjusted, the machines would start back up, coughing and blatting slowly at first, burning either too much oil, through heat- and grit-worn pistons, or not enough, with dust-soaked filters starving the motors. The men would tinker with the engines, adjusting throttles, until the deafening race of the engines was saturating the small clearing and spreading into the damaged forest, shaking the ground with the throbbing, and the howl of the timber being planed to foursquare beams, slabs of lumber falling away in bouncing clatter as the men resumed their attempts at making a living. Shouting at each other to be heard over the roar of the sawmill, but unable to make themselves be heard. Shaking their heads and resorting to crude gestures and, when those failed, shaking their heads further in frustration and waving off even the attempts at communication. *Forget it.* Heads down, back to the focus on work. The bright leaves of the lumber falling away from the blade like sheafs of hay being cleaved. A fountain of sawdust pluming from the sawblade, whirring gold dust in the sun.

The forest shrilled with the shouting chorus of the insects, which seemed to be endeavoring to imitate the roar of the mill. There were catfish to catch in the swimming holes, squirrels and deer and turkeys for Jim Ed to hunt, and rutted clay roads to explore, either on foot or on bicycles, the tires of which were long-ago worn smooth and multipatched — but as wonderful as the isolated, suspended world of their childhood was, it was far and away secondary to the world they entered when they heard, or created, the tempered harmony.

The children, with their backs to the mill, walked up the dirt road, talking quietly, conversing earnestly. Walking quietly a little farther on, then — the mill so faint as to be almost inaudible — and in that new silence, and having walked a short ways into that silence, the children would begin to sing, making little attempts at harmonies. They would stumble with the harmony only once or twice, but on the third or fourth redo, they would hit it perfectly, and they would walk a little farther on, raising dust, their voices somehow floating above them, as if coming from somewhere else.

HOW IT IS NOW

THE WORLD, OR the world of country music — the only world she cared about — had surrounded her for maybe ten good years, had swarmed around her and her family, once it was discovered that she and they were the epicenter and nucleus of it, the yearning and voice that gave rise to what would quickly become the highly commercial Nashville music industry.

Then that world went on past, leaving her withered and broken, like the dry husk of a shed insect skin. That part doesn't much matter to her anymore — she has become accustomed to the physical pain and diminishment — but what plagues her is how she has been forgotten. Being forgotten is a thousand times worse than the physical reductions, the body's humiliations and betrayals, and there is still just enough of the old curse that was placed on her almost eighty years ago to keep her wishing for more, wanting more, needing more.

Her wishes are a burnt-out gutted shell of vitreous sear — a lifetime spent burning with a fire, a hunger, no one should be expected to possess — and now that her body is failing, there's no fuel left for the Poplar Creek summons to feed on. It has feasted on her, has long since used up the sweet best of her and moved on, either searching for another or disappeared completely, perhaps, to wait for a while — a generation, or a century — before emerging again; and whether near the original site or much farther on there is no way of predicting.

She is still left with some of the sparks — crumbs of fire that seek to find the last of any fuel she can feed them — but there is no fuel; no one wants her, no one knows who she is or how it was.

She has a house to live in, and Social Security and disability benefits. Most don't even have that. Most don't have anything — country music using up its young entertainers the way nations use up young men for war. Hank Williams dying in his Cadillac, Patsy Cline's plane tumbling from the sky, Buddy Holly's likewise, with Waylon Jennings having given up his seat on that plane, deciding to remain behind.

Why has Maxine survived? And if she had not survived, would she perhaps still be remembered, rather than forgotten?

Her children, while not entirely estranged, are scattered to the winds. They remember her birthday sometimes, but not much more. They are busy with their own lives, and back then, the fire did not allow her to bond to them as she might otherwise have.

They don't blame her for that, exactly — it's just that her identity to them was more of an absence than a presence. She bought the house right before the divorce, and right before running out of the last of what little money there ever was. It's a 1960s-style low brick ranch house in the suburbs of West Memphis, green sloping lawns and shady streets, young suburbanites sudsing and washing their cars on their driveway every weekend.

She's lived in it for more than forty years, and none of the neighbors knows her. They come and go, one generation after the next, in the cycles of raising their children. She is the old lady down the street, nothing more. They wash their cars. They polish the chrome and buff the surface. They smile at her on the rare occasions they see her, lift their sponges and dripping chamois cloths to her and wish her a good day.

She is a recovering alcoholic — one day at a time — and has to have her tea, particularly in the morning, and again at that point in the day, usually around four in the afternoon (particularly in the summer, with the days so long) when the light finally begins to lay down its long shadows across the well-kept lawns.

To help hold electricity costs down, she keeps the venetian blinds in her darkened living room closed, and other than the weekly terror of driving to the grocery store (she's almost legally blind, but hasn't had to go in for retesting at the DMV yet), her outings are pretty much restricted to limping behind her clattery aluminum walker out to check the mail. The black plastic wheels scrape on the pea gravel of her front walkway. There's rarely anything in the mailbox other than a promotional flyer from Radio Shack or a circular advertising cell phones.

She returns with great effort and spends the next thirty minutes reading the flyers, pondering the electronic equipment about which she knows nothing.

At that time of the afternoon, when another day has passed, another day without what she once had, she limps back into her kitchen and with shaking hands fixes another cup of tea.

She fell and broke her hip on Christmas, hurrying to answer the telephone — rushing down the stairs, only to have her hip snap to powder-dust, tumbling her to the bottom — and as such she has not been able to make it back upstairs in more than nine months, has been sleeping on her couch downstairs since that time and living out of a box — sweatsuits and jeans, mostly. The best part of her wardrobe remains upstairs, hanging in the closet.

She had it all, in the beginning — a family knit more tightly, for all its flaws and complications, than the interlocked limbs and branches of the forest itself — and then she turned away, was lured away, at first, though once she set out on that path toward stardom, the force pushing her from behind was surely too great for her to have turned back even if she had wanted to, which she never did, and still doesn't.

And if she had ignored the summons? Would she still be enmeshed in the center of a loving family?

You reap what you sow, she thinks, whenever she considers where her children might be at any given point of the day and what they might be doing. Then she moves on from the thought: one of the things she has had to learn in order to stop the drinking is not to traffic in self-pity. She still occasionally engages in bitterness — the slow, simmering, steady hunger that can crank up into a rolling boil — but self-pity, never. She can't go back and be a mother over again, and she knows also that even if she could, she would probably do it the same way all over again.

More attentive to her needs, really, are her siblings, the other two-thirds of the trio. Bonnie comes down from the Ozarks to visit about once a month. She's so relaxed, so *happy,* a bright spirit entering the room. Bonnie's happiness is earned — she has passed through the crucible and then somehow stepped away, and survived — and as such, Bonnie possesses a quiet grace.

Maxine can still be cranky, rough as a cob—all the rough internal edges are not yet sanded off her, nor will they ever be—but Bonnie has already passed on through; has become, in essence, the songs that they sang, gliding smooth, light, unfreighted by the world's deeper concerns.

Jim Ed is in Nashville: still working, always working. Amazingly, he's got some miles left in him, can still take a gig anywhere, any time. A county fair, a bar, a tribute album of duets: anything. It's still easier being a man on the road than a woman. It always has been.

She drinks her tea, all day long, and waits. The days and nights pass through her like light through a pane of dark glass. Some of the ache in her is real and some of it is simply an unsatisfied heat. She falls into long reveries that are interrupted only by the teakettle's whistle. She waits for the phone to ring. She lived too much, too high, fame blew through her like a hurricane, she has spent almost fifty years coming down off the high, and is still coming down, but she will not drink. And while part of that stubborn struggle, that decision, is based on character and force of will, part of it is testament to the haunting that still inhabits her, even if so much more faintly now: for if she drinks, there's no way she can be famous again. She has to remain ready, in case the summons returns.

Instead of drinking, she tries to preserve what feels like the last few days of her mortality, her last few hours, and waits, and watches, and yearns for one more chance.

CRAWFISH

THERE WERE BROWN children everywhere, during their growing-up years — five of them, with Maxine the oldest, Jim Ed two years younger, Bonnie five years younger, Raymond, seven years younger, and, later, the baby Norma, twelve years younger than Maxine. The three of them — the trio of the oldest — went almost everywhere together, did everything together, sang and played together, but as Maxine remembers it, the other two, Raymond and Norma, had even better voices, and were luminous, as if selected also, though chosen only for grace rather than the yeoman burden that appeared to have been tasked to the three oldest.

Raymond, who by the age of five was already an incredible guitar player, was also the funniest and sweetest child anyone had ever known, capable with his jokes and impersonations of making any adult laugh — even the most dour, which was usually Floyd — and Norma, as Maxine remembers it, had the most beautiful voice of all of them, was able to sing the tempered harmony with the three older Browns, or solo, with a voice that by itself would stop in his tracks anyone who heard it. Norma's voice would fill a listener from the ground up, as if the listener were a vessel into which she would pour her voice. It filled the listeners quickly, steadily, and once filled, they could not turn away, but would instead keep listening, flooded with warmth and stilled as if by hypnosis for however long she would sing.

The Browns' tempered harmony was soothing, and it healed, for a little while, the wounds of whoever listened to it — but Norma's voice did more than heal wounds. It made people become someone better than they had been before. Wiser, for a short while, and more compassionate and forgiving, more patient. And, always, joyful. There wasn't an ounce of meanness or unhappiness. At such times, it seemed she was nothing but spirit, as was Raymond, while the older trio, for whatever reasons, seemed to have just a little more grit or earth in them.

The three older ones were pretty much normal, most folks would say, except for their gift.

On a few occasions, the older trio would separate: Jim Ed going off on his own, or with Raymond and Bonnie out into the garden early to help Birdie, who even then was not in the best of health, had developed diabetes, though she never let it stop her. She kept working, cooking and cleaning and running the household while also juggling Floyd's various personas and voices that might emerge. Floyd was a hard worker himself, but was malleable in his miseries, euphorias, sulls, and generosities. He was a family man at times and a carouser at others. Undecided, unfixed, unattached in the world, roaring through it when he could and creeping through it when he could not.

With Jim Ed, what you saw was what you got. He was neither simple nor stubborn, but was possessed of an easygoing nature, though was also capable of steady focus on whatever task challenged him. A willing workhorse.

As a child, before he got pulled into the music business — swept into it by Maxine — the thing he loved most was fishing. He was drawn again and again to the banks of Poplar Creek, where, even before he was old enough to use a cane pole, he would sit with a length of cotton string tossed into the creek, a scrap of raw bacon tied to one end, and watch like a heron as mud-brown crayfish inched slowly toward it.

He felt an extreme peace in deepening the practice of being cautious. The bacon sent out tiny iridescent ribbons of fat-sheen on the surface of the brown water. He pulled the string in toward the shore a millimeter at a time. An hour could pass in that manner, two hours. Sometimes he got the crawfish, other times not. It didn't matter.

But soon enough Maxine, up on the porch, would shout for him to come back to the house, made uncomfortable by being alone for too long and by not knowing where everybody was, and what they were doing, and what they would be doing next. Always adjusting, tightening a screw here or there. Even midnote in a song, raising the pitch a fraction or dropping it similarly, as if for sheer devilment, or possessed of a force, the amplitudes of which she sought to control or at least stay abreast with — and forcing her brother and sister to follow her, and stay with her.

She went out on the porch whenever they were out of sight for too long. She yelled to Bonnie to come in from the garden and help her with something, or to come play. She called down to Jim Ed at the creek, where he always went if he wasn't with them.

Bonnie would look up from her gardening and — in those days — dutifully attend to Maxine's beckonings. Jim Ed did likewise, rising on cramped knees — the crawdads bolting back into the deeper water — and starting back up the hill. He would rather have stayed a little longer, but it didn't really matter; he could always come back tomorrow.

SOME PEOPLE SEEM destined for the safe middle, while others appear to be wedded to the extremities of high and low. On their own, Jim Ed and Bonnie were pretty safely in the middle, but once they joined in with Maxine, she took them straight to the upper reaches every time, and then right back down to the bottom, every time. As if their lives had to follow the range of their voices, when they were together.

The youngest brother, Raymond, did not make it as far into history. Floyd and Birdie were having lots of fights in the evenings after the children had gone to bed — misery throughout the tautness of their isolation, their poverty — but Raymond, even at the age of five, helped more than anyone keep things all strung together, with his antics. For this, as well as his general spirit, his older siblings doted on him.

He died when Maxine was twelve. The last time she saw him, he had just trapped and killed an opossum in the henhouse and was chasing her around the house with it. Then he was gone, off into the logging woods with Floyd and Jim Ed.

It was the rainy season, and down in the bottom, the truck got stuck in the mud. Floyd was rocking it back and forth, gunning the engine and slipping, trying to power out, and Raymond was leaning out the window, watching the slick tires spin, when his door popped open and he fell out, just as the truck was sliding sideways.

The truck rolled across him, stopped on top of him, and they couldn't get it off. Jim Ed was ten, and there wasn't a damn thing he could do about anything.

Maxine was named Homecoming Queen for senior year. She was the most striking girl in the school (Bonnie, still at the middle school, had not quite yet begun to mature), and while there were days when Maxine thought she might be beautiful, there were also days when she was certain she was not, days when everything about her seemed wrong and off: her jaw a millimeter too sharp, her eyes set a fraction too far apart, her eyebrows imperfect, her nose too long, and her family something to be ashamed rather than proud of. As if she could not trust her own first impressions or instincts. There were times when she thought, with amazement, *I might really be beautiful;* but such thoughts were rare, and they were up at the surface, where they always vanished quickly, possessing the fleeting quality of dreams and as such, unable to be true.

Even after she received the distinction, she had trouble believing there had not been a mistake. She was haunted by the fear that there were votes that had been cast but were somehow missing and would be discovered — what humiliation! — or, worse yet, that those who had voted for her would change their minds and call for a replacement. That even if she had been moderately attractive on that one particular day of the voting, her luster would dim and the honor would be rescinded.

She considered not going to school, in the heart-pounding days immediately preceding the dance, but in the end could not stay away, for the terror of not being there to defend her crown should it come into peril outweighed her fear of losing it at all.

Her fear was not totally ungrounded; there had already been one near miss, when she realized that receiving the honor meant she had to get a new dress to wear for the coronation. She had assumed there was one that each queen wore every year, that the school had several sizes available and loaned them out, like uniforms or costumes — what kind of prize would require the recipient to descend further into poverty? There was no way — she knew without asking — that her family could afford the shimmering royal blue dress she wanted, from the front window display at Harrigan's on Main Street; nor could she afford any other kind. She had tortured herself once already by going in and trying it on — it would need only a little taking-in at the waist — and she had been overwhelmed by the slide of the silk on her bare skin, and the quiet rustle of it, and by the way all of her senses announced to her, for the first time with no ambiguity, *I am grown up now.*

Not even Birdie would have been able to support such a ridiculous dream, and Maxine spent days in misery, terrified by the approach of the calendar and discussions of dress rehearsals. Other girls, once they were over their own disappointments at not being chosen, were beginning to ask her what she was going to wear — might she choose the emerald or saffron over the blue? — and the younger girls, the junior and sophomore queens, had already bought their dresses and taken them home, had already modeled them for their friends, had coiffed their hair into a dozen different styles, and were simply treading water now, awaiting the event with delicious anticipation rather than cold terror.

Only Bonnie knew of her predicament, but was not much help, suggesting that Maxine ask Birdie to sew her a new dress.

"We can't even afford the material," Maxine said, "and even if we could, she's never sewn silk before. I don't know what to do. I can't go," she said. "I'm queen, but I can't go."

"There's got to be something," Bonnie said. "Maybe one of the other queens would let you share. Maybe she could come out and wave to the crowd, then go back inside and change, and let you wear her dress and come out and wave."

"It doesn't work that way," Maxine said. "There's no girl in the world who would do that. I sure as hell wouldn't. Anyway, it would look stupid. Everybody would know. It would be worse than not going. That's the dumbest thing I ever heard of. I just won't go. Dammit, I just won't go." Her chin trembled and tears welled, but she held them in; there was no way she would cry in front of her little sister.

Bonnie's own chin quivered, but she absorbed the criticism, tried to understand where it was coming from.

Maxine got her dress. The next morning before her own class started, Bonnie hurried across the street to the high school, found Maxine's homeroom teacher, and told her the problem. Maxine's teacher went to the football coach with her idea, which the coach presented to his team that afternoon, for the senior boys to take up a collection to buy Maxine the blue dress — and that first day, they had enough to put it on layaway before the school closed at six, and enough the next day to purchase it, so that the school bus was able to stop and let her run in and pick it up on her way home.

Maybe it was wrong, Maxine thought, to be made so happy by a material thing, and by a superficial beauty rather than the more durable soul within, but she was seventeen and to expect otherwise would have been ridiculous. Walking home through the crisp autumn, with the sound of the men's axes ringing and the scent of the wood smoke from their burn piles, and the dress box in her arms, she felt that every nerve in her body was more stimulated than it had ever been. As if she had passed through some thin screen or veil into a place where the world was unbearably beautiful, and where she would never know hardship or longing again. A lone red sweet gum leaf fell, twisting, and like a baseball outfielder she hurried ahead of Bonnie a few steps to catch it on top of the white box. Jim Ed trailed a few steps behind them, dragging a stick in the thick leaves, with his sisters seeming to him so old now as to essentially be full-grown adults, and he wondered if they would go off and leave him behind.

The girls stopped now and again to lift the lid of the box and peer inside at the silk, still not believing their luck, as if worried that the dress might somehow escape them. Running, then, the last distance to the house, to show Birdie and Floyd, and to go try it on, each of them. If her life had ever been better, Maxine didn't know when.

I can still be a good person and like this dress, she thought. *There's nothing wrong with being so happy.* She wondered if this was how Floyd felt when he drank.

Birdie started crying when she first saw the dress on Maxine, and then again when she saw it on Bonnie.

"You're sure it's yours? You don't have to take it back?" she asked, and when the girls told her how the senior boys had pooled their dollars to buy it for Maxine, Birdie cried again.

But the old Brown luck returned later that same day; the best day of Maxine's life turned sour even before nightfall, as the last of the dim light was leaving the forest and Floyd came in from the mill, smelling of diesel. Maxine couldn't wait to show him the dress, and she and Bonnie went back to their room to dress her up again. Getting her hair right, holding the mirror here and there. The dress seemed to fit better each time she put it on, as if her body were learning to fill its curves. As if she were learning to become the kind of person who might wear such a dress all the time.

Floyd wasn't prepared for the story Birdie told him while Maxine was changing. Rather than being touched by the generosity, he was embarrassed, and he wasn't prepared for his oldest daughter to be wearing what he viewed as so revealing a dress before so many people; with Maxine's slight build, it wasn't quite like there was cleavage showing, but almost. It was just too much skin, and the beauty of the skin, and the dress itself, and the radiant young woman wearing it was too much, as was the sudden freedom and power she assumed in that wearing. He looked at her not with pride but shock, and could only think *No:* no without reason, only no, and he forbid her to wear the dress.

Maxine thought she might have stepped into some dream world where words, though familiar to her, no longer made any sense; a land where people, even those closest to and beloved by her, spoke gibberish.

"No," she said, "you don't understand. I'm queen. I have to wear it."

None of the children had ever told Floyd no to anything before. This, on top of the humiliation of the gift and the surprise of seeing his daughters dressed up like movie stars, accenting rather than hiding their beauty, was all he needed to know and hear.

"If you go to Homecoming," he said, "you won't be wearing that dress. I forbid it. You can take it back. You can give the football boys their money back. You can thank them," he added. "That was nice."

Birdie was still and silent in the cabin, frozen as if with foreknowledge. There was only one way this could turn out, and Jim Ed and Bonnie knew it. Birdie willed Floyd to soften, set her mind straining toward that wish like a woman shoving uphill on a boulder, but she could feel no movement in that regard, and she felt sick, and thought, *We just have to get through this.*

"No," Maxine said again, quietly but firmly, "it's mine and I've been named the queen. I have to go."

"You can go," Floyd said, his anger quick in him now — the drinking voice — "if you don't bring it up again. But you can't wear the dress.

You'll have to wear something else. Wear your church dress," he said. "Wear one of your mother's dresses." He stared Maxine down, but was troubled by what he saw and sensed, a fury little different from his own. He turned and went to the cabinet, got his jug down, and to show that he was not rattled, that he was supremely in control, poured only half a glass, and sat down by the fire and took just one sip before rising again and going into the bathroom, where Birdie had hot water waiting in the porcelain tub. The steam coming from the door as he opened it, and him disappearing into that steam. Birdie and the girls not looking at one another, chastened not so much by his temper or ultimatum but by the strange unspoken collaboration of their betrayal-to-come. No words needed to be passed.

Maxine glided through the remaining days before the dance largely unconcerned; she had made up her mind, and there was no force on earth that would change that. She took the dress to school two days before, left it with a friend, and the afternoon of the dance, went straight from school to her friend's, where she changed out of her Sunday clothes and into the blue dress.

A little of the pleasure was gone — Floyd had sullied that — but the other girls' gasps and adulations strengthened something else inside her. It seemed better than a fair trade.

She moved past the feeling of secrecy and gave herself up to the honor of being queen. Was it her imagination, later that night, when the royalty court was presented at halftime, or were the cheers loudest for her? And whether because of her beauty or the magnanimity of the community's gift, no matter; the cheers for her were loudest, and her breath came so fast during those cheers that she could not have spoken if she had to, could only wave.

The presentation passed, the game resumed, and the evening stretched out. She knew it was ending, but no matter: something else was beginning, and she felt she had somehow imprinted herself upon the world — as if she had only now just entered it. This was who and how she was supposed to be, and now that she had crossed over into that place, it did not matter whether she took the dress off or not, for she had become that person — she was safely over on the other side, and realized only then that she had even been laboring to cross to some other side.

After the dance, she and Bonnie hurried back to her friend's house and she changed back into her regular dress. She and Bonnie got a ride to the end of their road with her friend's parents, and they walked down the moonlit lane, scuffling leaves and remembering the night, listening to owls, blowing delicious silver smoke from their lungs, and they marveled at how wonderful the world could be.

They were back a full half-hour before curfew — it was not yet ten thirty — but Floyd had been drinking all evening. He was not yet incapacitated, only belligerent and plague-ridden; the humiliation of the gift had become mythic in his mind, the one heavy stone to which he clutched in his descent, like a diver seeking ballast to help him make it all the way down to the bottom of where he felt he needed to go.

Jim Ed was in his room, playing his guitar quietly, pretending to be someone else, and Birdie was by the fire, rocking and knitting and waiting, listening to Floyd's tirades about pride and work, listening to him with passive detachment, knowing it wasn't Floyd speaking, but a stranger — the Floyd she knew was a good provider and hard worker, an honest man who knew right from wrong and who would do anything for his family — and as she rocked, she hoped Maxine would have the good sense rather than saucy rebellion — now that her perfect evening was over — to hide the dress rather than to still be wearing it.

Maxine would one day become the woman who would have worn the dress right on into the cabin, but the seventeen-year-old Maxine did not. Instead, she peered in the window, saw Floyd with his jug, and set the box down on the porch to come get later after he was asleep, and then she and Bonnie went on inside, bright and cheery and radiating pleased guilt, duplicity, relief, joy.

Birdie saw it all and smiled but felt a heaviness at the same time. Her needles clacked a bit faster now, as if she might somehow be able to weave a different outcome.

When Floyd drank like that, he reminded Maxine of a snarling dog, and it went unquestioned by her that on the best night of her life it was to that dog which she returned. She and Bonnie lingered a bit, not wanting to be in his presence but not wanting to abandon the box on the porch.

When he rose to go outside to urinate, they could only hold their breath, and were relieved to see how drunk he was, weaving and cursing, muttering. He looked at Maxine as he passed, assessed her plain dress, laughed, then went outside.

He found the box while stumbling around trying to bring in a piece of firewood. Sickened, they could hear him dropping the firewood, then the silence, then the sound of the box being opened.

He came inside carrying the long blue dress like a sash, eyes glittering, and went straight to the woodstove. Maxine shouted *No!* and grabbed his arm, but he threw it off, opened the stove door, and shoved the dress in, where the silk plumed immediately into brilliant crackling flame, flooding the cabin with a brief, fierce heat.

"I told you not to wear it," he said. "I told you no."

Strangely, it was Bonnie who cried loudest. Maxine didn't cry at all, simply went silent and cold — refused to acknowledge, in that moment, what the dress meant to her — and focused instead on hating Floyd. If she missed the dress overmuch, it might take away from energy she could spend hating him. She went and picked up his whiskey-smelling work jacket and brushed past him and opened the stove quickly and began shoving it in, amid the charred and flamed sheets and curves of her dress, but he snatched it back out, the sleeve afire, stamped it out, ashes and coals scattering all over the floor, and with the foul scent of burning silk filling the cabin.

Birdie had gotten up and was protesting, "Floyd, Floyd, please," and was patting his arm, trying to change his course through words alone — *"Floyd, Floyd,"* — and he was laughing now, pulling on his still smoldering jacket and laughing. With his sleeve still smoking, he turned to lecture the children about obedience, but then passed out, pitched forward, hitting his head hard on the cabin wall as he fell, and Birdie hurried to tend to him, and to extinguish the burning.

"I'm sorry," Bonnie said that night, thinking that she might have heard Maxine crying in the bed next to her. "You sure looked pretty.

You were beautiful." The scent of the burning fabric was acrid throughout the cabin, stinging their faces, and they could hear Floyd's snoring below, beneath the blanket with which Birdie had covered him, and could hear more clearly the sounds of the night, from where Birdie had opened the window to try to clear out some of the smoke. An owl calling that night, sounding just like it did in good times; the slow autumn-chilled trill of crickets. The girls reliving the good part of the night, not the bad.

"It was just a dress," Maxine said. "I wore it, and was queen, and the sonofabitch can't take that away. I wore it," she said.

Now she thought she heard Bonnie crying, and she sat up and told her not to worry, to stop it, that she had gotten to wear the dress, and that that was what mattered, but still Bonnie kept crying.

"What is it?" Maxine asked, and Bonnie whispered, "I don't know. I just miss Raymond."

This same year, a handsome country music disc jockey, Dick Hart, drifted through town, stopped in Sparkman to sign autographs, noticed Maxine's looks straight away, and invited her to come up to Little Rock the next night to meet him at a radio station he was bound for. He said he could get her plenty more autographs, that there would be all kinds of stars there.

Maxine and a friend snuck out that night, borrowing Floyd's Model A, pushing it a quarter-mile down the road before starting it, then driving up to Little Rock. A year before she wouldn't have dared, but now she felt she had less to lose.

They met Dick Hart at one A.M., and he was not in the least bit interested in getting autographs for them. The girls resisted his attentions but were thrilled with their adventure. They flirted, giggled, pushed away his pawing, then drove back home in the night, only to have the Model A overheat and break down just before daylight a few miles outside of Sparkman. She'd run the radiator so dry that it had melted a gas line and caught on fire, and they had to put the fire out by tossing handfuls of dirt on the engine.

Maxine and her friend walked on into town, and had to call Floyd to come get them at dawn. Floyd harangued her with vigor, accused her of going out to meet a boy, called her a tramp. Maxine cried and called him a sonofabitch. Floyd slapped her, and the strange fury between them got even worse. They raged at each other harder, over the smallest things, or were cold and indifferent, up or down, as if their relationship depended on nothing more than the variances of the moon. As if some larger force, far removed from their own influences, held governance over them all.

⌐ THE TRYOUT

THE BROWNS HAD moved in a little closer to town. Floyd had idled the mill, tired of the brutal labor and low profits, and opened a restaurant, where Birdie worked nonstop. People came from a long way off to eat her pies, made with her own pigs' lard, not storebought shortening that had been shipped great distances in the August heat. Musicians, in particular, drifted through on their way up to Nashville: that developing stream of young musicians in earnest hopeful exodus from the Deep South up to Nashville. Birdie's cooking reminded them of where they had come from, and what they had left behind in pursuit of glory.

Before and after meals, there would be jam sessions. Sometimes Bonnie and Maxine and Jim Ed would sit in the back of the restaurant and listen; other times they would shyly come forward and play and sing. One of the many elements of greatness is confidence, and they began to get just the faintest first hints of it — as if the breath of the god within them was choosing to blow gently on those embers. Dooming them. How might their lives have turned out if they had stayed there in town — had never gone back to the woods, but had remained there, in the center-stream of the music that was flowing through on the way to Nashville? Birdie in particular, despite the long hours, was pleased to be in town.

Floyd, however, had more than a little of the Browns' swooping up-and-down fortune in him, glittering in his blood like gold and red leaves. He missed the woods, too, especially in the fall, and so after the restaurant burned down one night, he took the insurance money and his family back into the woods and started the mill up again. He hired a few of his old friends and family back on and resumed his old ways, pushing farther on into the forest.

By this time — 1952 — there were little regional spinoffs of the Grand Ole Opry scattered all over the South — the Louisiana Hayride down in Shreveport, which was nurturing Jerry Lee Lewis, Loretta Lynn, and Jim Reeves, and the Ozark Jubilee up in Missouri, which was developing Willie Nelson, Webb Pierce, and Porter Wagoner.

Just up the road from the Browns, another radio station, KLRA, had started a program called *The Barnyard Frolic,* which staged a local talent show before a live audience each week. Everyone in Poplar Creek listened to it religiously, and kept telling the Browns that they were better than anyone who went on the show. Jim Ed's imitation of Hank Snow sounded more like him than Snow himself.

Unbeknownst to Jim Ed, Maxine borrowed a tape recorder and made a copy of Jim Ed imitating one of Hank Snow's songs and sent it in to the radio station. No light, she told herself, can be kept beneath its bushel forever.

All that next week, the first week of June, Maxine insisted that Jim Ed and Bonnie accompany her when she walked up the long clay road to the mailbox. Bonnie and Jim Ed protested, but then one day there it was, the letter addressed to Jim Ed, the script of the typewriter skewed and weak, the two-cent stamp canceled by hand, and inside, the warm invitation to an opportunity he had never dreamed even existed.

Just for a moment, he grinned when he first read the envelope, but following that, he had a strange reaction.

"Don't control my life that way," he said. "You should have asked. I know you meant to surprise me, but you should have asked."

Maxine was incredulous. "Do you mean to tell me you don't want to do it?" she asked. The three of them were standing around in the yellow heat of summer, Maxine and Jim Ed arguing as if over the tally in a game of hopscotch, rather than inhabiting a moment that would change so much. As if their arguments or decisions had any bearing on the turning of the world anyway, now that it had begun.

"No," Jim Ed said, his anger fading, "that's not what I mean." He smiled again, uncertain as to what he was feeling and why he had experienced a moment of pique, and then they turned and went running back down to the house to tell the others the news.

He stole the first show he played, became the established favorite within a month, and after only two months brought Maxine and Bonnie onto the show. They decided to call their group the Browns,

nothing fancy, and that evening they received their first standing ovation, more powerful than any drug. The strange pulse of satisfaction
rippled through each of them, waves of applause that were indistin-
guishable from love. Jim Ed devoured it, and even Bonnie, already secure and level-headed for a beautiful young woman who had just been
anointed a star, enjoyed it enormously, lark though it was for her.

It was Maxine who was most strongly affected, however. After that
first show was over, she couldn't stop thinking about it, nor could she
live without it. It was as if her soul had flown out of her body that
night. When would it be back? Even now, she wonders.

FABOR

THERE WAS A HUNTER who was drawn to *The Barnyard Frolic,* and who sought to exploit the local talents that passed through there. His name was Fabor Robinson, and he had made a fair amount of money by signing the various starry-eyed backwoods country youth who played for the *Frolic.* The Browns should have known better, as should have the hundreds who preceded them, though none of the others possessed what the Browns held.

It was like a slaughterhouse. Fabor would greet the young artist backstage immediately following his or her performance, while the adrenaline was still shimmering so strongly in the blood that it was as if the singer or musician were in an altered state. He would congratulate her, would compare her favorably to whatever icon she had been imitating that night, and he would say that he had an association with whomever she most admired or revered; that he did business with that star, had connections and access; and that he could envision that star becoming a mentor to the young talent.

He would have papers at the ready, and because the singers were desperate and starving and in love with what they were doing, they always signed. He signed them under the age of eighteen, no matter, with or without parental consent or witness, and then he went to certain radio stations and bribed the disc jockeys to make a hit of this-or-that single — one of the songs to which he now held all the titles — and while a star might be born, a star would most assuredly not get paid.

It shames Maxine to remember how gullible they were. For a long time, things had been simple, and any hungers they ever had were physical, but once the world discovered their sound, they knew a different kind of hunger. The size and magnitude of it, she realizes now, was precisely the size of the world's hunger, though for what, even now, she cannot say for sure.

"Did you grow up raised by Hank?" Fabor had asked Jim Ed, that first night. "Are you his bastard son? You're better than Hank Snow," he said. And after Fabor came to understand that Maxine made the decisions for the Browns, he began working her, putting a hunger into her — or building a pathway by which the world's hunger could enter.

"Incomparable," he said, "a siren, a star. Enchanting." He didn't compare her to anyone, for there was no one to whom she compared; but neither did he dwell on the fact that some of the beauty of her sound came from being a part of the whole.

"I hope you're ready to become a star," he said, "because you already are one. Look at you," he said. "You're smart, you're beautiful, and you've got the voice of an angel. Look at you. Are you ready to be a star?" Gazing at Bonnie then, before turning to Jim Ed. "Young Mr. Snow," he said, and he was aware of Maxine's new-kindled ravening, the gust or gasp of it when he turned his attention to another.

It was like shooting fish in a barrel. He got the Browns, though they certainly didn't need him to bribe the radio station: once the station managers heard their harmony, they wanted to play them anyway.

And just like that, they were owned for life. He had taken their power, had stolen their magic as surely as if capturing three fireflies in a glass bottle. They were so naïve, they didn't even recognize the wrongness of it: as if they were lambs looking up with twitching tails and stepping toward the approach of the lion.

Most of Fabor's stable of slaves for life — his contracts, legal and binding, owned everything they would ever do; any disbursements by him to them were to be at his discretion, following adjustments for his overhead and administration — were non-talents, church choiristers and nickel-balladeers, barely worth the trouble of recording, much less promoting. But over the years he had managed to snare a few big fish, the largest of which was Gentleman Jim Reeves, who had already been enslaved by a personal services contract to Fabor for years, and who was utterly miserable, despite his success on the radio playlists and in the hearts of those who sat around their radios every weekend listening to his gentle, steady crooning. No one would ever have guessed at his anguish beneath the surface, or the drinking. His persona was that of Gentleman Jim, and he kept it up in public, no matter how awful his life was.

Reeves and his wife, Mary, were only about ten years older than the Browns, but were pretty hammered by the road when they met the Browns, playing with them at a show in Shreveport that Fabor had set up. It was in a high school auditorium, the most people they had ever played for before, and looked as glamorous to them as it did dispiriting and run down to Jim Reeves, who at that time was just beginning the downside of his career — still riding fairly high on old hits but not making many new ones.

Mary Reeves was elegant, thin to the point of a knifeblade, like Maxine herself, and a wearer of furs at even the least of opportunities: any faint breeze from the north that might drop the temperature below fifty. Jim was as carefree as Jim Ed, and they hit it off right from the start. "So you're the one Fabor's been talking about who's going to put me out of business," Jim Reeves said. "Do me a favor and do it quickly." He took out a flask and handed it to Jim Ed. "To the next Hank Snow," Jim said, "and to the Browns. Welcome," he said. "You're in the family now."

Jim went onstage first, then called the Browns up, introduced them on the heels and good tidings of his own performance. He handed his audience over to them, stepped back, and played backup the rest of the night, and laughed when he saw that the Browns did not really understand how good they were, and that for now at least they were just running on the power of youth, that they knew nothing, and that everything was new.

Jim remembered those days, and so did Mary. They had signed with Fabor ten years earlier, but it felt like a hundred. They had both long ago traveled beyond any notions of or hopes for newness; but when they were around the Browns, they could remember it; and when they heard them sing, they definitely remembered it.

They took the Browns under their wing and helped take care of them as best as they could. The venues were small and the paths leading to them roughshod; cars rode so much stiffer in those days, and the shows usually required the use of back roads, with the stars driving their own vehicles — and while Fabor stayed in luxury hotels throughout the South, the Browns and Jim and Mary slept in their cars, huddled in blankets, when they slept at all. Usually, they were driving, pushing hard to arrive at the next gig just in time to take to the stage.

It was hard work, but it was no sacrifice; the Browns were in a groove, and despite the physical hardships and the emotional toil of being Fabor's slaves, it was for each of them the best time of their lives. They had found the steel rails laid out for them and were proceeding with great verve. None of the other mattered. They were fitting the world and yet also traveling just above it, creating a newer and alternative world—making adventures each day that paralleled the world below, but which were brighter, sharper, more deeply felt.

Maxine was getting her nightly applause, the soon predictable standing ovations. Jim Ed was sleeping with different women every night, and Bonnie was content with the beauty of the sound.

None of them was in it for the money, and that was fortunate, for there was none. They had a song soar right to the top of the charts, number one on the country list—"Looking Back to See"—and for this Fabor doled out a whopping $170 that year.

They were puzzled by the accounting, and Maxine called Fabor up in California and asked where the other checks were.

"That's it," he said, "but you should consider yourself lucky: it takes most artists two or three years before they earn back their expenses and even get their first check. You can ask Jim Reeves about that."

She did, and Jim grimaced and shook his head and said, "He's right; you're pretty much screwed."

On the surface, it looked glamorous—driving all around Arkansas, when before they'd rarely been out of Poplar Creek, and receiving applause every evening, no matter where they played, and doing what they loved. It would have seemed glamorous, too, and perhaps it was.

But in between those two places—the glamorous surface and the beautiful core of the heart—the miles were hard, maybe not as hard for young people as for those who'd been at it for years, like Jim and Mary, but tough nonetheless. It wasn't a life you would want for anyone you cared about—and if someone did get into such a life, you would want them to get back out as quickly as possible.

Fabor was a lecher. It was rare to find a young woman back then willing to tour. It's hard to imagine that only one lifetime separates the difficulties experienced by a handful of trailblazers like Maxine and Bonnie. Back then, it was so outrageous and outlandish for a woman to leave home — much less to get up on a stage for the express purpose of entertaining a largely male audience — that the basic assumption was that that woman was cheap and easy and desperate. Even some of their male counterparts in other bands made that assumption and pressured them relentlessly, but always, the audiences and promoters did.

It was Bonnie upon whom Fabor set his relentless sights. Subtlety was not his forte, and he was after her from the first moment he saw her, telling her, among other things, that a woman who was a virgin had a different, weaker voice than one who was not, and that it was his duty as her representative and agent to help her strengthen her voice to its fullest potential.

She wasn't going to sleep with him, of course — not to improve her voice or for any other reason — but she worried about it, was made a little insecure by the gnawing that she was somehow holding her siblings back.

Fabor used them hard that first year; toured them all over hell and back, barely paying them enough for meals, and on the nights when audience numbers were low — playing in a club where ten or twelve people showed — he would berate them, calling them lazy. They turned out another number one hit, "Here Today and Gone Tomorrow," but then, afraid that their success would skyrocket too fast and that he might somehow lose control of them, he began releasing the worst cuts of some of their studio re-takes, including a wretched song called "Itsy Bitsy Witsy Me," which they had sung just for fun, in falsetto, with off-key piano work. It was never meant to be recorded, much less released on the radio.

"Why in the hell would he do that?" Maxine asked Jim. "It's an embarrassment. Why would he want to sandbag us?"

"It's complicated," Jim said. "Part of him wants to be rich and part of him wants to be king. I can't even say he's got a split personality, because I've never seen anything good in him. It's a bad deal," Jim said, "but we're healthy, we're doing what we love, and we're having some good times. Am I right? Are we having some good times?"

"You're right," Maxine said. "We're having some good times, but that doesn't mean he's still not a sonofabitch."

"He is that," he agreed. "It takes some getting used to." Jim was silent for a moment, then picked up his guitar and played a few melancholy chords, spacing them far enough apart so that gentleness, if not peace, might fill in, and fit.

It was as if Fabor viewed them all as he would a herd of sheep, or goats, or cattle. Floyd was controlling, but nothing like this; Floyd's destructiveness was turned inward, while Fabor's seemed only to radiate outward, burning with menace.

At larger venues, where Fabor made each of his musicians play only two or three songs, presenting a dozen or more musicians to an audience on any one night, he insisted that each and every performer remain onstage after his or her last song, for the duration of the evening—on display but no longer performing, sitting there in a chair onstage with a stupid smile—the adrenaline from the musicians' own performances leaching away quickly now while the newest act played and sang and received the next round of applause. It was brutal, it was ridiculous, and even the audiences were discomforted by it.

Fabor advertised his traveling show as "The Fabor Robinson String Music Act," but the performers and audiences began calling it the Fabor Robinson Strange Music Act.

He was tone deaf; he favored loud over soft, fast over slow, surface over depth, style over substance.

Still, the Browns were able to tolerate him, for a while. It was a piece of rotten luck, they told themselves—before signing with Fabor, they had sent a demo tape to RCA, but that letter had gotten lost in a pile in New York; less than a week after they had all three signed with Fabor, an offer had come from RCA, but it was too late then.

It didn't matter, at first. They had come out of the woods, their gift had maneuvered them from out of the most desolate obscurity into something resembling the larger world or a crack or fissure leading out into the larger world — and in the beginning, their being hostages did not yet matter so much, for they were being heard, and everyone who heard them loved them, would love them forever. There were, they believed, far worse things than being imprisoned.

~ BUDDY

THE LITTLE DOG is the light of her life, or is to the extent that she'll allow another to hold that much power over her. She pretends that a large part of her days are not centered around his regular appearances. He comes over to see her in the morning, not long after she's gotten up and has made her tea and is sitting in the kitchen reading the paper, scowling at the news but somehow pleased also by each day's verification of her views on the disintegration of culture. The entitlement of affluence, the aversion to hard work, the immodesty and promiscuity, the greed and selfishness, the savage civil wars and collapsing environment . . . It's all there and she scans it quickly, pretty much knowing what the gist will be, while she waits for Buddy to show up at the back door, with a presence to which she is so attuned that she imagines she can discern his approach through the synchrony of their two hearts beating as he draws ever closer, yard by yard: stopping at each of his signposts to scent-mark, investigating each garden and every sandbox, trotting primly along his route, through gaps in the miscellany of sagging chain-link fences and cedar-split rail fences, working his way toward her through a fairly convoluted routing, so that it is not as if Maxine's backyard is merely another stop along the way but is instead his sole destination.

How her heart leaps when, in the accruing stillness of her waiting, she hears the distant scold of a blue jay in the Millers' backyard, indicating that Buddy is passing through. She smiles, takes a sip of tea — *He always comes to see me.* Such pleasure, or, if not quite pleasure, satisfaction, will never end; his arrivals and their effect on her are as constant and mythic as those of each day's rising of the sun. And five or six beats later, she hears the fussing of the mockingbird in the yard next door as Buddy crosses over, ceaseless in his predictability. She's all but deaf, but she sits with her better ear turned and tuned to his approach, and it seems that she can still occasionally hear what she wants to hear.

She rises as quickly as she can from her chair — how did it get to be this time in the morning so fast? After so much waiting, why is time moving so quickly now?

It was precisely this way when she was drinking: the fearful yet delighted edginess in her blood, and the delicious pretending that things were otherwise — that the edginess was not there. Trying to control it, but only barely, and in the end, not.

The visual aura — certain things at the periphery dimming while others become more illuminated, even gilded — and the tightening also of aural intensities, with some sounds becoming so much sharper as to be almost painful. The quickened heartbeat, to the point of palpitations, and the rush of anticipatory endorphins: always, the best part about drinking was the very last second, right before the first sip was taken.

But the sip had to be taken in order to complete the cycle. In order to begin it all over again and start the journey back toward anticipation.

So it is with Buddy's daily arrivals. Maxine gathers the little scraps she has been saving for him (sometimes she splurges and opens a can of dog food, though as fond as she is of him, she tries not to do this too often) and opens the door to see him waiting there, just a tad impatient, but otherwise a perfect little gentleman, a silver-frosted little wirehaired terrier looking utterly distinguished, his eyes bright with his own waiting.

He cocks his head and listens as she speaks to him, tells him *Good morning, Mister Buddy,* lavishes a few old-woman's endearments on him — "Aren't you a handsome fellow this morning! How is your day going, what have you seen?" — and then lowers the paper plate to where he is waiting, the place where he always receives it, next to the water bowl that she always keeps filled; and he drops his head quickly then and eats steadily, though neatly, spilling nothing.

When he is done, he lifts his head and licks his lips and beholds her for a moment, waiting for more — she laughs but never gives him more: "You've got to stay trim, Mister Buddy" — and then he is off, and Maxine, through long practice, has become accustomed to pretending that she's all right with that, and that she doesn't wish he were hers or that she had a fence around her yard which, after entering, he could not exit.

She pretends that she does not want the responsibility of having him around more often than he is, that his brief daily visits each morning are just right. She pretends that it's exactly the way she would have designed things if the choice were up to her.

Then he is gone, and the long day begins. With some luck she will see him again, later in the afternoon, when he passes back through her yard, hurrying toward his home to arrive there before his owners' children get in from school—but those passages are fleeting, and rarely does he have time to stop, even on the occasions when she sets out enticements.

What to do with such long days, and such longer waiting? Sometimes—even now, after nearly fifty years of being forgotten—she sends handwritten notes, in old-woman shaky-scrawl, to the addresses of nightclubs that she remembers, or to music companies, requesting work, asking for another chance, another gig, another audience, another anything; though there is nothing, only a terrifying absence. The letters almost always come back unopened, Return to Sender, though occasionally there will be a form rejection or, ever so infrequently, a short personal rejection.

She doesn't mail the letters out as much as she used to—stamps have gotten so expensive—but now and again she still does: she just can't help it.

She knows she could still sing. Can still sing. She sings to herself. Hers is an old voice now, but she still feels a power in her. It's trapped down in there. It won't ever leave, not while she's alive.

She sings as long as she can, until she becomes dismayed by the diminishment—five, ten good minutes, with rests—and then falls quiet again, putters around in the dark house, waits for the mailman, and in the afternoons, looks out the back window at the bright heat of the day, hoping for a glimpse of Buddy passing by.

THE NEW BUILDING

THERE IS A BALANCE in the world, and no work is ever wasted. Fabor had imprisoned their careers even as they were first blooming, and there would be others who would trip the Browns up as they were ascending, who would pull them down just when they had gotten a leg up — but it worked the other way too. Whenever they got too far down, someone always happened by to give them a hand back up. Along with the unpredictability and controlling nature of Floyd came the unconditional love of Birdie, and her ceaseless work on their behalf and on behalf of the nuclear shell of their family.

Life at the mill was getting hard again. Floyd loved being in the woods, but always, the work eventually proved to be incompatible with his alcoholism. Inattentive due to drink, he lost two fingers on his left hand, a match now with the two he had lost on his right hand some years earlier, and so he packed his family up and moved up to Pine Bluff, began building another restaurant on the foundation of the old one, and named it the Trio Club in honor of Maxine, Bonnie, and Jim Ed.

Floyd milled the lumber for the restaurant and drove it into town, and the whole family pitched in with the construction, with Birdie working hardest of all, up before anyone else and staying out on the job long after the others had worn out.

She got tired, but she didn't know how to quit. *It'll be beautiful,* she kept saying. Floyd and Jim Ed did the wiring and plumbing, and, spurred largely by Birdie, they had the place open a month after driving the first nail. As there was always a balance, or a striving-for-balance, in their up-and-down lives, so too was there a similar meter in their family. Whatever Floyd and later Maxine put at risk, or even damaged or sought to destroy or turn their back on, Birdie and Bonnie would always be ready to help put back together. The oscillation in their lives was remarkable, though as close as they were to it, they never noticed it, but instead simply continued to move forward each day, always looking one day ahead.

Floyd and Birdie put a new sign over the threshold, brightly painted light bulbs made to look like neon, arranged to represent in crude silhouette the profiles of the three oldest Browns, with a treble clef and three notes next to the glow-in-the-dark dazzling illumination: red, green, gold, orange, pink. Moths swarmed the lights, fell in thick clutters to the ground. Birdie swept them each morning, kept the light bulbs dusted and clean, unscrewed them and painted them anew every two months, sometimes experimenting with the arrangements to give each silhouette a slightly different effect — one more lurid, one more ebullient, one purer. It was amazing what a little variance could achieve, even with the borders of the illumination remaining unchanged and unalterable.

People came to eat Birdie's pies, but also to listen, in the evenings, to the Browns' soothing harmonies: singers and musicians who would go on to become the stars of the next decade. There was just something so *slick,* so smooth, about the up-and-down registry of the sound. Johnny Cash, Jerry Lee Lewis, Patsy Cline, Buddy Holly, and the Davis Sisters came to hear them. It was a tight little core; the seeds of what would become the multibillion-dollar Nashville country music industry came through there and were touched by the Browns — coming like the lost young people they all were back then, coming more to touch the Browns than to be touched, like animals in the wild forest coming to crouch and drink at the head of a fountain, the only wellspring for miles around, and doing so in a time of drought, and with fires burning all around.

They came, they brushed up against the Browns, and then they went on their way — magic-brushed, and forged from a fire they sometimes didn't even realize they'd touched, though others of them understood right from the very beginning the nature of the raw talent they were witnessing.

The new restaurant had been open only a few weeks when the one who would change everything, and who would never be forgotten, drifted through. He was nothing, just a kid with a guitar — one of maybe hundreds who traveled that path up through Pine Bluff — and those inclined to disbelieve in predestination might do well to reconsider the path that took him straight to the Browns. He had been born only a hundred or so miles to the east and had lived his seventeen years with some passion, and some magic, but nothing like what would come after his life intersected theirs.

As if for all of the short seventeen years beforehand he had just been treading water, waiting—not unlike Fabor, though with a good heart, if a wounded one—to come straight to them, brush against them, take from them what he could, and continue on, possibly without even knowing he had taken anything.

For Elvis, it must surely have been like something from a dream, in which the sleepwalker does not question his or her route but is drawn and moves easily, traveling not with ambition, for once, but with only the milder things for a while, such as hope and curiosity.

If anyone were to ask him about it afterward, he would certainly not have described his approach like that of a moth to a light but would instead have said that he was simply pulled by the scent of Birdie's cooking. He was whistling as he walked, guitar strapped to his back, walking up the dirt road carpeted with the soft straw of pine needles, as if such fronds had been laid on the road in advance and expectation of his arrival, though there was no such expectation, it was only a day like all others, with chicken being fried and pies being baked.

Mourning doves called lazily from the tops of pine trees and fluttered in pockets of sand or red clay worn down to the finest powder, taking baths. Grasshoppers clacked. Elvis was just walking, maybe knowing he was stepping into history, maybe not. Maybe just hungry. Seventeen years old. Still essentially just a boy, whistling. His old car out of gas. Walking, ostensibly to look for nightclubs where he could play, or churches—he had it vaguely in mind that he wanted to be a gospel singer—but mostly just walking, and moving, as best as he could tell, toward the odor of that chicken frying, and the rolls baking, and the pies cooling on the windowsills.

Walking right on through that curtain. Maybe he was dimly aware, or maybe he was still unknowing, just hungry, always hungry. Maxine and Bonnie and Jim Ed's mother's restaurant just right up the road: the exquisite timing of history. Early spring. He could see the restaurant coming into view. Surely he had no idea what awaited him. Surely he was just out walking. Maybe daydreaming about fame a little, but not overly much.

He saw the light-bulb silhouettes of the three young musicians — unignited in the daylight like that, they appeared unprepossessing, but he was intrigued by the garish possibility of the display, and delighted to imagine what it looked like at night. Seeing it, something in him calmed and became centered, almost as if he had found a lost sibling.

Birdie had just finished the last of the breakfast menu. There were still a few cathead biscuits left, and the cream gravy, with its flecks of bacon and chunks of ham, was still warm if not steaming — not yet chilled to the consistency of pudding — and now she was starting the lunch menu, whacking the chickens (which she had killed and cleaned only the day before) into pieces for frying, the cleaver striking the ancient chopping block with reassuring authority: a sound he remembered from Tupelo. After disassembling the chickens and heating the frying oil (dropping a match onto the surface of the oil and waiting for the tip to ignite), she dipped the chicken pieces into a bowl of egg and buttermilk, then into a sack filled with flour and red pepper and salt, and shook it to coat them. Then she put the chicken, still in its sack, back into the refrigerator — one of her many secrets — and set about peeling and slicing potatoes, also for frying, her big knotted hands working the little knife as deftly as any banjo player's worked his instrument.

The pies were already made, some late the night before and others first thing that morning, long before sunup. Strawberries canned from summer, blackberry, rhubarb, apple, lemon meringue.

"Do you have chocolate, ma'am?" he asked when he came into the restaurant. As polite a set of manners as she had ever seen, and something else, too. He introduced himself, though back then the name didn't mean anything. It was the last time it would mean nothing. She didn't know any Presleys. She didn't make chocolate pie every day, but she had made some that morning, they were not yet even fully chilled.

"You can't start with pie," she said. "Pie is for dessert." She eyed his back-slung guitar case, his shoulder bag with its one change of clothes, the sandy pants cuffs and dusty shoes. "Have you even had breakfast today?" His old belt was cinched beyond its last hole, nail-riven new holes stippling it; but not a whiff of depression or sadness that day, nothing but joy, possessing no idea, really, what he was walking into. Maybe having a little idea, a vague picture, of the general size of the fame he desired — the fame roughly, or so he would have guessed, commensurate with the size of his appetite, which sometimes thrilled him and other times frightened him.

He would know the fame when he saw it. But of the inexplicable and damning sadness that would one day begin to roughly parallel it, he had no clue whatsoever.

"No, ma'am," he said. "But I sure would like some pie."

Occasionally she could get the sense that one of them might be worth something. But that first time, she had no real sense that he would be any different. She didn't even ask him to play. She just fed him, brought him his pie, and then all the rest. She thought it strange how already and immediately he seemed to view her as a mother, but such a thing did not displease her.

"Are those your children, ma'am?" he asked. "Are they singers?" Adjusting his guitar strap, the instrument still strapped to his back.

They became fast friends. They played music together, but also played like children. On occasions when Fabor did not have Jim Reeves and the Browns booked, the Browns would tour with Elvis, if it could be called touring, drifting and wandering to whatever club would have them. Playing for fun and essentially playing for free: working below radar to keep from having to hassle with Fabor. Sometimes a club owner would fill their cars with gas, would get their hotel rooms, would buy them drinks.

The girls would line up all night outside Jim Ed's and Elvis's rooms, some nights a dozen or more, as if waiting in line for a sale to open at a department store. Ten, fifteen minutes a girl, and Elvis and Jim Ed never sticking his head out the door to see how long the line might be, or exercising any real form of quality control — just grinding on until he could go no more, the girls outside fighting one another to cut in line.

✤ ✤ ✤

It was as if already they had two lives. The boys would engage in their all-night revelry, breeding away like bulls, too amped up from the performance to sleep or in any way descend from their high spirits — while Bonnie and Maxine would hole up in their room and talk about the show and engage in catty comments about the harlots.

Sometimes they would watch television, an utter novelty to them, and other times they would listen to the radio loudly while Elvis and Jim Ed thundered on in the adjacent rooms. Sometimes they would read or write letters; sometimes they would drink. Always, by that point, they would think about fame and would remember the applause.

The girls didn't get to sleep around. That was the boys' task, the boys' duty. Bonnie didn't want to — was saving herself for marriage — and Maxine, though she wanted to, didn't, mostly just because she wasn't supposed to. More smoldering. So much waiting. Still believing she had a hand in this matter of her life — in any of it.

In the morning the party-life would be gone entirely, passing like a wonderful storm for the boys, and they would all four reconvene for breakfast, bleary-eyed and wrung out, but filling back up, the well recharging from what was surely a limitless reservoir.

Did Maxine and Bonnie want their own partners, as enduring and steadfast as were the boys' liaisons fleeting? Bonnie, certainly; Maxine, less so. By that point she would bury any ten lovers if it helped her get more of the drug she needed. She told Bonnie she was "horny as a two-peckered billy goat," but her real hunger was for something far below.

Was it her fault that she was that way, or anyone's fault that two sisters of the same parents could be so different? There was no right or wrong in it. It was all only an elemental force blowing through them. It was all requisite for the world to turn as it turned.

In the beginning, Maxine and Bonnie started out riding home in the back seat, with Jim Ed and Elvis up front. After a few months that would change — one day Elvis and Bonnie would be in the back, tender and quiet and shy, almost as if it was not courtship at all, but as if Elvis were simply doing Maxine a favor, letting her have the more comfortable seat up front, or as if Elvis himself were seeking a more comfortable seat. And then after a little while longer, the new dynamics came to seem just as they should be, and Elvis and Bonnie did not need to be so quiet and serious, were laughing more in the back seat, not as if either or both or any of them were going to change the world in any way but instead as if they were just kids.

As they drove through the Arkansas springtime, breeze-blown dogwood blossoms lined the roads like flowers tossed at a wedding. They gunned the car up the hills, gliding down the back side, gravel loose under their thin tires, their guitars stacked in the trunk, in need of retuning after every stop, and the memory of the last show and the applause wrapping them like a warmed blanket on an otherwise chilly day. The spring sunlight flashed through the windshield, the windows rolled down despite the mountain chill, the boys smoking cigarettes. They were all four, back then, passionate about music — Elvis was only just beginning to let go of his dream of becoming a famous gospel singer, was just starting to get an inkling of what rock-and-roll was, and where it could take him.

On the drives back home they would stop and picnic in out-of-the-way places. A little waterfall with mossy limestone caves, beside which bloomed purple and gold violets. A meadow where wild turkeys gobbled back in the shadows while the Browns and Elvis spread a blanket to sit on and fixed sandwiches from bread that Birdie had baked for them and sliced ham from a hog Floyd had killed and butchered and smoked.

A cold beer each for the boys. Bonnie laughing, demurring again when offered one; Maxine taking a sip of Elvis's, however, then a sip from Jim Ed's, before opening her own bottle.

The four of them napping afterward in the lengthening slants of sun. Waking up a little later and playing some music. The distances were not too great, back then, and their calendars were not overly scheduled. There was still plenty of time to get back home, and back then, they all four still knew the way.

⟋ SHINING ON

IT'S THE LITTLE things she remembers best. Helping Bonnie with her makeup in the incredibly tense moments before a show. The simple pleasure of practicing; the first perfect chord from Jim Ed once the guitar was tuned. The brief and tiny space between banter and earnestness when they first leaned in and announced themselves, and released their voices, each time: an action like stepping across a little stream, a stream so small as to be crossed entirely with but one step.

The glances of respect whenever she first entered a room of her peers back in those days. Even if someone didn't like her or approve of the Browns' sound, there was this certain quick look she saw them give her. It was always there, even at the corner of her vision, and she was reassured by it, as might be a woman who, in checking her appearance in a mirror, sees that everything is just as she wishes it to be and has no need to adjust anything.

Best of all, of course, the stages: in London and Frankfurt, in Hot Springs and Nacogdoches, in Memphis, New Orleans, Knoxville, Nashville, Savannah, and Jackson. The particular pleasure of a new stage, the flooring unfamiliar, and the curve of walls and arc of roof likewise not yet known. The strangest details impressing themselves upon her, in that heightened state of awareness, that hyperacuity, as the adrenaline began to burn and the pupils constricted. Noticing a bat-shaped swirl in the growth rings of the oak flooring beneath her feet, or a dent in the steel mesh of the waiting microphone. The usher in Fayetteville who looked so much like Floyd, with his red jacket and slicked-back white hair. The WPA mural of John Henry on the high wall of the Cactus Theater in Lubbock. Her heart terrified, beating a million times a minute as she wondered what the audience would be like, wondering, *Will they love us?* Terrified, and grateful to her brother and sister beside her, as she stepped forward to find out.

Of the time that ensued once the lights came on her and the applause began all memory leaves her, if ever it was in her in the first place. Unconscious, owned, possessed, they sang, moved through their repertoire unthinking, giving themselves over to the audience with a complete selflessness.

What she does remember, beyond the first shine of the lights, is the end: the thing she lived for, the moment of perfect stillness when, after the last note had fallen upon the audience and was still settling over them, loosening, spreading out and then disappearing, there was the sweet and hallowed space in which the audience, saturated and bewitched, realized the songs were over but, entranced as they were, could not yet quite lift their hands to clap.

It was almost like a moment of confusion, as if the audience had been caught deep in some middle place between the dreaming and the waking and did not want to leave, though finally, like divers surfacing, came back up to the top, reluctantly at first, but gradually and — as if realizing only then where they were — enthusiastically.

Those full three or four seconds of silence, and the delight of her terror — *What if they do not clap at all? What if they do not rise to their feet?* — were more powerful than anything she had ever known.

Only when it did come — the first few waves of applause, then the sea roar, and then the rising — would she relax a tiny bit, and glance over at her brother and sister. The three of them somehow closer, out there on the stage, than they ever were in so-called real life. Relaxing, finally, after so long a wait and so long a journey, for a short period, before winding up tight all over again on their way to the next show, next audience, next state.

She remembers too the parties afterward. The ones she remembers most are those that took place in winter: the warmth, the heat of so many gathered together inside on a cold night; the post-performance excitement, the echo of it lingering. There was nowhere near as much as there had been in that perfect, single shining moment at the end of the song, but still, some of that same lingering.

She understood that it would go away — was going away — but she stood there at the parties, or moved through their midst, keen-eyed, determined to milk every last bit of it. A trawler far at sea with an immense net, never stopping, pushing farther.

THE MOVIE

FOR AS LONG as she can remember — which is to say, since she stopped drinking almost thirty years ago — she has been wanting a movie. It is a desire that burns in her every bit as intensely as did once her ambition for making music, for getting her voice out into the world, but she doesn't have any idea how to go about it. Mostly, she thinks, she has to just sit quietly, desiring it, burning, and wait for it to come to her. Waiting for her old contract with the world to reassert itself.

The silver screen, she calls it, whenever she talks to Bonnie on the phone. Wouldn't it make a marvelous movie? She fantasizes about the three of them being at the premiere, imagines various outfits she might wear, and is certain that at such a gala there would be a request for the three of them to sing again. She's certain they would comply, and certain, also, that it, the tempered harmony — this otherworldly phenomenon — would excite an entire new generation, and that once again, as always before, the audience — a thousand, two thousand, all in evening dresses and tuxedos — would leap to their feet, leaping as if summoned by violent jerks of invisible strings from above, and that the waves of applause, of love, would roll over and through her again: always, one more time.

Everyone else has a movie. Johnny Cash had a couple. Charley Pride had one, Loretta Lynn had a couple; the Beatles had twenty or more. Patsy Cline had one, Hank Williams had one. Elvis had maybe half a hundred, which, though she understands it, gnaws at her; for when they first started out, they were bigger than he was, and then — for a while — even when he was big, they stayed even with him on all the charts, for a while.

Even their best friend, Jim Reeves — Gentleman Jim Reeves — had a movie made about him, as did their record producer, Chet Atkins, with *The Chet Atkins Story.* A movie at or near the end of one's career or life is simply de rigueur in country music. Where's her movie? It's like going out onstage without shoes, or like the recurring nightmare in which, while playing in a huge and elegant venue, her voice comes out but the microphone isn't working, so that only the audience in the first few rows can hear her.

This is how it was in the old days, this fever, this feeling that something immense had entered the world and was shoving her, pushing her from behind, urging her toward a life of great consequence, with the wind at her back; and now, as then, she is eager to accept that assignation.

That the fame has been gone fifty years now does not register in her. In her mind it has only been gone one day. Sometimes she imagines the actors and actresses she would like to see in her movie. They change, decade by decade. In such imaginings, she tries to stay current.

How can fame not equal a movie? The fame came so quickly. Almost everything they touched went to number one. After having lived through a World War, then a Depression, then another World War, and finally an economic expansion, and the ascent from poverty into middle class — after all that, there was an excitement and a yearning to feel sophisticated, and a dissatisfaction or even embarrassment about those earlier days and generations. The Browns' voices were shiny and elegant, and utterly controlled; the spirit of their voices had the Appalachian hillbilly music as its rootstock, but without the nasal whine and twang. People had never heard anything like it and could not get enough of it. Every song the Browns released in 1955 and 1956 hit the top ten. Never in the history of music has any group had as many Top Ten hits over a two-year period, nor as many number ones.

It was a smaller world — fewer radio stations, and smaller audiences — and television had not yet assumed full primacy in the culture. Radio was still king. Companies such as RCA were only just beginning to merge the two media, using variety shows as a bridge. It was still an aural rather than visual culture with regard to how people entertained themselves and how they relaxed after a long day at work in the factory — exhausted from having trudged a day closer to a relief if not an affluence that finally was beginning to seem possible. They sat down on their couch, opened a beer, turned the music on, and listened to whatever was playing, as if awaiting instruction on how to live the rest of their lives, or to be encouraged to get up and keep going — to live more engaged lives, heroic lives — though sometimes, too, they sat there after work just listening.

The Browns flooded the market with their songs, which were written mostly by Maxine: stories of small-town growing-up, cruising the drag, dressing up for boys, cruel betrayals, longings for love — the standard fare of what would become American music. Jim Ed penned some of the drinking songs, and within about an eighteen-month period, they had essentially created the country music market, had provided both a template and a path for all the other musicians, many almost exactly like themselves but lacking only the strange assignation.

It could have happened to anyone; it could only have happened to them. The Browns — led largely by the firstborn and fiercest and hungriest — broke trail, and quickly, like escapees; all the others poured through right behind them.

And as if creating or colonizing all that new territory — the idea of country music — wasn't enough, the Browns spilled over, within that same short time period, into other adjacent markets: pop, rock, folk.

And just as quickly, Fabor became a multimillionaire, one nickel at a time, and whenever the Browns had the temerity to inquire about royalties, he scolded them for even thinking of such matters and told them that the greats — Hank Snow, Roy Acuff, Little Jimmy Dickens — never bothered with such matters but focused instead on holding on to the special thing they had, and that consideration of monetary advancement — indeed, considerations of anything other than the purity of their sound — were a distraction, and would over time create fractures through which their magic would slowly drain away.

Their window of opportunity for stardom was, Fabor warned them, very small, and he worked them like mules. On this count, he was right; it was the sole piece of truth he ever gave them.

It cost him, Fabor told them, to send them on all their tours and to develop the market they were building. *Hell,* Fabor said, *you're still in hock to me for all that, you haven't even paid out yet. I'm taking a chance on you,* he told them, *I'm taking a big gamble.*

The most money the Browns ever got paid during that two-year period of their first blossoming, their incredible incandescence — the same years that, like a fire's backdraft sucking oxygen, they pulled Elvis along behind them, and into the fire — was $13,000, in 1957. The check looked like a lot when they got it, but it didn't go very far, split three ways and across two years. It seems so easy now to cry foul and to counsel lawsuit or litigation. But it was not easy then, for a man's or a woman's signature meant more. It was a raw deal for the Browns, but it was a deal.

What Maxine remembers from those times, however — the beginning, if not the middle and the end — is not the wrongdoings, betrayals, and chicanery, but the high points.

In the beginning it seemed that was all there was. She realizes now that there must have been an undercurrent of lows running slow and deep beneath the surface, but she could not hear them or chose not to acknowledge their existence, though she is beginning to understand now that those very undercurrents — the lows straining to rise and attach themselves to, and bring down, the highs — might well have been among the many intangibles that gave them their temper, their meter. The promise implicit in such a sound that everything would eventually meet in the middle; and a bittersweetness, yet for some maybe a comfort in that promise, that contract.

Restricted to the downstairs section of her house as she is, Maxine longs for the day when she can climb the steps again and shower in her own bathroom, can select clothes from her bedroom closet, rather than sleeping on the couch and living out of the cardboard box that Bonnie brought downstairs for her. No one ever thinks they will end up this way; yet neither are there any plans that can be laid to prevent such steady approach of darkness, when it is darkness's time to come.

She fixes tea with hands that always shake now. She looks out the window. She tries not to make too many phone calls. Jim Ed, over in Nashville, is always on the road, and Bonnie, in the Ozarks, is always out in the garden with her husband, Brownie. Floyd and Birdie are long gone, and her children have moved as far away, it seems, as possible. Her relationships with them are neither sour nor severed, but instead, just never took full root. She did raise them, did provide for them; there is that bond, that gratitude, at least.

It seems strange to her, given that for all its stresses, her attachment to her own parents, and home, and childhood, was significant, and remains with her still.

Sometimes she goes into her tiny office, where all her memorabilia is stored neatly in cedar chests, and where framed photographs cover every inch of wall and occupy every portion of desk space: photos of her and her brother and sister with all of the old greats: Ernest Tubb, Vassar Clements, Doc Watson, Dolly Parton, Porter Wagoner. Elvis, of course, and the Beatles, and the Mamas and the Papas, even Dylan. Pictures of her with senators, governors, and presidents. A newspaper from London that reported them to be the number one musical act in all of England. Pictures of her throwing out the first pitch at the All-Star Game in 1956, when the Browns were at the top of both the country and pop charts simultaneously, the first time that had ever been done, and also the last. She was dating the Washington Senators' third baseman, who was playing in the game; they were a couple in the era before the proliferation of tabloids dedicated to chronicling such movements. He suggested that she throw out the first pitch, and that the Browns sing the national anthem, which they did.

A clock somewhere ticking, melting away, back then, but they had no idea.

She doesn't go into that back room often, but instead keeps it sealed off from the rest of the house — ready to display to a visitor, or perhaps an archivist, should one ever appear — but it spooks her and depresses her to go in there alone. Too many ghosts, and, strangely enough, too much hope, for she cannot look at a single one of those pictures —

her youthful glitter, her shimmer — without thinking, *I can still do that.*

None of the ghosts have had to face what she faces. They are all frozen in fame, still and forever reveling in it. Johnny Horton ("North to Alaska" and "The Battle of New Orleans"), whom she dated briefly, prior to meeting Tommy, gone by the age of forty.

Bill Black, Elvis's bass player, whom she also dated before meeting Tommy, dying of a brain tumor at thirty-nine. Johnny Cash, with whom she had a fling, during the waning horrors of her years with Tommy. They were all drawn straight to her, stars circling her, for a couple of years, maybe three. They came to her, heard something that spurred them on and that somehow etched new pathways in their creativities, and then they went on, while she remained.

Her sound altered them. Her sound remains, but they went away. It was more of her pioneering: often the only girl in an all-boys' club, Maxine, lonely and on the road, up for anything, not always making the best choices, all in the name of entertainment, hunger, fire.

It's lonely in that room. The historical footnotes, the photos and yellowed clippings, mean nothing. The only thing that ever mattered, and that still matters, was and is the applause.

The sealed-off back room is a Fort Knox of country music history, but it means less than nothing, is a kind of black hole that threatens to suck away even the last and faintest dying embers of her once bright vitality.

It confuses her, why going into the room depresses her so much. As if what is on the walls is not proof but a mockery, and an indictment of something — though of what, she cannot say. How can such a full life add up to nothing? How can such fullness yield emptiness?

How can such a feast increase, rather than sate, a hunger? Day by day, though still only dimly, the nature of it becomes more apparent to her. As if some incomplete accounting yet remains, some awful and immense cost commensurate with all that momentary bliss.

Far more often, rather than going in to look at her memorabilia, she goes into the front room and sits on her couch and watches old home movies of her and her family. She doesn't have cable or satellite, but has half a dozen old VCR tapes that she transferred from the silent sixteen-millimeter reels, gotten from the camera that Birdie bought for the Browns back when their career was first taking off and they were traveling to so many places — places that Floyd and Birdie had never seen, and never would.

For some reason the old movies don't discourage her the way the museum room does. The celluloid seems to possess a different power — as if in the flickering light and the grainy, jerky movements of the young people in those frames, time has not yet gotten the upper hand. There's no sound, but watching some of the footage of their early shows, and seeing their mouths move, she remembers what it was like, and imagines that she can still hear it. She watches the camera pan to the small audiences back then, hands clapping wildly, as if in fast motion, and imagines she can hear that, too.

Sequences of Elvis mugging for the camera, and of him running up behind Bonnie at a swimming pool, the summer light so brilliant, and pushing her into the pool with a giant splash. Maxine remembers the heat of the day, Bonnie's shrieks, the smell of chlorine. She remembers how time wasn't moving, back then.

Frames of Jim and Mary Reeves, the one time they all five went on an extended tour together, traveling out to the Pacific Northwest, a two-week journey, and the mountains and plains and dense rainforests as exotic to them as if they had traveled to Mongolia. Maxine did all the filming, and there are long stretches where she filmed the era's myriad construction projects — dams being built, gaping dry reservoirs not yet filled, and roadbeds excavated but with their foundations not yet poured — Maxine filming such things to show Floyd, who could never have imagined such industry. Though the footage is incredibly boring now, she watches it all and marvels at, and tries to recall, the enthusiasm she had back then for everything — even the sight of a bulldozer digging a ditch — and of how everything was new and unfamiliar.

There was not a trace of her depression, back then, and not a trace of weakness; and again the clock of the world was utterly frozen: for herself, surely, and yet also, she thinks, for everyone else, or at least everyone with whom they came in contact — even if only for a very short while. For two or three beats, maybe; for the amount of time it takes to draw a deep breath.

It *was* frozen, for a few moments, she is certain of this. The old movies remind her of this, they are her proof.

A JOURNEY

ELVIS WENT BACK down south and then over to Texas on a solo tour, and the Browns went on their Pacific Northwest tour with Jim and Mary. Ten years of Fabor, and ten years of touring, was beginning to take a toll on Jim and Mary. Had the Browns cared to see such a thing, they might have been able to peer into the short near future that awaited them, with the paths of nearly all mentors establishing as if through ancient negotiation the same trails down which their disciples must travel — but the Browns chose not to observe those diminishments, that underlying wobble, and instead, in the power and exhilaration of their youth, observed only the joy.

Sure, Jim was drinking a little more, and Mary seemed to be strung a little more tightly than even a year or two before, but there was still great fun to be had at every show, and in every mile traveled, in every breath taken in, and in every exhalation.

It was all so incredibly new — as if they had just been born. The air in the Colorado mountains was cooler and drier than they had known air could be, and they noticed that sounds traveled farther, and held together longer.

To save Fabor money, they camped out as they traveled, and built campfires to stay warm, and sang and played music far into the night, while Jim Ed and Jim drank from their flasks and watched the sparks cascade into the stars whenever they tossed wood onto the fire. Bonnie and Maxine weren't yet drinking much back then, but under those cold stars, and in the spirit of the party, they would have a warming sip now and again whenever Jim Ed or Jim passed the flask.

For a country music singer, Jim wasn't much of an outdoorsman, and the Browns sometimes teased him about this, calling him a rhinestone cowboy and telling him he would have to come visit them at their home someday, spend some time with them in the woods, before he could truly call himself country — but there on that trip, Jim began to learn a little about such things and was not displeased with a life he had previously viewed as uncouth.

The endless sky of Wyoming, and then, farther up into the mountains, the foreboding yet exhilarating forests of spruce and fir. The sulfurous exhalations of Yellowstone, the fantastic roiling belches of the mud pots, the hissing vent-hole aspirations of fumaroles. The impatient ninety-three-minute wait on the boardwalk for the spray of Old Faithful, with the brimstone taste of it in their lungs. Tourists rushing out afterward to reclaim their scattered laundry, having stuffed it down into the maw of the geyser some moments before the turbulent ejection.

Bears walking the roads and leaning up against their car with dagger-claws, nose-smearing against the glass, mugging for snacks. Jim trying to put some of Mary's lipstick on one bear, and the bear snarling and snapping at him, Jim pulling his hand back just in time, milliseconds away from the end of his guitar-picking.

Pelicans floating overhead, as ghostly white and slow moving as if in a dream, and seagulls drifting and squealing, no matter that they were still a thousand miles from any present-day ocean.

The tattered clouds of the Pacific Northwest, then — all the way to Puget Sound — where the slate and metallic sheen of the skies, bruise purple and storm green, was beautiful, but seemed to attach its leaden colors to Maxine's blood in a way that she found dispiriting. Too far from home, was all, perhaps, or maybe it just wasn't her place on earth.

In her home movies from that trip, she can see hints of what was to come, in those few frames that she inhabits, in the moments when Bonnie grabs the camera and turns it back on her. Not quite yet a worry or a fretfulness, but instead maybe just the beginnings of a kind of stillness or wariness: the dawning, perhaps, of an understanding of the nature if not the name of the thing — the blessing and the curse — that was in her. The realization that she probably wouldn't be able to slow it down or moderate it, even if she ever desired to. Which was just fine, more than fine, at the age of twenty-three. But not in control. Apace with it, but not in control of it.

Seeing those beautiful pewter skies in the Northwest and feeling the first tug or bump of depression: as surprising an emotion to her then as if a large ship far out at sea, floating serenely and confidently above a thousand feet of water and with no sign of a shore in any direction, was to suddenly bump hard against something just beneath the surface.

In the Pacific Northwest, she saw a killer whale. She was sitting by herself after their last show, out on a porch overlooking the water. She was lulled by the ghostly white shapes of the big sailboats in their moorings on the dark water, masts stark against the sky without their sails, the water lapping almost but not quite rhythmically against the dock. The male musicians were still inside the bar, drinking. Maxine kept turning and looking back in from the darkness at the yellow window squares, and at the mirthful, vibrant figures moving around within those frames. She wanted to join them but for some reason could not.

When the whale surfaced she saw only the back part of it, going back down, gleaming wet in the night. She thought at first that it was a sailboat turning slowly over. When she realized what it was, she ran inside to get the others — her sorrow or sadness jolted out of her, burned so clean and free, it was as if it would never return — but the whale did not reappear, and they teased her and accused her of being drunk.

Once they were turned away and headed back, Maxine quickly felt better, headed back downhill. The continent as vast as her dreams, and thrilling for that, but unsettling; it was as if the physical detachment from her home, one of those fractures that Fabor had counseled them about, had opened up, and everything she was, and everything she might be, was draining out.

They ran out of money in Idaho and Fabor wouldn't wire them any, so they had to wait tables and wash dishes in a truck stop, and play live shows in the parking lot each night, selling autographed black-and-white glossies of themselves afterward to raise enough money to get back home; but no matter, they were pointed in the right direction, and because of their youth, it was nothing but fun, only an adventure.

They were driving two cars, the Browns in one and Jim and Mary in another — they traded drivers and passengers — and Jim and Mary pulled a little homemade shell of a trailer that was stuffed with all their gear. Passing back through Colorado, they detoured to go see Pikes Peak, where, frustrated by how hard the trailer was to maneuver, Jim Reeves unhitched the trailer, took their luggage out, and gave the little trailer a shove with his boot, sent it catapulting over the edge of a thousand-foot cliff just for laughs.

At another point in the journey, still in Colorado, Jim and Mary's car ran out of gas in an autumn snowstorm in the middle of the night. Jim Ed hiked down off the mountain in his dress boots while the others stayed with the cars and struggled to build a wretched little fire with comic books and wet branches. They were on a back road, and no traffic passed by — they imagined they might remain stranded there on into the winter, and the next spring — but fortune favored them and Jim Ed found a cabin at the bottom of the mountain at daylight and got a ride back up to their cars with a can of precious gasoline. They continued on their way, back down toward the flatlands, back down toward warmth, back down toward home. Driving hard now, nonstop, with no more gigs scheduled, and the strange and intensely bittersweet pull of home aching in all of them.

They did not regret the tour, but each felt as if he or she had somehow gotten away with some great risk or gamble, in the adventure of their outing — had sought to pull away from the directive of where the larger world most wanted them to be and what it wanted them to be doing, and that although the freedom of that pulling away had been exhilarating, they were getting back home only just in time. What the consequences of not getting back home and reattaching might have been, they could not have said, but they knew instinctively that those consequences would not have been in their favor.

Almost as if each of them had been guilty, while on that grand trip, of spurning their various gifts, and were made uneasy by the strange thrill they felt in that betrayal, that willful destruction of the vague contract they each held. A contract that, unlike the one with Fabor, they had never signed, and never requested.

They drove day and night, heading south and west, down out of the mountains and across the broad plains and then back up into the hills and hollows. They took the good roads straight on toward Memphis, arriving south of there just before dusk. They stopped and looked down at the Mississippi and were reassured by the force and mass of it, as well as by the deceptive leisureliness of its pace. The muddy color of the river, as well, was calming—prior to their trip out west, that color was the only one they had ever known a river to be—and with the last of the sun glinting off the water it looked like a winding path of bronze, passing with strength through a seething velvet jungle, and they relaxed further, watching it and considering the things they had seen.

Jim offered everyone a drink from his flask. There was a hand-carved sign in the pull-out area where they were parked that told the story of the New Madrid Fault, over which they were sitting. Back in 1811, the fault—which underlay the Mississippi River from Cairo, Illinois, down through Memphis and Tupelo and Jackson and all the way down to New Orleans and into the sea—had cracked like an eggshell. The Mississippi had run backwards for days in what everyone, slaves and slave owners and freemen, believed with deepest conviction was the end time, with the bodies of men and animals riding those frothy, muddy waves, pitching and tossing amid the timbers and rootwads of forests and the rooftops of houses. Horses, some dead and swollen from hundreds of miles ago, others still saddled and swimming hard, as if riding to war, but with no riders. A terrible harvest from what used to be downstream but was now upstream.

The Browns and Jim and Mary sat on the back bumpers of their old cars and watched the river until the glint went away. Then they got in their cars and continued on, following the river south for a while before stopping to call Floyd and Birdie. They gave them an estimate of when they'd be in, and proceeded on, a tiny caravan, winding now on the familiar country roads and back roads of their youth, drawing ever closer to the feast.

And when they passed the old sawmill, which was shut down again, and pulled into their dark yard and saw the lights on in all the rooms, saw the figures of their mother and father and Norma inside, saw those figures come out of the light and into the darkness to greet them, they were received as if home from a war. They introduced Jim and Mary to their family, and celebrated with music and Birdie's cooking all night long.

A fire in the fireplace, the smell of pies baking, and a pot roast cooking in the oven. Sweet potatoes, carrots, potatoes, turnip greens: *home,* warm and yellow lit and safe and intimate. *Home,* never leave, never leave. Bonnie laughing the loudest, glowing, exuberant and radiant. A glance by her over at Maxine, who, though smiling, seemed almost at one point to be wearing a stage smile, seemed somehow to be curiously distracted. *Home,* never leave.

⟨ LITTLE JIMMY DICKENS

By 1956, there was no one bigger. They were as big as Elvis; Elvis was as big as the Browns. They had won every major award there was in country music, and the Browns had been at it just long enough that they were beginning to get comfortable with their good fortune. Ascent was all they had ever known; how could there ever be anything else?

Few if any mapmakers can mark the precise moment of highest fame or pleasure in any life, whether an ordinary one or extraordinary; and rarer still are the travelers' own abilities to do so. Maxine, with the alcoholic's force of denial — and no matter that she is in recovery — still believes her apogee has not been reached, that all which has come before has been but a false plateau. A more detailed observer, however, might suggest that the peak came very early, and quickly: on the first night they appeared on the Grand Ole Opry.

In typical Brown fashion, it was a night of their highest high, and yet one of the lows that would most gnaw at Maxine for the rest of her career.

They had been chosen to share the headlines that night with Little Jimmy Dickens, one of the original stars of the Grand Ole Opry. How they had adored him, had spent their childhoods crowded around the static of their one radio listening to him on Saturday nights, and counting the days and nights until the next week's performance.

Meeting Jimmy Dickens then, backstage, the first time they made it to the Opry. Approaching him with stars in their eyes — this little man, this icon — but being rebuffed by him even before they could shake his hand. Already, he had seen more change than he had bargained for in his life, and the high nasal whine that was his trademark must have seemed to him the antithesis of these three attractive young people, and their own sound, and their sudden fame.

He sneered at them, wouldn't shake their hands, and instead snarled the one most cutting greeting anyone could have designed — *"Y'all ain't country"* — then turned on his heel and walked off.

There was no one from whom such rebuke could have been more painful. They were too young, too heartbroken, too desperately professional to do anything but smile and pretend nothing had happened and move on to their next greeting. The curtains about to lift. The biggest night of their lives.

The curtains lifting, then, to the applause. Not a single face was distinguishable to them on the other side of that wall of light, but such radiant love emanated from that place. It was only two minutes and thirty seconds of love, to be sure, but it was love nonetheless, and something else, too — not just power and voice and control in a hard world, but some other beautiful thing that they could not quite reach or touch.

The sound pouring out of them and the audience roaring, rising to applaud their youth and originality. Giving them a welcome, an ovation, the likes of which Little Jimmy, in all his years of trailblazing, had never known.

Drinks backstage, afterward. Little Jimmy glowering, shunning them, leaving early. Able, in his fury, to see something that no one else yet could: that they were attempting to leave behind forever the place they had come from in a betrayal, a disowning, that was to him of biblical proportions. Harlots and blasphemers. He knew they were friends with Elvis, and though Elvis was not yet as huge as he would soon become, Little Jimmy knew all he needed to know about Elvis, too. Jimmy Dickens knew that once the Browns had crossed one line — leaving Poplar Creek behind, and leaving it so quickly, and making that strange sound — there were surely no other lines they would not also cross. The sound, once unleashed into the world, flowing downhill, spreading and pooling. Powerful, beautiful, treacherous, unmanageable. He didn't want anything to do with it, and he understood that it would destroy all that he was about.

⟳ DEER HUNT

JIM AND MARY CAME out to visit them that next November, after the northwestern tour, so that Jim and Jim Ed could go deer hunting. Jim had never held a gun before, and had been putting it off, but Jim Ed had been hounding him about it for years, and Jim saw it as a way not only to take a rest, but to reconnect with the Browns, whom Jim had not seen so much since Elvis had entered their lives, and to maybe even recapture some of the vitality that he remembered the Browns having when he had first met up with them.

Because Jim was family now, they brought him home to hang out and go hunting along the high bluffs of Poplar Creek, where the men sat in rickety stands up in the limbs of oak and hickory and ash trees and waited and watched for the deer that were the same color as the dried leaves. Jim Ed had hunted along the bluffs above Poplar Creek for all his life, as had Floyd, as had Floyd's father.

Jim Ed knew the places where the deer were likely to travel. It seemed mysterious, and from day to day, it was; but across the span of years, the movements of the deer compressed to a predictability that was surprising and yet reassuring. If you were willing to wait long enough, you would get a chance — as if the paths of the deer, over the long haul, were governed by decisions made by larger factors.

On their first hunt together, Jim Ed gave Jim his prize spot, the stand that overlooked the central corridor down which deer passed regularly. Jim had wanted to take his flask up on the stand with him — it was to be an afternoon hunt — but Jim Ed surprised him by saying that he didn't want to do that. Jim Ed had had uncles and cousins fall from their tree stands while drinking and be killed or injured. "Plus, it's just better without," Jim Ed said. "It's great. You'll see."

"You're talking like some kind of prohibitionist," Jim told the younger man. A pause, and then a tease that was not entirely a tease. "Are you forbidding me to take my medicine up there with me, especially on such a cool autumn afternoon?"

"Hurry — we're late."

Jim eyed his flask. The forest dark and strange before them. "How do you know we're late?" he asked.

"I can just feel it," Jim Ed said. "It's going to be a good day. Come on." Jim shrugged, left the flask on the table untouched, picked up his gun, and went out into the autumn light with the younger man, and felt immediately how right Jim Ed had been.

They walked side by side down the clay road that sloped into the bottomlands, the sky blue and cold above them, with the brayings of Canada geese overhead. They talked about little things at first but then transitioned smoothly into the larger things that lay beneath them. The road left the field and went down into the forest, past the places where Floyd and the crews had felled individual trees over the years — past giant stumps in varying stages of decay — and into the area that Floyd, like his father before him, had kept reserved for hunting. The trees were immense, the mast crop plentiful. The quality of light was different, and the soil, closer to the creek, was richer from the many floods. Sounds were muted; there was a greater stillness among the big trees.

That first time, Jim Ed directed Jim to climb up into his favorite blind, a platform nailed to the fork of an oak tree thirty feet above the ground. Dry leaves blanketed the earth, with only a few red and brown and gold leaves still clinging to the branches above. If anyone had looked up at the fork in the tree, they would have been able to see Jim sitting up there — but the deer never looked up, keeping their eyes alert only for threats down at eye level, and the blind was high enough up that any currents of human scent were carried farther away.

Jim, as sober as a judge, climbed up the crude plank ladder to the favorite tree and nestled in, pleased with the world and the time of day, and feeling like a boy again, a boy in a tree fort watching the horizon for pirates or dragons.

Jim Ed walked quietly along the ridge that led to the next tree stand, passing through shafts of copper light. He could sense he was a little late, that already the deer were moving, but he could tell also that everything would turn out all right: that things were just as they were meant to be. Some days were like that, and when they were, they resonated within him so deeply that it was as if he heard a voice speaking to him, assuring him of how things would turn out: that his wish, his desire, would be granted.

He found the tree he was searching for and, slinging his rifle over his shoulder, climbed carefully up the board ladder, each step a single slat nailed to the trunk. The steps had grown slick with moss since the last hunting season, and he had not had time to check any of the boards for rot or mildew. Even as he was ascending, one board pulled free in his hand, leaving a gap in his climb that made his reliance on the next board all the more critical. When he finally reached the security of the platform above, his heart was beating quickly, and he sat there, still and silent, for some time before it finally slowed.

He looked over and saw some hundred yards distant the hunched shape of Jim up in his tree, as motionless as a gargoyle.

Jim Ed looked farther out then and saw the buck long before Jim noticed it, even though it was coming straight at Jim. It was as large a buck as Jim Ed had ever seen. Its antlers were dark brown, burnished by polishing them against saplings, sharpening their tips for battle, though one of the tips was broken off from such battles. The buck's coat was already winter dark, and he was fat from eating acorns. His face was streaked with gray and latticed with scars, and yet he was still muscular. There was a white patch around each of his eyes, a perfect O of snow whiteness, giving him a look of permanent startlement.

The deer's neck was swollen thick with November rut, and when he stopped from time to time and looked around, searching for a doe to breed, his breath came in puffs of vapor cloud if he paused in the shadows, though when he was in the mild slants of sunlight, no such breath-clouds arose.

It was Jim's deer, coming straight at him, but Jim did not see it; to Jim Ed, it appeared that Jim might be asleep.

Now the deer paused again, as if it had been seeking a rendezvous with some mysterious stranger in this approximate place and at this approximate time, and, finding no such appointment — looking carefully everywhere — decided to abandon that interior directive, and turned and began drifting instead toward Jim Ed's tree stand; and still Jim gave no sign of seeing the great deer, or of even being awake.

The deer was close enough now that Jim Ed could hear the rustling of dry leaves as it strode through them, coming like a gift, and still Jim Ed waited and watched, from the corner of his eye, to see if his guest might stir and yet take this deer.

The deer was almost too close — only thirty yards out, so that any small movement by Jim Ed might be seen or sensed — and now the deer stopped again, as if dumbfounded that here, too, the appointment toward which he had been summoned had failed to materialize. The deer stood there waiting, and Jim Ed understood that the gift was his, not Jim's, and that, as he had come hunting in search of a deer, to scorn or reject such a gift now would be disrespectful.

Jim Ed lifted the rifle carefully and put the crosshairs of the scope just behind the deer's left shoulder. The deer was so close that it filled the scope. Jim Ed waited for a moment, and then squeezed the trigger as he had on so many deer before.

In the echo of the blast, the deer hunched its back and hopped as if bee-stung, then whirled and galloped off like a racehorse, its tight-tucked tail the only indication that it was injured.

Jim awoke with a shout and watched the deer sprint past, its wide tall antlers bobbing. To him, in his grogginess, it looked like a deer running through the woods with a chair tied upside down above his head. If he had been able to fire a shot at the sprinting-away deer, he would have, but he was too disoriented; he could only watch the strange dream, then the half-dream, and then the deer was gone.

Figuring that the hunt was over — dusk was but an hour or so away, and he could not imagine any more deer coming through after the uproar of the shot — Jim climbed down from his ladder and began shuffling through the leaves toward Jim Ed's tree stand. Jim Ed frowned — it was his habit after shooting a deer to sit quietly for half an hour, so that the wounded deer — confused and not knowing exactly where the shot had come from — would, if unpursued, run only a very short distance and then lie down to bleed out and die. Left untended, a hole in the heart would not heal itself, and the deer would die quietly, sinking back down toward the same soil that had briefly animated it.

Even now, Jim Ed heard a faint crashing in the distance, and knew that his deer had already bedded down and was looking back, watching to see if the hunter might be stirring. And upon seeing Jim sauntering through the forest, the deer had leapt back up and plunged down into the ravine.

They set off to look for the deer. Jim Ed searched a long time for the first drop of blood and the first sprinklings of hair.

It was slow going, reading the deer's last history drop by drop, and grew harder still once they entered the ravine. They soon ran out of light, but Jim Ed had brought a flashlight, and they continued on. Jim Ed could not help but think that if Jim had stayed in his tree stand they would already have the deer cleaned and hauled out and would be back home, maybe nursing one of Jim's beloved whiskeys, but he was too polite to let Jim know of his mistake. He wanted to build an enthusiasm for the hunt in Jim, and so he pushed through the brush without comment or criticism, intent instead only on finding the tiny drops that would lead them to their trophy.

In older times Jim Ed had carried a lantern, the dull but democratic glow of which was ideal for casting an equal light that served well the search for the anomalous spatterings, the red drops drying to brown and splintering already into little fissures and fractures, like mud cracks in a dried-out pond — each speck of blood on each random leaf but a single drop, and nothing that seemed capable of killing the deer — but he had no lantern this evening, only the flashlight with its narrow beam, and with so much darkness on either side of that beam. It was slower hunting, and they walked carefully. It was always Jim Ed who noticed the next drop, and the next. Jim was just out for a walk.

When they finally came to the end of the blood trail, the giant deer was piled up like an accordion at the very bottom of the ravine, and somehow not looking like quite the same animal. Huge, and power-ful, but not quite as vital.

Jim Ed cleaned the deer, fastidious as ever — when he was done, he washed his hands in the trickling creek beside which the deer had died — and then the two men took turns pulling the heavy animal up the long hill. Jim congratulated Jim Ed on the size of the animal, and how strange it was that the deer had almost walked right up to Jim Ed.

"I've always been lucky that way," Jim Ed said, panting. He knew of no harder work in the world than dragging a big deer uphill.

Eventually they reached the clay road and left the deer there — its antlers seeming even larger in the scan of the flashlight than they had in the daylight — and they walked to Floyd and Birdie's house in high spirits. Back at the house, everyone was excited to hear that Jim Ed had shot a big deer, and they all climbed into Floyd's truck to go see. A Saturday-night outing, an event of great festivity.

All the time in the world was theirs, suddenly; the world slowed to a creep, in hunting season. Timelessness — after having been gone all the preceding year — returned.

Hanging the deer from the ancient pole between the two oaks, be-neath which they had always cleaned their deer. Butchering the deer the next day in the autumn sunlight, perfect temperature, cool enough to keep insects away, but with the workers able to feel the warmth of leisurely, attentive work to a task. It would be hard to call it work, it was just a life.

Bonnie and Maxine played guitars on the porch and sang, as did Norma, still just a child. The girls baked pies with Birdie, put them on the windowsill to cool. It could easily be said these were the happi-est times of their lives. That week, Jim Ed and Jim did not stop with hunting deer but went after ducks, too, walking along the banks and bluffs of Poplar Creek, jumping the flamboyantly colored little wood ducks, which were the best-eating duck — the birds' breasts swollen from a diet of acorns — and later in the day walking back home with a burlap bag of the iridescent birds, each as fantastically colored as a parrot.

They would lay the birds out on the porch for everyone to admire, and then they would all pluck the ducks—the beautiful, brilliant feathers swirling, the miracle disassembling—and when they had the birds all cleaned, they would cook them that night on a grill outside, roasting them slowly over hickory coals, with an onion slice and strip of bacon laid over them.

Afterward, they would play canasta or hearts or bridge, and then, further into the night, they might or might not play their guitars; it did not matter—the days and nights were unending, and they did only as they wanted. They still talked about fame, a little bit, but mostly in those times between tours they simply hung out at home and prospered, and remembered that there was so much more to life than work. That almost everything—including their own brief popularity—was vastly overrated. There on Poplar Creek, in the midst of their family, they could not say why such a realization, a remembrance, brought them such happiness, only that it did.

Perhaps that was their second chance, and Bonnie and Jim Ed eventually took it. Everyone gets a second chance, but perhaps Maxine never saw hers.

Jim and Mary went home then, back to Nashville. All were invigorated by the return of sweetness—the recalibration of their lives—and each felt rejuvenated by the time spent with old friends: the Browns by their long visit with their mentors, one of their initial touchstones in the business, and Jim and Mary by the elemental isolation of the Browns. There was no name for it, but there was no denying that whatever they had was something that could be tapped into, something that rubbed off on a person, and helped.

But then they left, went back to work, and back out on the road: partly as if pushed once again by some larger destiny, and yet, were they not already also inhabiting an existing destiny?

As if two or maybe three destinies exist for all travelers, a twisted helix, with one path shining more at different times in the traveler's life—better illuminated and more attractive to the traveler, though not always the smoothest or most seamless path; and from those two or three different destinies, over the course of a traveler's life, a sound is created, if not always a harmony, which, while not audible to the travelers themselves, might possibly be heard by others who follow close enough behind them.

The harmony falling away, after that, the sound waves dissolving back into nothing, as if they had never been.

BOAT RIDE ON POPLAR CREEK

IT WAS AN OLD metal flatbottom boat that Jim Ed and Floyd had used for duck hunting and for checking trotlines. Elvis knew nothing about paddling, or rivers, or nature, but plenty, already, about romance. He volunteered to take Bonnie on a picnic. Despite his touring schedule, he was still finding ways to get back to Poplar Creek, even if for but a day or two. He was drawn primarily to Bonnie, but he received sustenance from all of them. They never quite knew when he would appear, or exactly when he would have to go away.

It was Maxine's belief, whenever she thought about it, which wasn't often — by that time she was pretty much all business, all ambition — that Elvis was a little frightened of her. And she could understand that. There were times when even she was a little frightened of herself. A temper — Floyd's temper — was emerging in her, whereas Bonnie had been gifted with Birdie's sweet temperament, and only Birdie's; there had been no twining of the two, no crossing over.

Maxine and Elvis were friends, nothing more. She was older, and as fierce about her music as he was. They were both going places. They weren't competitors — there was too much of a strange allegiance between them for that — and in those years, they moved in smooth and seamless parallel, with no electricity between Maxine and Elvis, only concerted striving from both of them.

When Maxine thought about it, it made sense. She was almost all work, while Bonnie was more play. Certainly, Maxine had plenty of suitors; there were many who didn't mind her drive. But Elvis didn't need anything she had; when he looked in her eyes, he could very well have been looking in the mirror.

Birdie packed Bonnie and Elvis a lunch that first time they went down the river. Jim Ed and Elvis drove Floyd's old logging truck several miles downstream, to leave at the take-out at Taylor Branch, then came back up to the house in Jim Ed's truck, so that Elvis and Bonnie would have a ride waiting for them at the end of their journey.

There was enough food to last them three or four days, and a picnic blanket, a straw hamper, and canning jars of lemonade. It was
springtime, and Bonnie rode in the bow and paddled a little while
Elvis stroked clumsily in the stern, banging the paddle against the
gunwales, pinching his fingers and getting annoyed with the boat
when it swirled and drifted sideways, not going where he wanted it
to — bouncing slowly off the sides of logs along the shore — until he
figured it out and found the creek's invisible but powerful centerline.

They rounded the bend, the river murmuring, the birdsong riot-
ous, even in midday.

Elvis noted the faint sheen on Bonnie's neck, the top button of her
shirt unfastened in the warmth. Elvis was excited, hopeful, and, for
a little while, not thinking about music or fame, but only the joy of
life — though they did have their guitars packed in burlap bags, to pick
a little when they stopped for lunch.

On the river, it was easier for him to open up. The current seemed
to pull from him all tensions and worries, all fears and doubts. On the
river, it seemed he could say things he wasn't even sure he believed,
though why else would he have been opening up, confessing them?

Telling her he never felt like he belonged to the world. How he
never felt connected or attached. How he always felt as if he were falling, drifting. Except when he was up onstage and holding the guitar.
That was the only time he felt in control, he said, the only time he
felt like the world stopped long enough to keep from shoving him
through it.

Bonnie listened. There were times when she wondered why Elvis
was drawn to her instead of Maxine. She pointed out a patch of black-
berries on the bank, and the two of them maneuvered the boat over to
shore.

They tied the boat off and took one of the now empty jars into the
blackberry patch. Once off the river, Elvis tried to hedge his earlier
outpouring, tried to disown it. He asked her if she had any worries,
any fears of her own, and he laughed at her when she thought about it
and then said no, and he felt better, laughed again.

Train tracks ran parallel to the creek, and Bonnie and Elvis followed the berry patch out to that slash of light through the woods.

It was even hotter there in the berries than it was on the creek. They walked along the tracks for a while, the jar quickly full and the two of them dropping the berries into his old shirt, which he had taken off to use for the berry gathering, his skin as pale as the cream Birdie would ladle over the berries later that evening.

The scent of creosote in the sunlight, and the heat and brilliance reflecting off the steel rails. They moved down the tracks steadily, heads down, intent, neither of them like anyone who would change the world, but like laborers. Getting scratches on their hands reaching for the biggest, juiciest berries. Laughing, racing to get to the biggest and best berries ahead of each other, whenever they saw them.

Wait, anyone who saw them might have said — an observer in the future, gifted, or cursed, with the ability to look back. *You don't have to leave yet. You don't have to leave at all.*

THE RESTAURANT

IT'S HARD FOR Bonnie to get away now, particularly in the spring-time, when her garden is in full roar. She can't drive anymore—something is wrong with her inner ear so that she gets unpredictable spells of vertigo and has to lie down immediately—but she tries to get over to West Memphis to see Maxine once every month or two. Brownie has to drive her, and his hearing is shot, worse even than Maxine's, and he's still recovering from his open heart surgery of less than six months ago—but what else is there but family? It's all Bonnie knows how to do—to stay attached, connected, even if with the faintest tendrils of her visits, with the two of them, Bonnie and loyal Brownie, braving the elements to go see Maxine.

Usually, once Bonnie arrives, the three of them go to a catfish parlor out in the country: Maxine's big outing. Brownie, a physician, is retired, but is still able to dispense medication, and he brings Maxine whatever pills or shots she needs.

They dress like royalty for the occasion; they bustle in Maxine's downstairs bathroom, applying makeup, adjusting their jewelry just so, and plucking silver hairs from each other's black sweaters. It's springtime, but sometimes the air conditioner at the catfish house runs cold. In their career, they hardly ever knew elegance. Once a year, at the Grammys. The two years in a row they beat Elvis, then the two years they finished second. The year they lost narrowly to the Beatles. The time they won in country one year, then rock the next. Everyone's gone now, dust, it no longer matters to anyone but them, and among the three of them, really, it only matters to Maxine.

They enter the restaurant slowly, regally, looking around as if expecting to be recognized—if not by fans, then at least by the waiters and waitresses remembering them from their last visit a couple of months ago—but there is no such recognition, only the busy workaday comings and goings of food tray-bussing. A young woman at the front asks if they're here to see someone, and when they say no, she leads them to one of the long picnic tables at which the diners eat in family-style seating. She places them at the far end, in a corner, but that's all right: it allows Maxine to look out at all that is going on.

Bonnie and Brownie talk a little about their garden, but Maxine doesn't ask any questions about it and soon enough succeeds in moving the conversation back to music, asking Bonnie and Brownie if they've heard anything new, anything good. Neither of them has; their hearing, they say, gets worse by the hour.

"I haven't either," Maxine confides, and then sniffs. "The entertainers of today dress like paupers and streetwalkers," she says. "I don't like that." The first time they went on *The Ed Sullivan Show,* the producers had to sew a piece of cloth over Bonnie's ample figure just before the Browns went onstage, to obscure even the hint of cleavage.

The men these days are no better, Maxine reports. The country rock star with frayed jeans, beard stubble, gold earrings. What would Little Jimmy say?

"We broke the trail for them," she says, a spike of the old bitterness rising quickly. "We made it where they could succeed, and now it's like they don't respect any of that."

Bonnie and Brownie glance at each other. There's the good Maxine, calmer and more mature, just taking life one day at a time — recovering from fame — and then there's the old Maxine, with her hard and hungry heart, never sated.

Bonnie leans forward, eyes alight — suddenly she looks twenty-five years younger — and she attempts to temper Maxine's sulk, as Birdie once and always sought to address Floyd's.

"I like the old-time lyrics better," Bonnie says. "Even the silly ones. Willie Nelson's 'Stay a Little Longer'!" she exclaims, and begins to parse the song out, speaking carefully to emphasize the words' nonsensicalness, but the habit of song pulls her in, and she begins to sing.

The music of the song spills from her with silver beauty — the description of a narrator sitting in the window above, the saga of the slop bucket tumbling down, and then the seamless shift to the joy and whimsy of a mule and a grasshopper eating ice cream, the mule getting sick, and laying him on the green. She sings it as she always sang every song, as if it had always existed for her voice and hers only.

People at surrounding picnic tables look up from their plates, slightly startled by the clear belling of her voice. Fragments of fried fish dot the plastic checkered tablecloths around them. Although the diners have all been issued silverware, their fingers are shiny from the fish as well as the hush puppies. They look over at the two elegantly dressed old women and the mild old gentleman sitting with them, who is smiling as if he can still hear perfectly his wife's singing, and they stop eating for a moment, confused — all movement and motion in the restaurant pauses, then ceases, as Bonnie's voice does not so much fall over and envelop all others but instead cuts through all other sound, and best of all, in that molten, illuminated way, flows into the spaces between all other sound.

They came to dine on catfish, to eat all they can on a Friday evening, but for ten or fifteen seconds, they are treated to something else, something the likes of which they've never heard before, and they stop what they are doing, bathed by the voice, which is still clear and beautiful after all these years, and the diners are mesmerized, spellbound, bewitched.

Bonnie finishes her little lilt — "A mule and a *grasshopper?* What can that *possibly* mean?" — and in the silence that follows, the sated, exquisite stillness of an audience spellbound, Maxine and Bonnie both are reminded of the power of their gift. And though Maxine still carries more regret than is healthy, she too feels healed, briefly, by the beauty of Bonnie's little song. Strangely, Maxine is not gripped by the lesser, baser response of envy, but is temporarily elevated.

It was hard for Maxine not to jump in when Bonnie started singing spontaneously. She would have, in the old days, without a moment's hesitation. But not now. Her pride's too fierce, her clamant insistence on perfection. She's unwilling, even in so ignoble a venue as a catfish parlor, to step into the slipstream of Bonnie's sudden grace without being fully ready, fully warmed up.

The hunger was there, though. That night, she remembers that they've made a pact with one another: that if they ever do perform again as a trio, they will quit the first time they fail to get a standing ovation.

Bonnie does not get one that night in the restaurant — there isn't even any applause, but instead, just that confused kind of brief attention from the other diners, recognizing they're hearing something different, and something special, but not knowing what it is — but this doesn't really count, for it's not an official performance, or even a full song; and most important, it's not the trio. It was just Bonnie making a bewitching little sound.

The diners resume their dining. The nice waitress comes back over with her pitcher of iced tea and tells Bonnie that that was real pretty and asks if she used to be a singer.

On their way out of the restaurant, Bonnie and Brownie walk down the wooden steps, gripping the handrail but walking steadily, with the gift of their youth, only five years younger than Maxine on the calendar, but much healthier.

Maxine can't negotiate the steps. She pauses at the top of them and then makes a game try, but she simply can't see the ground on which to place her feet; it's too dark, and she's too weak. She grips the handrail with both hands, shudders a bit, trying to will not just the necessary strength into existence but all the other things she needs but can no longer have — better eyesight, better hips, better balance. But she cannot control those things any longer, and no blazing lights come on to illuminate her path, her brave attempt; instead, she turns and calls back to one of the waitresses, asking if she can get help down the handicapped ramp, while her sister and brother-in-law proceed, seemingly unfazed and unfettered by time.

The handicapped ramp, while descending more gradually, winds away from the restaurant and parking lot at first; eventually it switches back toward Bonnie and Brownie, and their parked car — but for the time being Maxine and the waitress are heading off into the darkness, toward a grove of woods, shady oak trees with long trellises of Spanish moss hanging down.

The handicapped ramp is more poorly lit than the regular stairs; only three lamps punctuate its entire length, so that they have to move through the darkness from one pool of light to the next, as if swimming. It's terrifying to Maxine, with her night blindness — limping toward the dark forest with her newly mended hip, the fractured seam of it throbbing and threatening to snap again, every step a miracle — but worth it, maybe, for that night out on the town, and, best of all, for the waitress's touch, her hand on Maxine's arm for a little while. *Should I have joined in with Bonnie,* Maxine wonders, *when she sang her little ditty? No, absolutely not; it's imperative to have absolute control over one's voice* — and yet, how many more chances are there?

She grips the waitress's arm with both hands. She holds her chin up as they ease down the ramp, walking away from everyone, walking straight toward the dark woods. Only the tremors — as powerful as electrical currents, and with her quivering like an Olympic gymnast — belie the fear that is raging within her as she proceeds regally down the ramp with the waitress, into the darkness, chatting quietly all the while.

Bonnie and Brownie take her back to her dark home, the lone porch light burning. Bonnie and Brownie are staying at the nearby Motel 6. It's a late night for all of them, and Bonnie and Brownie want to be up and traveling early in the morning, trying to make it back to Dardanelle and then north in time for that day's watering. Worried that already the plants will be parched.

They embrace, tell her to call if she needs anything, then go back down the walk slowly to their car.

JIM REEVES'S FREEDOM

JIM AND MARY JUST couldn't do it anymore. Jim had been ridden hard and put up wet too many times, he told them. To get out of his personal services contract with Fabor, he had to give up full interest in all his previous hits — eleven years' worth, including a dozen number ones, along with $10,000 cash — but he was free, by God, and got to start over. He didn't have as much bounce in his step as he used to, he said, but there was enough to keep going.

"I feel like I got out just in time," he said. "Maybe I stayed a little too long, but I think I got out in time." Ever the gentleman, ever their friend, he offered to loan them the money, if they wanted to try to cut a similar deal.

"No," Jim Ed said, shaking his head, "we couldn't. That's really nice, but we couldn't. I can't borrow that much from you."

Maxine's eyes went dark, thinking of Fabor. "Do you have that much?"

Jim laughed. "No," he said, "I'd have to borrow it myself to loan it to you. But at least, by God, I wouldn't be borrowing it from Fabor."

"No, pal," Jim Ed said again, gently. "But thank you. It's sure been a good ride."

"It sure has."

Another drink, and another. The Browns thought that indeed he did look free — liberated — but not so fresh. As if there was not so much left to liberate.

Floyd and Birdie continued to marvel at — to revel in — their children's ability to make a living doing what everyone in their family had always done, playing music and singing — and marveled too at the celebrity. Only Norma remained behind now, still in school, but in some ways it was almost as if the others were still at home, for at almost any hour of the day or night, they could turn on their radio — a gift from their children — and, if they listened long enough, one of the Browns' songs would always come on. It was almost like it had been when they were still living at home.

To Floyd, in such moments, lying on his back beneath the maw of a tractor, or mucking out the mules' stalls, it was almost as if they were still right there, and occasionally he would stop in his labors and just listen; and though they were his children and it was a sound he had known all his life, even he, with his familiarity with their music, and his gruff demons, would in those moments know a balm. He would lie there looking up at the blue sky through the underside of the old engine, or would lean on his shovel and just listen, with a strange and wonderful mix of emotions; the old fevers draining away as if never to return, and pride swelling in him, and the core thing, the thing he didn't even think about much: love.

The radio was scratchy but the sound was pure. Sometimes he liked to pretend that they were just around the corner of the house, practicing. If Birdie was nearby — if she was not farther off, down in the garden — he would call to her, sometimes identifying for her which song was playing, other times just shouting that they were on; and in those early years, she would stop what she was doing and hurry up the hill to hear the miracle of it. Committing the ancient error of wanting things, good things, to stay only just the way they were. Wanting to stop time in its tracks, even then, with their lives pretty much behind them by that point; loving the scroll of days, now that their children knew comforts that Birdie and Floyd had never known.

When times were good like that, and Floyd was in his cups but not yet despondent or bitter or frightened, he had a saying, a little joke, that indicated how pleased he was with such rare moments of calm and cheer and fearlessness. He knew such confidence was foolish, which was why it amused him, on the occasions he felt it.

"We might get out of this alive after all," he would say, grinning, enormously pleased with life, and the moment. Laughing at himself, mostly, knowing how quickly that moment of optimism was fading even as he briefly inhabited it.

✤ ✤ ✤

Maxine has so much time to think now. She tries not to live with regret, but if you're hungry for something and you don't ever get it, then how else can you live? It makes no sense to her; it seems dishonest to pretend there's no longing. Some people are just lucky enough for it to finally fade away. She was lucky in other ways, but never that way.

When they first got famous, but before Elvis and the Beatles found them — back when they were just a little famous, even though it seemed like a lot — her parents had diverged in their opinions of the fame, as they did on so many other issues.

Floyd, for all his criticism and distrust of Maxine, was finally proud — or so it seemed — and urged them only to push on harder, to take every venue offered to them; to make hay while the sun briefly shone. It was Birdie who in her quiet way first suggested moderation or caution.

When Birdie told her how she sure enjoyed having her children around the house now and again, Maxine had seen only a clinging old woman more interested in her own needs than in the opportunities that lay before her children.

It had surprised Maxine a little, for never before had she known Birdie to be that way — but Maxine had paid it little mind and pushed on, hurried on, saying yes to everything. There had been no balance, no tempering. What was it Birdie had said? *I hope you'll remember to leave room in your schedule for how things used to be.* Maxine had bristled at the intimation that there might be anything in her life that wasn't good, and had been further exasperated by Birdie's ignorance as to what her life was like. Irked by Birdie's intuition, and her simple ways. Maxine had grown past all that, had put away the childish things of her youth, and was irritated that Birdie wasn't necessarily overjoyed by and utterly approving of the new Maxine, the famous Maxine.

And if Birdie had explained it further — that risking the cutting off of Maxine's foundation entirely might eventually render Maxine's gift lifeless — would Maxine have listened? In all honesty, almost surely not. And in the meantime, there was Floyd with his unfettered enthusiasms countering Birdie's temperance. What did Birdie know about fame, anyway?

It was nobody's fault but her own, Maxine tells herself, that she is where she is now. Certainly, she's too far down the road to turn back.

What if we hadn't signed with Fabor? What if we had managed to buy back our freedom sooner? Things moved too fast, back then. And anyway, what did Jim Reeves really do with his freedom? By the time he got it back, it was too late—the good was already past. He felt better, was all. The tension of being owned by a cruel person was gone, but his freedom had come so late in the game that, in Maxine's view, at least, it might as well have not come at all.

FABOR RETURNS

FABOR CALLED FOR them to come to California under the guise of needing to record some new songs, but the real reason was that he was in lust for Bonnie. It was the first time they would travel without the protective custody of Jim and Mary, and because Fabor owned the Browns, they went to him.

He told them they could stay in his mansion, and his interest was clear from the moment he picked them up at the train station, when he saw Bonnie get off the train, accompanied by Maxine and Jim Ed, who though older were no match for Fabor, so far from home, and so gripped by his power, and with the obstacle of him between where they were and where they were going.

Fabor started in on his play for Bonnie that afternoon, in the recording studio, having successfully isolated her for a solo while placing Maxine and Jim Ed on the other side of the glass. They watched in disbelief as Fabor circled the crooning Bonnie, placing his hands on her hips and then around her waist as she fidgeted and twisted and sidestepped — still singing, still recording — and finally, with tears streaming down her face, wrenching free from his grope, the song catching in her throat only a little. Her voice so powerful that even with that little catch, it was a good recording, and the cries of protest from Jim Ed and Maxine, and the thumping of their hands and fists against the window, were as muted to the recording as would have been the movements of insects under a glass jar.

By the time Maxine and Jim Ed spilled out of the control room and hurried down the hall and into the recording room, the song was done, and Fabor, with the disease to which he was hostage, had been rejected by Bonnie yet again — she had had to physically shove him away — but was still pursuing her.

"I'm just wanting to be friendly," he was saying. "I'm just wanting to help you become a better singer."

Bonnie was shaken — she had been pursued before, but never with either such insistence or madness — and the Browns retired to their rooms, unnerved by their host's way of doing business.

"I don't care if he is the boss," Maxine told Jim Ed. "If he tries to touch her again, you knock the hell out of him."

"Don't think I won't," Jim Ed said, but Bonnie put her hand on his and said it was okay, she could handle it.

They thought they might catch a break at dinner, served there in the mansion, where Fabor's wife would be joining them, but they were wrong. Fabor, shameless as a goat, continued to pressure Bonnie, discussing all the different forms of sex, and which ones were his favorite, and, again, his graphic desires for Bonnie, while his wife smiled and nodded.

The Browns ended up leaving the table. Jim Ed was confused, Maxine was furious, and Bonnie was in tears. They went back to Maxine and Jim Ed's room, despairing at this circus, or prison, that they had gotten themselves into.

"We should probably leave," Maxine said, and Bonnie, pale, didn't disagree. "Our songs are all recorded; he got everything he needed from us. We can just camp out at the train station. At least we'll be away from him."

Jim Ed hesitated. "I think we can protect her tonight," he said. "I know we can. Let's just stay the night, then leave in the morning before breakfast. I don't think he'll bother us again tonight."

Maxine disagreed. "He can't help himself," she said. "He's an asshole and a prick, but beyond that, he can't help himself. He'll be back."

"I'll be okay," Bonnie said. "Our rooms are right next to each other. I'll lock the door. We'll be okay. We can leave in the morning, before he even wakes up."

No one could fool Maxine in such matters. She had an alcoholic's innate understanding of the nature and possibilities of deceit as well as desire. She told Bonnie good night, walked her to her room, and made sure she locked her door, then lay there in bed, listening and waiting for what she knew would be coming.

It only took a couple of hours. When she heard the click and rattle of the key, she jumped out of bed and ran down the hallway to Bonnie's room, where she found Fabor, clad only in a multicolored floral-pattern silk bathrobe, advancing on Bonnie, who was standing up in her bed and shrieking.

Jim Ed came rushing down the hall behind Maxine, and they shoved Fabor out of the room. Jim Ed took a swing at him and knocked him down. Fabor got up and slunk down the hall.

Maxine stuffed Bonnie's clothes and belongings into her suitcase, she and Jim Ed stormed back to their room and packed, and then they went out into the night, off the grounds and into the darkness, hauling their suitcases. They would walk the eight miles to the train station. Fabor reappeared on the lawn, in his ridiculous bathrobe, and followed them a short distance, shouting, "I still own you!"

Maxine and Bonnie cried the whole way. They stopped only to switch arms in the lugging of their suitcases — it was a humid night, and they were sweltering — and they reached the train station in the last wedge of darkness before daylight. They slumped on the station benches, their heads on one another's shoulders, and slept for an hour or so, with the calls of the dawn birds entering their sleep. Maxine twitched, rousing herself every so many minutes to make sure Fabor had not followed them, before they were all three awakened by the nearing of the train.

By eight thirty they were boarded and looking out at the golden morning, pulling away from the station and California, and once more headed home, being given another chance to get back on track and to make their stand together in the only place that really mattered, and the one place where they were always at their absolute strongest. Forged with the lows as important as the highs, and the world making them into something that they had not necessarily asked for. The world, not Fabor, owning them in that regard.

Home to Floyd and Birdie, who would always adore them. Home to Poplar Creek, and rich for having a place to return to, whether free or captive, or somewhere in between.

JIM ED GETS A JOB

JIM ED WAS ALWAYS the workhorse. It was the way he best fit the world, and there was a grace in that. It was he to whom Maxine and Bonnie turned when the Browns sought their own freedom. After the incident in California, there could be no turning back: better to quit singing than to continue as hostages to Fabor.

Jim Ed put down his guitar and went back to work in the mill. It was risky business, and all the more so for his having been away for a couple of years. During that time he had gotten a little soft, not so much physically, but mentally. The economy was starting to warm up, the country was hungry for lumber again, and Floyd had started the mill back up, had knocked the flakes of rust off the blades and oiled the machinery and cleared out the clamor of brush that swarmed in over the machines whenever the mill paused.

Town and the woods, back and forth; Floyd and Birdie boarded up the Trio Club for a while and retreated to the place they had come from, the place that had kept them alive, though sometimes at such high cost.

Jim Ed figured that if he worked double shifts, he could get close to the debt in about six months, and could maybe borrow the rest from Floyd. Birdie was glad to have her children back home.

All Jim Ed had to do was take care of his hands. He asked Floyd to keep him away from the planer as much as possible, and to instead assign him the harder tasks, such as sorting and stacking the newly sawn lumber. It was backbreaking labor, but all he had to do was be mindful of splinters and of falling stacks. In a way, the work was a kind of freedom in itself, allowing Jim Ed the ability to lose himself in the repetitive symmetry, and in the brief waiting for each next plank, and in the exhaustion, the limber ache of being utterly spent at the end of the day.

Like his father, he loved the roar of the mill, the shrill, exciting clamor of the alchemy by which twisted trees were made into straight

Nashville Chrome

and shining lumber. He loved the green scent of the trees, and the sharper scent once it was planed to lumber, and the bright whiteness of it that was particularly dazzling within the first few moments of being planed — before the first fading oxidation — and he loved most of all being back home, with his full family.

Like all the workers, Jim Ed avoided even a single beer at lunch. He listened, just as he had when he was a child, for the sharpener's midday call to find the ringing, tempered harmony. If Bonnie and Maxine were around — and usually they were — they would walk down to the mill to help him listen. It was a game for them now, to see which of them could hear it first, and yet, still, they took it seriously, and always, each was quieted almost to the point of hypnosis when he or she heard it — as a Border collie or other herding dog might feel when, even if ever so briefly, perfect order was established within a herd.

Bonnie and Maxine would bring their own guitars and Jim Ed's down to the clearing. They would eat lunch with Floyd and Jim Ed and the rest of the workers, and when they had finished, they would play and sing quietly there in the shade while the rest of the workers listened and finished their lunches.

It went like that day after day, all through the summer and into the fall.

They were already free, and just didn't know it.

The mill's operation was ragged in the first weeks after being restarted. Flecks of rust fell from every cog and gear and even from the blades themselves in those first days, so that little plumes and clouds of shimmering orange-gold dust attended the whine and shriek and roar of the mill. An asymmetric ringing in Jim Ed's ears, the resumption of tinnitus, those first few weeks, until his brain learned how to block out the roar and the echo of the roar that followed him in his head even after the mill had shut down at five every day. Floyd enjoying his second chance.

A one-legged man, still out in the woods, still felling trees! Everywhere in the Browns' lives there continued to be this surface symmetry, surface functionality, girded below by the muscular knot of asymmetry, the tense and conflicting roil of things being always just a step off-balance, and in need of correcting.

After work Jim Ed would go fishing with the other men from the mill; other evenings he would go to a campfire with them out in the woods, in a clearing of their own making, and would drink and tell stories. Still other evenings he went straight home, eager for dinner and to see his family, and after eating went out on the porch with all of them and played and sang. His hands were still intact, his voice still miraculous. Of the three of them, he was the most malleable, able to adapt to any sound and imitate any voice, even while slowly developing his own — but also, in a remarkable way, he was the foundation for the three of them.

There were fireflies in the meadow. No one was rich and it couldn't even be said that everyone was fully healthy — Floyd's ghost leg bothered him, particularly in the evenings, and Birdie's heart was beginning to beat irregularly — but it was all still good, all still a dream. It was as if they had not quite yet been called out onto the stage where they would leave behind the place that had given them their gift in the first place. They had been to the Opry but had come back.

Out in the fields, between their porch and the woods, and at the edges of their vision, the sparks drifted, rose and fell, blinking on and off. As soon as they got free they were going to Nashville on their own, they had decided.

Jim Ed had had some close calls, had gotten some nicks on his hands here and there — but now he was two-thirds of the way through the debt. He only had to run the planer occasionally. For his part, Floyd was enjoying having his son working with him but was starting already to get worn down by the labor and was beginning to get that itchy, cautious feeling that something not all good was about to happen; and despite the better income, Floyd was missing the restaurant business, with the daily surprise, or potential surprise, of almost anyone coming through the door, at any time. Wherever he was, he hungered for elsewhere.

At the mill, the camaraderie with the same group of men, their duties and gestures and habits so familiar to one another, was a comfort, as was the pleasure of the physical exhaustion at the end of each day and the tangible expression of product, of material rendered or stacked — the scent and touch of the newly cut boards, and the roar of a saw ripping them, and the trembling in his chest, the whole mill shaking as the planer buzzed — but the older he got, the more he liked the restaurant, and liked particularly the chance it gave for him to show off his children, there on top of the hill, with the faux neon sign blinking.

He was drinking too much again. It was what he did when he was near the edge of great failure, but also what he did when he was far less frequently at the edge of success and peace. That old part of him, that ancient part, that could not look at a forest without wanting to burn it down, if only for the excitement. Stepping in closer to such destruction, as if trying to feel a warmth he could not otherwise attain.

As Floyd grew older he was less inclined to put more money into the mill. He kept thinking about the restaurant. He didn't replace his equipment as often as he used to, and used the blades for longer than he had in years past. And sometimes, even if a tempered harmony had been able to be achieved from a blade in days and weeks past, it would one day not be that way for the same blade. No matter how much the sharpener worked on it, the harmony could no longer be found. One day it would be as if it had just gone away.

The better the steel, the easier the harmony was to find, but some of the blades he was buying now were cheaper, and although the Browns could always find whatever harmony there was to be gotten from each blade, it began to seem to them, over the summer, that the sound was leaving those blades faster than it used to.

The green forest beyond, shimmering in the heat, a thousand shades of green, and the muddy creek that gave it life, wandering slowly through that forest, seeming to promise them that nothing would ever change.

The day Jim Ed hurt his hand, he wasn't even working the planer. He had been stacking boards and a tree length had gotten stuck in the blade. The planer operator had hollered to him to come help, to get on one end and pull. The wood was in a bind and needed to be rocked back and forth.

It was just bad luck. He could have been more careful, should have been — especially knowing that he was almost done with his shift — but it was late in the day and both he and the planer operator were hot and tired and thinking of home. Jim Ed in particular had been day-dreaming, thinking of past concerts and envisioning new ones — and for whatever reason, he got things backwards, they both did, so that when Jim Ed pushed, the planer pulled, and the tree wrenched free, kicked back out of the blade, and he found himself leaning too far forward, outstretched, with his good hand, his right hand, pulled right up into the shrieking saw.

It took only two fingers. He thought it was going to take the whole hand. It didn't even hurt, just felt like a bump, and he thought at first the fingers had gotten folded under his hand.

There wasn't even that much blood at first, but then there was, and though the sawdust absorbed a lot of it, it was still all over the planing table, and running down his arm.

All of the men had seen such things before, but never with it happening to the boss's son. The planer operator shut the engines down and gave a call to the others to come start looking for the fingers. The protocol was to find the fingers, clean them and wrap them in ice, if possible, though if no ice was available, then cold water — and get to a hospital and sew them back on as quickly as possible. Sometimes it worked. Sometimes with young people amazing things were possible.

Floyd was down in the woods, working with the sawyers. He heard the mill shut down, and when he didn't hear it start back up, he wondered what all might be going on. But he and his crew were way down in the bottom, and he kept thinking the engines would probably start back up at any minute, and didn't want to waste a trip up the hill out of simple curiosity.

He and his men started back to work on the tree they were felling, an immense water oak, and the sounds of their own saws and axes filled in the silence, the men working steadily beneath the shade of the old tree that would soon enough be toppling over and flooding the men's work space with light.

The planer operator, hunting for the fingers as if his livelihood depended on it, found them both quickly. He knew where to look and he hurried Jim Ed into his truck. They sped off just as Birdie and the girls were walking down to see what was going on. Other than the initial call to the other men to come help look for the fingers, there had been no outcry, no turmoil, though once Birdie and the girls got down there, that changed. Bonnie and Norma began to cry, Birdie was keening, and Maxine was cursing like a sailor. Wanting fiercely to go back in time even a few minutes so they could do things differently. As if believing the outcome would have been different.

The finger reattachments didn't take, and in the end, the doctor said, would be more likely to cause an infection that could compromise the rest of his hand, or even his life, and would at the very least delay his recovery, and would never be functional anyway. The doctor took the fingers back off just two days after putting them back on. Floyd had been drinking since the accident and was out of commission himself for a while. Bonnie and Jim Ed and Maxine conferred in the hospital room and made a vow to keep going. The magic was in their voices; Jim Ed's guitar playing, while adequate, had always been a bit of a prop anyway. They would adjust their voices yet again. He would still be able to play, just not quite as deftly.

Such ragged disynchrony in their lives below. No one knew. Anyone who heard their voices from that time, so polished, would never have imagined mud or heat or blood or sawdust. Would certainly never have envisioned despair, captivity, furor, confusion. All would have continued to be serene above, ordered and calm, always in control. Sleep, just a little longer.

Floyd took a loan out on the mill, gave Jim Ed the money. The Browns were touched by his generosity—his insistence that they take the money—and did not turn it down. They thanked him profusely and promised they'd get it back in no time, that once they started touring again, and without Fabor doing their accounting, they'd be back on their feet before they knew it. Maxine had been writing some new songs and they couldn't wait to try them out. They would be even better than before, they said.

They weren't bragging or bluffing. It was just a truth, like a wide-open lane. They could see it, could still feel it moving through them, carrying them with it. It was just the way it was.

They were neck and neck with Elvis now. As incandescent as had been their trajectory, his was even slightly more so. His number one hits were beginning to score more on the pop charts, and theirs on country. While Jim Ed had been at the mill and the Browns back at Poplar Creek, Elvis had released "Hound Dog," "Blue Suede Shoes," and "Don't Be Cruel."

The sales for the Browns' last three hits — "Rhythm of the Rain," "You Can't Grow Peaches on a Cherry Tree," and "I Heard the Bluebirds Sing" — were the same as for Elvis's last three, but the audiences were different now. Some of the listeners were starting to cross over from country to pop. They might be back one day — they would be back — but there were larger cultural forces at work. The audiences were crossing over, following another now. The thing that had made the Browns so revered — the ability to tamp down any unrest and present a smooth surface — would ultimately be their weakness, but they would be the last to know it. It would take Maxine fifty years to figure it out, the faintest breeze beginning to make little ripples on the surface of that smooth water.

Elvis was touring like crazy while the Browns treaded water, waiting for Jim Ed's hand to heal. They were starving for the stage. Elvis wasn't rich yet but was beginning to enter and map the territory of rich. He wasn't Elvis, Inc., yet, but a lot can change in six months at that age, and with such uncontrollable power surging up through so flexible and malleable a vessel as the human soul and the mortal body.

Whenever he got to within a hundred miles of the Trio Club, he would detour, drawn by sweet Bonnie, and by the lights on the hill. He would drive through the night to get there, would call up Bonnie and tell her he was coming in, then would get on the phone with Birdie and ask if she was cooking anything special.

He'd get in after midnight and would be back on the road shortly after daylight, after breakfast and a short walk with Bonnie. Then he would be gone, while the rest of the Browns stayed behind, believing that they still had everything they had started out with, that nothing was going away.

And Elvis, on his drive back north, feeling reinvigorated, refreshed, more powerful, more illuminated. Driving east back to Nashville, into the morning sun, a song playing on the radio, listening to one of his own songs sometimes, and laughing. It sounded pretty good.

ANOTHER MISTAKE

NOW THE HARD TIMES really began — the first truly swooping lows. They were terrified, not yet understanding that the lows were only the setup for the highs. Instead, they held on tightly, and just rode — not in control, but holding on.

The army drafted Jim Ed despite the injury to his hand. Maybe he wouldn't be able to fire weapons, but they could find some use for him. He would be in the service indefinitely. Floyd went to his congressman, argued that he was a one-legged sawmill operator, that he was just about to reopen the mill and needed his son to help run it, and that the mill was needed for the war effort — but there was no war; they were between wars. At least let him stay in Arkansas, Floyd argued, but the army sent him to California.

Elvis got drafted as well but was able to get a gig performing for the troops and was able to keep his songs out in the market. It was not an insubstantial fork in their paths.

Back home, Maxine didn't give up. She and Bonnie practiced with Norma, tried to play a few shows like that, but it was hard: Norma was still in school, and they needed Jim Ed. Their sound needed him to stabilize it — to temper Maxine's hidden despair and Bonnie's unadulterated cleanliness. They waited, and Maxine wrote songs. It wasn't the end of the world. People still knew who they were. They were still famous; their songs were still playing on the radio.

How durable would the gift be? Should they have guarded it more carefully? They cannot be blamed for thinking it was indestructible, beyond the ability to just fade away.

In Pine Bluff, there was a handsome small-town lawyer, hard partier, heavy drinker, and womanizer, Tommy Russell. He started hanging around Maxine during her downtime between tours. She thought he would settle down, would stop chasing other women, would love only her, would stop drinking, would provide her daily and nightly with what she was missing, not being up on the stage. She was wrong.

Nashville Chrome

MARRYING TOMMY

ONE OF THE THINGS she's noticed about getting older, about being so old, is not what she would have expected — the cascade of memories — but the opposite phenomenon: a vast forgetting. Sometimes it feels like a walling-off, the creation of one compartment after another, into which she sequesters one imperfection after another, until finally her mind has become a house in which every room has become filled, every closet jam-packed, every drawer stuffed with all that she does not want to remember and never wanted to have happen.

She doesn't know what the source of her talent is — she understands she'll never know that, until maybe right at the end — but she has come to understand the nature of the talent, which is the ability to inhabit, with grace, the blank spaces between old established things. To fill that empty space with the sound of longing and, paradoxically, the sound of assurance — of calm satisfaction.

There never really was any assurance, but that was what people wanted to believe.

Maybe there had been some assurance. Maybe there had been calm satisfaction, too — fragments of it, at least, that she accidentally walled off in trying to cover up all the disappointments or mistakes.

Carefully, some days, she begins to go back into some of those walled-off areas to search for those little moments in the missing years that she overlooked, passed by or never noticed. The good that went unacknowledged, and that got shoveled over with the bad.

Was she moving too fast to notice anything, in those middle years, or was she simply too drunk? *My God,* she thinks, *if I could have those thirty or forty middle years back, I could have been somebody, I could have done something. Not Raymond- and Norma-worthy, but something. Not perfect, but better than I was.*

In a fight, she always went straight to the biggest person in the room, the one who could do her the most harm — getting in an argument with the president of a record company, or the owner of a regional network. She didn't back down from anyone. She couldn't bear to think of being frightened of anything.

She opens one of the most distasteful walled-off areas. She remembers Tommy. She remembers the wedding, remembers what she thinks might have been brief satisfaction, though even now she's not quite sure, and looks back at it as if watching an old movie with no sound, a film in which she thinks she recognizes one of the women as herself, younger but no longer quite young.

She's been so careful to keep the unpleasant and even horrific years of her marriage — what a dumb-ass idea that was! why didn't someone stop her? — walled off that she covered it all up, good and bad.

Why work so hard to get rid of something only to then risk bringing it back? It makes no sense, and she wonders if she's dying, if this is what happens near the end. Perhaps certain chemicals begin to dissolve those walls so that all those hoarded or safeguarded disappointments come spilling back into the rest of the architecture. Or maybe a person doesn't have to be dying for it to happen. Maybe the disappointment and bitterness begin to rot and fester and ferment once all the storage space is jam-packed. It creates a sweet acid that begins to slowly erode the integrity of the structure that housed that disappointment until finally one day all the walls are gone and life comes flooding back.

Is this what it's like for Bonnie? Maxine wonders, and for the ten thousandth time she wonders why Bonnie gets to be so damned happy all the time, while she, Maxine, has to always carry the heaviest load.

She's not envious of Bonnie, she tells herself. That would be a bad thing. You're not supposed to be jealous of a sister. That's common, and she's anything but that. She's mostly just amazed, is all. She marvels at how Bonnie — and, for that matter, Jim Ed — got all of it while Maxine got none of it.

Courage. The box, the compartment, is spilling out now, so why not open it? She's too tired to run from it and there's nowhere left to go anyway. She moves closer to the spoils, curious, having almost forgotten that which she worked hard to forget.

She's fidgety, but is surprised, for as the first wave of swamp muck comes oozing over her ankles — vaguely warm, as if made that way by some innocuous chemical activity, like blood or urine, or the sea in sunlight — she can find in the ferment none of the terrible memories she's been keeping boxed up, but instead something interesting, something positive. It is a thing that, as best as she can tell, is mildly pleasant, bittersweet, and she considers the recollection with no small amount of suspicion.

Is it a trick, and why hadn't she noticed it the first time it went past?

She hadn't been looking to get married when she met Tommy Russell, a small-town lawyer working in the big city of Pine Bluff, pop. 28,000, some fifty miles north of Sparkman and Poplar Creek. She hadn't even been looking to date anyone, not steadily; her primary relationship was touring, singing, and songwriting. Anything else, and anyone else, would have slowed that down.

He was good-looking, though that couldn't have been all of it; she had seen handsome men before. Was he more handsome than Elvis? Certainly not, but handsome enough, and possessing a flair, a confidence — a sharp-edged self-awareness that, back then, she never imagined could hurt her. Tall and dark-haired, he had something else, a devilishness, and it was an old story: his attentions flattered her. It seemed to her that when the two of them were together they drew more attention than she did when alone. It wasn't like having Jim Ed and Bonnie on either side of her, but it was almost like that. He filled all available spaces with himself; he summoned attention.

He was a hard drinker but that had seemed like fun at the time, and there were few in her world who were not. Even Bonnie and Elvis would party with them on the road, though they were both pretty good about being able to make a drink last much of the evening rather than gulping it down. Bonnie was, anyway; there were some nights when Elvis was a gulper already, though others when he remained in control, merely took the smallest sips.

But that was Elvis, and it's Tommy whom she's trying to remember. All her life she's taken great pains not to speak ill of him, though there was so much about which she could have: the drinking, the chronic unfaithfulness, the verbal abuse. The source of so much of her great unhappiness during those middle years, or so she believed for a long time. An unfairness, a burden no one should have to carry, though he is long gone now, died ten years ago, carries no burden whatsoever; though still, she has kept all that toxic brew closed off.

What she sees and remembers now frightens her, however, for in the remembering, she sees it just as she saw it then: wonderful, exhilarating, intoxicating. She had thought it had been all misery and woe, and to realize now that for a moment, however brief, it wasn't, unsettles her; as if, given a second chance, she would make the same mistakes all over again.

For their first date, he took her to see a case he was arguing. A man had been accused — rightly, it turned out — of embezzling from the governor's office, then blackmailing the governor and his staff with details of various affairs. It was a big case, and there had even been threats against Tommy's client's life — bodyguards were present at the trial — and it thrilled her to see the power Tommy commanded, with not just the jury, judge, and spectators as his audience, listening intently to every word, but a further audience as well, call it the scales of justice or even God, with fate in the balance, fate held in Tommy's outstretched hands as he argued, pleaded, cajoled, scolded, declaimed.

Tommy won the case, and two weeks later, at a party, asked her to marry him, and she said sure, yes.

Bonnie, of all people, tried to talk her out of it. Her little sister! What did Bonnie know of love? It turned out she could not have been more right, but even now it rankles Maxine that Bonnie had given such counsel. As if, in her crush with Elvis, Bonnie thought she already knew everything there was to know of love. She had been right and Maxine had been wrong, but still, it rankles her.

The memory, however, has been modified while in storage. Maxine remembers the pride — a franticness in her heart — when, upon announcement of the verdict, Tommy shook his client's hand quickly but then sought her out, came straight to her, and with all eyes still on him. He had left his client too quickly in his eagerness to come see her, and his client trailed after him, moving through the throng.

Maxine heard the man expressing his thanks, mixed with disbelief — it had been clear to Maxine, at least, that they had had him dead to rights — and she was surprised by both the brusqueness and the essence of Tommy's answer.

"There's no need to thank me," he told his client. "I would have worked just as hard for the other fellow." He paused, his dark eyes almost black, and with adrenaline still surrounding him, dense and palpable. "I would have nailed you to the wall," he said, and the man withdrew his hand, wilted back into the crowd.

Maxine had totally misread things that day. She had not considered Tommy's anger to be that of self-loathing but had instead thought his was an anger of righteousness, that he judged and disapproved of his client.

She had not known sourness or ferment that day, only hope and admiration. There had been a power in the courthouse, and she had been a part of it, swept along with it, and best of all, for the first time she hadn't had to produce that power to keep things moving or get people to hear her. It was just happening, as if that was its natural and due course.

Was this how it was for Bonnie with Elvis? She imagined that it was.

She won't go so far as to acknowledge that such a thing might not have been healthy or the best possible course for Bonnie. But remembering her immense mistake and the decades of consequences, she experiences a glimmer of understanding of one of the people whom she should know best in the world but who is in so many ways her opposite.

Maxine peers into the box further, and is further surprised: there is only mild pleasure. The torment is gone. Where is the poison she had expected — where is the putrefaction? Has some bizarre alchemy occurred across the many years — one that has rendered, completely unbeknownst to her, disappointment into beauty, venality into integrity, loss into gain?

If so, what a double waste: the waste of the initial rotting, and then the second waste, in failing to witness the alchemy of rot back into sweetness. As if there are some in the world who simply cannot win for losing.

But for a while, there was nothing but winning. *Be damned,* she thinks. *I will get back to that.*

Neither she nor Tommy ended up being able to control much of anything, much less the directions or outcomes of their lives—but they put on a beautiful wedding. It's strange, she thinks, that she has the courage now to look back, and stranger still that she should see that it was beautiful.

The ceremony itself was a big church wedding at the Baptist church in Memphis, but it's the reception afterward that she's remembering. One of Tommy's bosses owned an estate north of town — there was no other word for it but *mansion* — and the wedding party went there after the ceremony.

Blue barbecue haze lay like fog over the green rolling hills, and the music of fiddles and banjos and mandolins drifted from beneath the big canvas tent set up for the musicians, of which it seemed there were hundreds. Guitars were leaning everywhere, and country people from the hills, identifiable by their informal dress — Maxine's people, in clean slacks and clean shirts and old leather shoes shined — wandered the grounds, rarely conversing with the attorneys and judges who stood in clumps and clusters, in their suits. Seen from afar, it might have looked like a battleground, with the two opposing armies arranging in slow combat, and the blue smoke from the barbecue appearing like that from cannons. The musicians' tent a gathering place for generals, and even the sleek horses that grazed in the fields beyond looking like the saddleless mounts of cavalry. A few men and women lounged on the hillsides with their straw hats pulled over their eyes, and from a great enough distance, it might have seemed that they were the first casualties of a skirmish that was only beginning.

There were, however, clues that it was not a war. Small children moved among the horses, petting them and feeding them handfuls of summer grass. Women walked arm in arm with other women, young and old, not as if in assistance of the injured, but as they had once done in a time before the war. And to such a faraway viewer gifted also with the ability to hear all sounds, no matter how delicate or muted, that spectator would have seen the band of chefs in their starched white aprons and high, billowing hats, looking like surgeons at first, coming out of one of the tents, carrying glinting knives and silver platters.

The pride and officiousness of the chefs as they carried plates to the long buffet table would have indicated to the viewer that maybe it was not a war after all, but merely a great feast, and when one of the chefs, after much consultation, was given the honor of ringing the great iron bell out in the yard of the mansion, the peal of it would have rolled out to that distant audience, and would have found freedom and a certain style in the great loneliness of space between that spectator and all those gathered below.

As the clang and ringing of the bell traveled across that distance, the sound waves would have spread out into greater and more relaxed amplitudes, then would have begun to waver and shimmer in their inevitable disintegration — the sound acting like a living thing briefly in possession of spirit and soul, but susceptible, like all else in the world, to the inevitable decay and sheer mechanical reduction wrought by friction and time, and with the listener feeling starved for more, as he or she first detected that wavering, that unwinding of the perfect sound as it began to first loosen, thread by thread.

Before that, though — just before that — there would have been perfection. Across the uncompromised and sculpted space of the landscape itself, the sound waves would have found a brief synchrony with the shapes of all the things below and over which they traveled.

The slopes and curves of the sound would have followed the slopes and curves of the hills, would have flowed gently left and right of any obstacles such as boulders or trees. There would have been a greatness to the sound, a fullness, in the freedom of all that space, and as the resonance of it filled the listener and began to act within the listener himself, there would have been confusion; for even though the sound of the bell was just now reaching the listener, the bell ringer had already turned his back and was walking away.

How long was it good before it turned bad? A month with Tommy, or six weeks, before she realized her mistake, but clung stubbornly to hope?

"There's not a skirt he won't chase," Bonnie told her. "You're not going to change him. He's just marrying you because you're famous. If you ever stopped, he'd be gone in a week. He'll be gone in a week anyway. Please," Bonnie said. "I know he's fun but you don't have to marry him."

There was still time for Tommy to get better. Hell, there was a whole long lifetime in which things could get better. Maxine laughs quietly, marvels at what she has found in the box. It was atrocious, it was unbearable, but for a long while she had withstood it. And look, now: she had been mistaken, it had not been all bad. Why hadn't she been able to enjoy what she enjoyed? Why had she let the imperfections corrupt all the goodness?

Who in her life ever told her she wasn't good enough, besides herself? It certainly wasn't Birdie. Every day of her life, Birdie doted on her; informed all her children that the sun rose and set on each of them. Tommy told her with his actions that she wasn't good enough — prowling after other women whenever she went out on the road. But he was just a two-bit fucker, she sees that now; at eighty, she sees what Bonnie saw at twenty.

Was it Floyd who told her? She doesn't want to acknowledge this, and though they fought like cat and dog, she doesn't ever really recall him saying those words *You're not good enough.* Maybe he did and she has plastered those words over in the gerrymandered architecture of her life, but she doesn't think he did. What she remembers is the pride — perhaps, too immense a pride — he took in their sudden success.

She remembers the fights, but he was her father: he loved her. There were times when he withheld his love, times when he turned away and was isolated from everyone, was only pretending to be present, with either his merry drunkenness, or his belligerence, or his sullenness, or despair, or euphoria. His mercurial moods were amplified by the bottle, and with the radiant waves of those moods suddenly and in no way echoing or imitating the contours around and beneath him — *the family.* Calm or raging, when he drank, he was center stage — and maybe it was that simple: when he drank, he wasn't quite himself, but was a performer of sorts, and in that manner, withheld his truer self from them all; and in that withholding, he told her, told all of them, *You're not good enough — I choose drinking instead of you.*

But did anyone actually ever speak those dreaded words to her out loud, or did they come from within?

Floyd was born in 1895. Parts of three centuries separate the then from the now, the beginning of his life and the trailing-away of hers, and yet the sound wave of him, the disturbed energy of his presence and actions in the world, will not fade. A hundred and fifteen years separates where he began and where she is now, and what she remembers when she thinks of her father is not so much the fights of adolescence over control and suspicion, boundaries and rebellion, or his heroic labors in the forest, trying to scrape together a living, but the quiet dark spaces of early evening, the relative silences when he would come in from the mill, smelling of sawdust and diesel, and would go to the cabinet and take down his bottle and pour his first small glass of whiskey.

The brassy twist of the cap, its first little squeaky sound. The splash, the short gurgle. The immense feeling of relief spilling from him as his homecoming filled the cabin. As if he had traveled a long way to make it back to them, and back to that bottle, and had arrived just in time, as darkness fell, and that it had saved him.

GRACELAND

SHE REMEMBERS THE first time she heard him referred to as the King. It caught her by surprise, but she didn't give it much thought one way or the other. She didn't think it would stick, thought it was just a nickname some local station used for him. She thought it was overreaching, a parody of ambition. Weren't they all, despite their surprising successes, still just local musicians traveling from one small town to the next, and occasionally getting to play a larger venue, like the Opry?

None of the Browns had a clue. They were like racehorses with blinders, thundering down the dirt track. There was a jockey lashing them and the horses were dimly aware that there were people in the stands, but they thought nothing of where the track was going—whether it was straightening or circling in a loop—or of the consequences of their efforts and accomplishments. They knew only that there was some flyweight jockey on their back, urging them on, directing them to do that which they already loved doing.

The flyweight rider therefore almost, but not quite, unnecessary, irrelevant. What rider? The horse in its blinders cannot see. The horse out on the track feels only the other horses falling back in groups of ones and twos, then clumps of threes and fours. Knows nothing of history, or of any arc beyond the moment of the next stride.

The promoters of Graceland hold a major festival each August to commemorate his untimely death. They celebrate everything about him, from the sweet country boy he was to the bloated extrapolation of insatiable American appetite and surface showmanship that he became. His worshipers prowl the grounds of Graceland with metal detectors that they've smuggled in before being accosted by security guards. They flock through in their pilgrimage, telling stories of connections in which they've participated—a toy stuffed animal signed by him, a comb he was alleged to have used once. As time marches on, the list of hallowed associates grows ever shorter, even as the pilgrims' zealotry grows more intense with the accruing distance. As if seeking blindly in their annual congregation to reassemble, like astronomical nebulae, enough of the strange burning to resurrect even a glimmer of what was. Of what he carried within him always, and of what he made them feel.

To such sojourners, anything he touched is sacred, and any person he touched, or who touched him, hallowed. They brought his parents out regularly while they were living and bombarded them with the most unthinkable questions, shoved to the front of the line to show them windowpanes in which the pilgrim thought she sometimes saw the King's profile. Asking Elvis's old daddy for a lock of his hair, a fingernail. As the years pass by, the organizers have invited his dentist — "Shake the hand that filled Elvis's cavities!" — to answer questions about the King's oral hygiene, what his tonsils looked like.

At these conventions, no small number of the attendees wander the grounds dressed like Elvis, or thinking that they are dressed like him. Some of them miss the mark by quite a bit, while the others represent him fairly accurately at all the different stages of his life. There are baby Elvises in strollers, clad in dark glasses, with grease-blackened hair. It's a clan, a cult willing to drink whatever Kool-Aid is put before them, but it's an audience, it's worship and acclaim, even if slightly indirect, and each year when the promoters invite the Browns, Maxine says yes, in the years she's well enough to make the journey.

Jim Ed is always working, and Bonnie doesn't dare go — among the faithful who even know about her early romance, there are many who believe that when she ended their relationship, she started him on his spiral — but Maxine always goes when she's able.

The promoters promise to set up a little booth where Maxine can sit and sell her CDs and sign autographs. Maxine has learned over the years to bring a pillow to sit on, padding the folding metal chair. She smiles, grimaces at the sillier questions, tries to answer the ones she can — tries to interject a little about herself, and her career, and that of her brother and sister, but only rarely gets the chance for that. With her diminished hearing, she often can't quite make out what they're saying to her, and so only nods politely and signs, in careful, shaky, spidery scrawl, her full name, Maxine Brown — she dropped the

Russell after the divorce — on whatever odd package or item they are shoving across the table at her. Usually an old album of his, but often anything — a tie, a gas receipt, the back of a hand. They must have contact, even if they don't know what it is they're contacting. They are lost, each and every one of them, and for a short while, she feels almost motherly toward them; it makes her feel considerably better, recognizing how lost they are, makes her feel as if she herself is not.

Napkins are the worst. No matter how careful she is, the pen always catches and tears the paper, leaves a blotted, unsatisfactory mess; though still they shove them at her, wanting to accumulate and gather anything and everything, starving and lonely and long adrift.

Each year they send for her in a limousine, which thrills her. She spends days, weeks, beforehand, anticipating, trying on different outfits, experimenting with different makeup, and humming, crooning, keeping her voice supple, in case someone should ask her to sing an impromptu song. The organizers will put her up in a garish suite: a king-size four-poster bed with velour curtains, cloying potpourri, Graceland ashtrays, photographs and velvet paintings adorning the walls, and shag carpet thick enough to lose a golf ball in.

It's the best time of year for her, August. She loves the vile and mismatched tasteless opulence of the hotel room — the Negro waiters from room service, the giant television screen, the air conditioner set on fifty-six degrees while outside the temperature exceeds a muggy one hundred degrees. She even loves sitting in the metal folding chair at her little card table, smiling brightly at the brief gawking of passing-by strangers, a few of whom stop to visit.

But best of all, she loves the ride in the long black limousine. She sits way in the back, all dressed up, and chats through the speakerphone with whichever affable chauffeur they have sent, telling him her life story while he listens with interest. Adjusting the air conditioner in the plush leather seat, and hurtling down the road, the big shark of a car, smooth and powerful, piloted by the elegant uniformed driver in utter control of the road, passing one ailing car after another on the too short drive up to Graceland: the fender-sprung sputtering old truck in front of them loaded down with green twisted firewood or piled high with the bric-a-brac of moving day, residue of a divorce sale or possibly a family still barely intact but seeking a more affordable rent; the bald-tired Bel Air or Impala muffler-dragging and low-riding with death spirals of blue-gray smoke blatting from behind; and cane poles lashed to the roof, hunter-gatherers setting out in search of the afternoon's sustenance.

Passing the fields and farms, the red clay visible like a scab on slopes of land that have been logged too hard, or grazed too hard, or farmed too hard and are now slipping away into gullies of erosion, the signature of poverty, of not enough . . .

Past the weathered farmhouses, in the yards of which lie scattered bicycles and tricycles, the toys from multiple generations of various offspring and relatives, and the trailers up on cinder blocks, sometimes attached to the old house and other times set off at some distance, inescapable evidence of the economic siege that had beset a family or clan for so long that the defeat and desperation is in their every habit, as if twined now into their DNA — the besieged inhabitants of such farms so at the edge, or so at the end, that they no longer even bother to buy lottery tickets, no longer even drink or smoke, for there is no money for any of it, only desperation. The household so poor and so common that the electricity has long ago been cut off, looping wires hanging in various stages of disassembly from leaning creosote-soaked wooden poles that will one day be cut up for firewood, and the dishwater having to be heated on a woodstove, even in summer.

And from the porch of more than one such encampment, one of the occupants, usually a woman, coming out onto the porch to toss out a tray of soapy gray dishwater, not looking up until the dishwater is already in the air, sailing in flashing heliograph-spray through August heat-haze toward the hard-packed, lifeless red clay shell of a yard that has accepted a thousand or ten thousand other such hurlings.

Steam rising from the shifting tossed rope of gray water, and steam then from the hardpan clay itself as the water lands — steam rising even in August, as if some volcanic activity, some nearing geothermal yearning, is stirring in that beleaguered and defeated yard. The woman only then lifting her head, mid-sling, to witness the long black car powering north, with the woman pausing to stare for a moment

at the distant sight not so much of celebrity or even power but of utter wealth — staring at the limousine impassively, with neither longing
nor scorn, only the mask of impassivity, as if there is now no setback or
humiliation, no misfortune or obstacle, that can affect her disposition
one way or the other, there is only the next chore to tend to, and this
life, this shortening life, to hurry up and finish . . .

And what does Maxine feel, passing such farmlands? Does she feel
the centripetal pull — the first twenty-one years of her life lived that
way, the life she escaped, the foundation of all that was to come later,
both the glory and the despair — or does she feel nothing at all, only
the satisfaction of great luck? Perhaps she falls silent in her conversation with the driver for a while. Perhaps she considers for a moment
that in such scenes she is looking at herself across time — not at the
woman she likely would have become, but in some way the woman
she still is, unseen and unknown and likewise waiting for the last day
on the calendar. As if nothing has happened, as if she was once that
dishwater woman and has always been, and must always be.

No. She clears her throat, just to feel the old familiar tingle of voice
being prepared. She could still sing if she had to. The voice will never
leave her. She is ensconced in the cool glide of the limousine, the thick
tinted glass protecting her from the hard scorch of the countryside.
This is how things are supposed to be: the world has corrected itself,
she is royalty, she was chosen for royalty, and while it's a shame the
dishwater woman has to suffer and know unhappiness and, perhaps
worse, the anonymity of time hurtling past, time that the dishwater
woman can in no way influence, Maxine, too, has suffered and known
unhappiness, and now, finally, it's time for such things to end. *Now, at
last.*

Pulling into Memphis, then, her far too brief ride in the lap of luxury nearing its end. Through the outlying industrial wastelands, and
roads as ragged as a war zone. Why is the driver taking her this way?
Isn't there a more elegant routing, a smoother path?

Onward, and back out into the country. Beads of condensation
trickling down her window, so great is the difference between her ride
and the terrific heat outside. Passing through the gates of her dead
friend's manor — cars everywhere, glinting in the heat — she leans for-

ward with the quick hit of anticipation — she almost imagines that she might see him again — and despite the heat, she cracks the window an inch to let in the true, untinted light and to better taste the real air of the experience, the summer-hot air of the pilgrims who once worshiped him and still do, or who never did but now do. *This is what I wanted,* she thinks. *This is what I deserve.* There was not a shred of difference between them, and her success came first. Why have things turned out this way, and might the inequity yet be salvaged or correlated?

Giddy as a teenager, she takes in all the heat and light through that inch-crack of window, and the sweet scent of new-mown grass in summer heat, all the lawns manicured in preparation for the throngs.

And she sees it, then, Graceland itself, no less than the Taj Mahal. The American Taj Mahal.

For two days and two nights, she imagines she is royalty. Because she and only two others — Bonnie and Jim Ed — know that she is the source and not the echo or shadow of her time. That it was Elvis and all the others whose voices splintered from hers, rather than the other way around — it is easy for her to bask in the hoopla and imagine that more of it is about her than is now really the case.

Some Augusts she's too beaten down to travel, despite it being the highlight of her year; or she is recovering from one surgery or another. In the years she can't go, can't make the short journey, the folks at Graceland are kind to her; they send her flowers and a nice handwritten note saying that everyone is asking about her, and that they all hope she can make it next year, and that they'll be waiting for her. *There's always next year,* they say. *We'll look forward to next time.*

HER NEW FAMILY

SHE WON'T SPEAK poorly of Tommy, or of Floyd, despite the disappointments they caused her — the disappointments she allowed them to cause her. As ever, she carries what she perceives as an unfair load, in part because it is all she knows; she is so unaccustomed to being without burden that she's more comfortable with burden's presence than its absence. And having succumbed for long years to their same disease, she has no stomach for judging Floyd or Tommy.

She was lucky, she thinks. She got out — even if with so many scars — while they did not. They loved her imperfectly, and she thinks that was better than nothing.

In Tommy's case, she allows she might have been wrong about that.

He was unfaithful and irresponsible, had been led to believe over the course of his young life, by the way people turned to notice him when he entered a room, that he was special, and deserving therefore of special rules.

They had been married less than a year when she found out for the first time that, with spectacular unoriginality, he was involved with his secretary. She can only shake her head now at the space that separates her from who she was then and who she is now. She found one of the secretary's notes to him tucked in his coat pocket, and confronted Tommy, not so much with anger as disbelief and confusion. It wasn't so much that she didn't understand men could be that way as instead her surprise that her will alone was not enough to control the situation.

Tommy claimed the relationship was left over from before he knew Maxine, that he would break it off, that he felt sorry for the secretary, that Maxine was the love of his life, that he was a fool, that he would never do anything like that again — and she believed him, forgave him, and was surprised by a vulnerability, a worry, she had not known she possessed.

The anxiety began to spread through her rapidly, like an illness, and the times she had to go back out on the road became even more stressful. She didn't tell Birdie or Bonnie, and though she tried to shove the concerns down into some nether compartment, she had trouble keeping them there. *Maybe it will be a one-time thing,* she told herself, and, in her more worried moments, *Maybe I can be better, maybe I can do better. Maybe I can change him.* Almost surreptitiously, she studied how Bonnie and Elvis were together, lighthearted. She tried to be that way, but it felt forced.

It was only a month after discovering Tommy's first indiscretion that she found out she was pregnant. Certain that this would help turn him back toward her, she could not have been more wrong. Before their first child, Tommy, was born, Maxine discovered two other incidents, one reported to her directly by the wife of the minister at the church she had sometimes attended as a child, and discovering the other on her own when she came back from a tour days earlier than planned — her pregnancy showing hugely by that point — and found the woman asleep in her home at ten in the morning. Maxine had pulled the woman out of bed and began kicking at her and pulling her hair, intent on killing her — if she had had a weapon in her hands at the time, she would have — and chased the woman from her house and into the yard.

Maxine left Tommy after that, went back to live with Birdie and Floyd without explaining why, but after the birth, she moved back in with him. Tommy made some promises, and was pleased with the baby.

"Scarlet Ribbons" came next, followed by "I'm in Heaven." It was a good year, and she eased back out onto the road. *We married too young,* she told herself, *but we'll get through this.* Something was hardening within her, but that was all right; in that hardening, it felt like strength, even if the feeling did seem to lack a certain flexibility.

The baby was a joy, someone different every time she returned home.

The second child, Alicia, saved her life. Knowing she was pregnant again, though seized with headaches and back pain that had not been present the first time, Maxine went to her doctor, who discovered a fast-growing tumor along her spine; soon enough it would have cut off blood flow and sensation. They didn't have much money by that point — Tommy had started going to the dog races in Hot Springs — and Maxine knew that if she hadn't been pregnant, she probably would have put off going to the doctor for weeks or even months.

The doctor said she had gotten in to see him just in time; that it had been a matter of days.

"Teen-Ex" and "The Whiffenpoof Song": it didn't feel like a trap, this narrowing into a weir from which there would be no escape. There was time for both; as long as Tommy did his part, there was time for it all. The divorce rate in the country at that time was around 5 percent; she would break trail on a lot of things, but not that. If Birdie could stay with Floyd, she could hang in there a little longer with Tommy, who, to the best of her knowledge, had been good then for two or three months in a row.

"Lonely Little Robin" and "Ground Hog": more number ones. The anticipation — the hunger — while out on the road, of wanting to return home to her babies, and then, as they started to grow, her children, was a sweet and delicious and haunting thing. In her imagination, she would be welcomed back by a loving and attentive husband, though the reality upon her return was always something less, with fights and accusations and, worst of all, cold distances. There was anything but lightheartedness.

The boy, Tommy, was a dreamer, while Alicia reminded her of Bonnie, somehow always bringing little gusts of pleasure into even the tensest situations. Birdie came to visit when she could, though not as often as she would have liked — Floyd didn't like to be left alone — and Maxine could tell sometimes that Birdie was concerned Maxine wasn't getting to spend enough time with the children, though to her credit, Birdie held her thoughts pretty much to herself.

"They grow up fast" was all she ever said about it, and though Maxine heard her, it didn't really matter. What was Maxine supposed to do, give up her life?

"They'll be okay," she said. She started to say *They always have Tommy around,* but didn't. "They're good kids. They'll be okay."

Bit by bit now, she was finally beginning to have some success in walling off the hurt over her failed marriage. There was a new stress now, however, one far more problematic than Tommy's philandering, drinking, and gambling. The children had started to cry every time she got ready to leave. Her memories of them from that time are of tears streaming down their cheeks, their arms outstretched, or of them clinging to her waist and legs, until finally, each time, she had to pull away.

The only positive thing about such pain was that it displaced the grief she had about Tommy. *Let him go,* she thought, and sealed him over as if with concrete over a crypt, and her hardened heart felt so strong as to almost be something she could be proud of.

At a show in Little Rock, she went blind. She had been having a ferocious headache for days, but had been pushing through. She had to be led from the stage and driven straight to the hospital, where doctors found an infected tooth; upon their removal of it, her sight returned, slowly at first, but then with full capacity, and for days afterward she marveled at how beautiful the world looked, and at the miracle of a second chance.

CHET

THE UPSIDE CAME back to them in the spring, like the turn of the season itself. Jim Ed was released from the service, was learning how to strum the guitar anew, and they started touring as a trio again. And in the same way that Jim Reeves had found them earlier, Chet Atkins now took up their cause; another, even more powerful guardian angel. Maxine still had her steady burning worry about Tommy, but still hoped that fatherhood would settle him down; and in the meantime, professionally and artistically, things were going great once again. Who could blame her for turning away from the one path, which would only have led further into irreparable folly anyway, and following the siren call of fame? What choice was there, really?

Chet Atkins was the most talented studio musician of all time, a genius guitar picker who had invented all manners of styles. There was no better ear in music, and no better judge of talent, and no better producer of albums. As modest and unassuming as Fabor had been flamboyant and self-aggrandizing, Atkins had always been in love with music, had worked his way up steadily through the industry — playing county fairs, touring, accompanying larger stars on the Opry, then playing on the Opry by himself, what many would consider the height of fame — before discovering that what he really loved doing was helping other musicians bring out the best in themselves.

He worshiped the music, not the self — he was a slave to a beautiful or compelling sound, and preferred the traditional to the experimental — and he was so much a creature of the auditory senses that the sound of a single quivering chord, a single plucked string, was for him almost a visual and tactile experience. He could discern the faintest sounds and harmonies that lay in wait beneath larger, quicker ones.

He could hear and see the small spaces between sounds, and he could hear and see also the collision of too much crowding of sound waves, rhythm, balance. With arpeggio and fortissimo governing his spirit, he moved carefully and quietly through the world, utterly without ego, wanting only the opportunity to serve music and musicians.

He never gave up on his own music but stepped smoothly and directly into the producing business, was desired by all the record companies that were springing up at the time, but secured finally by the biggest and best, RCA — the place the star-dreaming Browns had first desired to be only a few short years earlier.

Working with RCA, Atkins got to have his hands on any album he chose, with the greatest performers of that age. After he stopped performing so much and spent more time producing, the public began to forget who he was, but the people who loved music never would.

Neither of those things mattered to him one way or the other. He was comfortable enough with silence, but he lived for his work, and for that point each day when he ultimately found himself suspended in music, in its midst and supported by sound, and considering how he might spread out certain strands while tightening others, deciding how to best populate that silence with all the motion and resonance and spirit and sound that would begin when it began, following its best and most natural and heroic course, and then — sometimes quietly, though other times with emphasis and verve — ending when it was time to end.

Suspended in such dreaming, such beauty and drama and spirit each day, as a creator might have been while considering an unformed world. Where to put the rivers, where to put the forests? Where to place the wild geese, and when?

Atkins ascended into this already prepared world — the world of record producing — as if it had been made exclusively for him, and in that ascension he embedded himself in the heart of the culture-to-come, became the nucleus from which most great American records of that era flowed.

His greatest joy lay in fixing or improving the slightest flaws or subtle imperfections in a performance, and he sought out the Browns, as did anyone who possessed even a thread of greatness. They were the lodestone, and everyone else possessed only bits and pieces of it, like iron filings, all of which turned and aligned themselves toward the Browns, and then began moving toward them.

In their first year with Chet Atkins, the Browns rolled out eight number one hits, and half a dozen others that went into the Top Ten.

They had two albums that year. They actually made some money, and each bought a house, good houses: Maxine her house in West Memphis, and Bonnie her farm up in the Ozarks. They sent money to Birdie and Floyd, paid off their loan. They knew the lodestone within them would never go away, and so they assumed that the fame never would.

Everyone was drawn to them. Back before the Beatles had even decided to call themselves the Beatles — when Pete Best was still the drummer, before Ringo — they had declared the Browns their favorite American group and flew to Nashville to spend time with them, where they tried over the course of a week to learn how to produce a tempered harmony, but could never quite get it. *You have to be family,* the Browns told them. *The sound all has to come from the same piece of steel.*

There was no other way. They helped the Beatles improve their harmonies, but the Beatles couldn't get the exact sound they wanted.

The Beatles lined up tours for the Browns in Europe, and when the Browns came to London, the Beatles were waiting there for them in the hotel lobby, carried all their bags upstairs for them, taking the steps in bounds, two at a time. They spent a month there with them, playing in little pubs together, the six of them harmonizing the best they could, while Jay Best drummed.

It was the last half of 1959, the eve of the most turbulent decade the country would know in nearly a century. In the last little window of sleep, then, that was all there was at the top: Elvis and the Browns, with the Beatles only beginning to stir over in Liverpool. The Browns did a song, "The Three Bells," an old French folk song told in three parts; a stoic and yet also sentimental story about little Jimmy Brown, whose life passes by in a rolling three minutes. He's born, married, and then, as an old man, buried, all in the same little mountain valley, with the greater and larger world unable to intrude on his charmed isolation.

"The Three Bells" outsold Elvis, and the Browns were up for a Grammy, though Elvis edged them out. That same year, the Browns recorded "Blue Christmas" with Chet Atkins — the song was perfect for their harmonies — but they found out just prior to releasing it that

Elvis had also just recorded it and had his version scheduled for release: a fluke, a confluence of spirit.

You go first, the Browns said. *Maybe we'll release ours some other time.* It didn't matter. There was no competition, there was plenty of air in the room for all of them, the country was huge and the country's appetite for music was even larger. They were all in a great current, being carried forward.

Some were still falling out of the current. Betty Jack Davis, of the Davis Sisters, whom they had only just befriended, was killed in a car wreck on the way home from a concert.

The Browns themselves experienced a faltering in the current, like a shot fired across the bow — a reminder that although they had been selected to carry the immortality, the vessels of their bodies would not be allowed to exist forever. On their way back from a trip to Europe, ice began forming on the wings of their plane, so that the pilot had to descend to an altitude where the ice might melt. The plane was bucking and stalling. The stewardesses told everyone to put on their life jackets. They descended to within a hundred feet of the ocean, bumping along — a thousand miles from land, a thousand miles from anywhere, in the dead of night — but the ice melted, and they ascended again and continued on.

ELVIS AND BONNIE

ELVIS HAD TRANSCENDED burning. Compared to him, the Browns were still down at ground level, burning brightly enough — flaming like tapered candles, or like individual trees in a forest, lightning-struck, crackling with flame, scorching and scalding everything and ultimately altering anything within their reach — but after coming in contact with them, Elvis had taken on a different kind of burning, a conflagration that was now his own. Elvis taking on as his own fuel the best or most primal of what was in each of the Browns, but also in himself, and rising in that burning like a sheet of paper — rising quickly on the heated updrafts created by the fire's own fast burning.

Anywhere he went now, there were reporters following him. If a town had a newspaper, it dispatched both a writer and a photographer to get a picture of him and a quote, and usually he was happy to oblige — but whenever he came back to Pine Bluff or Sparkman, he sought to do so unnoticed, unwilling to share any of his time that could otherwise be spent with Bonnie and the rest of the Browns. His secret family, secret refuge.

He slept out on the porch like a hound, with nothing but a pillow and bedroll; the most famous musician in America now, and maybe in the world. There was no way the bond could hold; he was burning, he was rising, lifting away like flaming flakes of cedar-shake shingles detaching from the roof of a burning cabin, but he was trying to hold on.

Rising at dawn to the roosters crowing and the sun strafing straight through the old forest. Birdie already up early and cooking. Bonnie dressed and ready for the day, bringing him a cup of coffee. Doves calling, and nothing ahead of the two of them that day but whatever they wanted; and the world's inability to find them, even if it had desired to — which it did — was a reassurance and refreshment to both of them, if not to Maxine.

Maxine wasn't living at home anymore, had her brutish life with Tommy, who envied her success and was frustrated by his inability to keep her where he wanted all the time, out of sight yet available to only him. She wasn't exactly turning out to be what he had envisioned in a wife — certainly not like the other wives on the block. He was drinking as much as Floyd had — as Floyd still did — in order to ensure in part that he was always part of any equation, an unpredictable factor to be reckoned with: central, and therefore determining as many of the reactions of others as possible, forcing them to adjust to his every slightest gesture — the tiniest inflection, the sudden stillness, or even the clearing of a throat. The difference between Floyd and Tommy was that Floyd supported Maxine's success while Tommy opposed it. This was not an insignificant difference.

Bonnie and Elvis lounged all day, lay in the fields after their picnics, having loved and reveled in how each could feel the world going past, as if the world was passing over and searching for them but not finding them. It occurred to each of them that there was nothing to prevent them from staying hidden forever.

One night they went canoeing. Maxine and Tommy were over at Floyd and Birdie's, all of them having dinner together, and after they had finished eating and had sat out on the porch and sung and played music for a while, Elvis and Bonnie decided to take a boat ride. Rather than using the old flatbottom jon boat, they chose the little wooden canoe Floyd stored leaning up against the side of the woodpile. They didn't know if it leaked or not, but Elvis was suddenly bright with joy at the prospect, almost manic, and Bonnie became excited, too.

Jim Ed and Floyd offered to run shuttle — to drive the old truck down and leave it at their usual take-out spot, and set off to do so, while Elvis dragged the canoe out and cleaned the leaves off it, and Bonnie lit a kerosene lantern.

Within ten minutes of having announced their intentions, Elvis and Bonnie were setting off on their journey. Birdie counseled them to be careful and watch out for water moccasins, while Tommy hoorahed them, called them foolish, guaranteed they would tip over or be snakebitten. "Maybe a panther will get you," he called out.

Maxine smiled, kept rocking in her chair, but was fuming. It was the single most romantic thing she'd ever seen, and she was surprised by the roar of jealousy, and something else — a disappointment, almost a despair — that was so powerful it made her feel faint. She gripped the arms of the rocker and kept her smile frozen and willed herself to keep rocking even as she felt her face growing taut and pale with something that was inexplicably like sorrow.

Bonnie carried the lantern and Elvis the canoe, hoisting it over his head as if it were but a single plank of lumber. His waist tiny, his shoulders strong enough, in his youth. They walked side by side, and as they proceeded through the forest in the domed glow of the lanternlight, following the rutted clay road down to the creek, frogs leapt across the trail in front of them, splashing through puddles. As the road narrowed closer to the creek, the limbs and branches of trees scraped against the underbelly of the uplifted canoe. In one such scraping a little green snake, as slender as a length of twine and the color of a jewel, fell from the branches above and wiggled briefly on the road in front of them before slithering off. They could hear the riffling sound of the creek's little current before they got there.

A half-moon hung in the tops of the trees. Owls were hooting, and Elvis and Bonnie embraced, then kissed, and then Elvis slid the boat into the water and held it while Bonnie, with the lantern and its swirling halo of moths, climbed in.

Elvis jumped in and shoved off.

They felt something severing between them and the world as the current caught them and the buoyancy of the boat asserted itself in the creek. As if something huge had happened, some change that was as powerful and final as the turning on or shutting off of a switch.

They got lost. It had been raining hard in the uplands, so that the water was higher and quicker. They took a wrong current, veered into a little oxbow that normally wouldn't have held enough water, and though still in the Poplar Creek drainage, they found themselves in a system of moonlit rippling threads, each and all of which would eventually flow back into the main stem of the creek, but which led them through new parts of the swamp they had never seen before.

The swollen side waters wandered excitedly through the trees. In places, the current carried them through the tops of willows, the green branches of which shook and thrashed as if seized below with some great electrical jolt, and they passed through and between the forks of leaning trees, not experienced enough to know the real danger of such a journey.

It was easy paddling, and they rode as if riding on revolving plates, shifting scales and lozenges of water that were alternately made bright by the half-moon and then dark by the shadows of the shuddering forest. Elvis and Bonnie barely had to paddle, and didn't even need to steer much; they needed only to flex the blade now and again as the swirling puzzle pieces of water coalesced, then separated, then merged again.

Soon Elvis and Bonnie were able to differentiate where the deeper and more enduring lines of current ran — the creek's true course — and which shining paths were merely temporary braids. The real creek ran steadier and faster even though it did not always have the most waves and riffles. The air above it was cooler, for some reason — perhaps there was simply less forest overstory, above the creek's center — and there was less acorn and soil scent and more of a clean-scrubbed, ionized kind of smell.

They tried to get back to Poplar Creek and to stay on it rather than getting off into those side channels, and sometimes they were successful, though other times off-course. Again, it didn't matter; in the end they had only to keep going forward.

From time to time there would be a large rolling swell in the middle of the creek, as if they were passing over a log, or, alarmingly, as if something immense were struggling to rise from far below — something that had traveled a long way and labored hard to get there.

In the tight stretches, where one of the tributaries passed through brush and swamp, Bonnie would set her paddle down and hold on to the lantern to keep it from being knocked over and leaving them in total darkness, or half-moon darkness. The moths continued to stay with her, fluttering against her, and she in turn waved them away, brushed them from her black hair.

They paddled for only a couple of hours, though in the dark forest it seemed much longer. With the current strong beneath them, it seemed possible that they could travel all the way to the Gulf of Mexico — following Poplar Creek to Honey Creek, and Honey Creek to the Mississippi, and then all the way down, where eventually they would be able to see dolphins finning in the moonlight, and white sand beaches, palm trees, and calm glinting waters.

Soon enough, however — too soon — they came to their bridge, the one Floyd had sought to cross back when Bonnie was a child, and they splashed out into the shallows and hauled the boat up to where the truck was parked and waiting, Jim Ed the most dependable person in the world.

They drove slowly. Fireflies floated through the woods and crickets chirped steadily. Neither of them wanted Birdie to be kept up late worrying, but theirs was another world, and they moved through it slowly, as if unable yet to leave it, and as if looking out at or down upon the other world, the real one, from some considerable distance.

When they finally got back, Birdie was waiting out on the porch, shelling peas, rocking. Tommy and Maxine had long since driven home, and Floyd and Jim Ed were asleep, Jim Ed half listening, in his sleep, for the rumble of the old truck returning home.

◠ AN OUTING

Every time that Maxine has had bad luck, there has been good luck right behind it. Even as recently as this last injury, her broken hip, it was the right thing at the right time, because the hip x-ray revealed another tumor. She had a hysterectomy to remove it, the tumor was benign, she kept on going.

It's little coincidences like these, all of them connecting across the length of her life, that remind her that she's chosen, and that suggest to her, even if in but a whisper now, that she isn't done, isn't finished, that something remains. The calling is so faint now that she can't help but wonder if she's not just imagining it, hearing only what she wants to hear. Hearing a barely audible shimmering, like the echo of sound, or the harmony above the harmony that Chet, and so many others, always insisted was there.

Was it really there? It was — she knows it was — and all it took to achieve it was a little concentration.

What would Chet say, she wonders, *what would Chet counsel?* He's been gone for almost a decade, but while he was alive, there was nothing she couldn't ask him for help with, nothing he wouldn't do for her or any of his musicians.

Is it her instinct — the summons, the hand of fate — or only her ego that keeps pushing her desire toward a movie? How can so surficial a medium, *Hollywood,* be the answer to anything, at or near the end of what has been an extraordinarily long and eventful life?

She watches for Buddy, as if he might have some answer. As if despite having had no answer and being no help in all the days before, he might one day — the next one — come trotting up to save and rescue her.

And in what manner? A scrolled-up list of instructions fastened to his collar, like a miniature keg of brandy for a stranger lost in the snowy mountains? The contact number for a moviemaker?

She understands she will be the last to go — she has understood this for decades — but still does not understand the meaning or significance of it, or what her responsibility is in this matter.

The staying is so much lonelier than the leaving.

As punctual as the rising and setting of the sun Buddy comes trotting into her yard, and her heart makes its same little leap as she beholds him, looking as frisky and engaged and interested as ever: running his same route, making sure everything is the same, then continuing on.

She bends down and scratches his ears as he eats her offering to him. "You're such a handsome little fellow. What have you seen today? What all is going on out there?"

She needs to go to the grocery store — she doesn't eat much, but is out of everything now — but is too tired, and too cowed by the idea, the knowledge of all that she must pass through, all that awaits her: the noise and brilliant summer-shimmering heat, the asphalt and clamor and bustle. She spends two days preparing herself for the journey, making a careful list — she has nothing left in the house but Saltines and dog food for Buddy — and deciding what she will wear, and at what hour of the day she will plan her entrance, her gambit, the presentation of herself, she whom she still believes, despite all suggestion now to the contrary, to be luminous, chosen.

She leaves at nine o'clock on a Thursday morning, after Buddy has been fed and traveled on, and after she has finished her tea — lemon, lavender and ginger, for nerves — when she is still at her strongest, and after the rush hour of school buses and carpools has abated. It's a seam of quietness that she's noticed, keen as a hunter, one in which she's most comfortable — or least uncomfortable — going out.

The morning is still tolerable, not yet too hot, as she gets in her car after folding her walker carefully and placing it in the back seat. The power of her old car — a '78 Malibu — is daunting to her as she thunks the transmission into reverse and begins backing out slowly, terrified that she can't see all that she needs to be seeing, or hear all that she needs to be hearing. She taps the brakes nervously to be sure they're still working. Is she really in control of the machine? It feels to her that the car's power is a restless one just beneath the touch of her frail foot.

She stops and starts in cautious hitches out onto the street, and relaxes ever so slightly — so far, so good — and puts it in drive and carefully begins her glide, driving as slowly as is physically possible, with the sun bright and the neighborhood trees flashing the light across her in a slow, dreamy scroll. *Am I really doing this?* she wonders, and marvels at her courage, her daring. The audacity of still being alive.

It takes a while, but she makes it to the Piggly Wiggly without incident, or none that she's aware of. At that time of morning, the parking lot is nearly empty, and she sits there in the hot car for long moments, congratulating herself on her success and girding herself for the next phase of her adventure, her bird's heart pounding furiously beneath paper-thin skin.

Exiting with dignity then, after making certain she has her list with her, she unfolds her walker and scoots it up the slight incline of rough blacktop toward the electric doorways of the store's entrance, the glass doors hissing open and shut like the jaws of something hungry, some mindless thing that seeks only to consume whatever passes near it, irrespective of fate or plans.

She reaches the rubberized tread plate, hesitates — the door hisses, widens, and waits — and then she forges ahead, moving as quickly as she can.

Inside the store it's cool and pleasant. She's losing some strength but feels better mentally. Still, it won't do to dawdle. Much remains expected of her for the return home.

She leaves her walker at the front and navigates the grocery cart up and down the aisles, half frightened by its unpredictability, its size. She gathers her meager groceries — TV dinners, raisins, sardines, prunes, tea, milk, cream, bananas — and circles back around to pay. A tremor in her hands as she does so. A nap would be nice. The glare of the parking lot, and of the day outside. The nice young black woman at the cash register is surely still a teenager. Maxine remembers being sixteen like it was yesterday.

Another young woman helps her with her bags, but before going out through the electric doors and into all the light and heat, Maxine pauses at the bulletin board on which are posted handwritten offers of services provided or services needed. *I need a movie,* she thinks. *Even a little one.* Is it too much to ask, she wonders, for some kind of hobbyist — not even an expert, but just someone with passion, someone who believes and understands that her journey was magnificent — to produce *something?* Some marker, some proof, that she was ever here.

Even a technician, a worker from a photo developing booth, could make copies of her old home movies and could interview her, could listen to her stories and resurrect the past and stir to life once more the now stilled columns of dust that were once in motion, and the people and times she most loved in the world . . .

She asks the young woman who is pushing her cart out to stop and get her a piece of paper and pen. The girl does so, and in her most careful script, Maxine begins writing her ad: "Wanted — moviemaking volunteer for producing film about famous musician" — she starts to write the word *legendary* instead of *famous* but decides to be understated, even modest — and then gives the square of light blue paper — lilac, really — back to the girl, who looks at it for long moments, completely unsure of the next step, so much so that Maxine herself has to direct the girl, "Go on, go ahead and put it up there with the others," and so the girl takes one of the unused pushpins and tacks the ad into an available square of space, claiming its territory in a way that pleases Maxine immensely.

They push on then, like pioneers, out into the glare and heat, and the girl, who has been so jolted out of her routine — she'll have something to talk about to her coworkers for the rest of the day — only now begins to make conversation with Maxine. "So, you're looking for a famous musician?" The girl asks her question quickly, having learned through deep experience how to time and adjust her queries and her banter to the precise distance remaining between her and the traveler's car, whether near or far, and Maxine has to correct her, smiles at the girl's inexperience in the world and tells her, "No, I'm a singer; I'm looking for someone to make a movie about me and my sister and brother."

Maxine knows better than to tell the girl her name and ask if she's heard of her. It's happened too many times, is too painful. And she's still and always too proud to traffic on Elvis's name — to do so would threaten in but a moment to crush the friendship they had, the special quality of it — and she's too proud also to list any of the others. She was on top, dammit, not them, she thinks. She opened the gate for all that would come, not just Loretta Lynn and Dolly Parton, but for the whole crossover industry — for the young men, too, guitar wizards like Keith Urban and Brad Paisley, multimillionaires like Kenny Chesney and Garth Brooks. She sees their pictures in the magazines and anguishes over their torn jeans — not a one of them is presentable — but she covets their easy fame and feels that every one of them owes her a thank-you note, that it was she and her family — no one more so than they — who opened that gate and let the past and the present spread into the wider bright future.

They look like grandmother and granddaughter, the girl with her grocery cart and Maxine with her walker. They reach the car with questions unanswered and answers that have raised more questions, but all the girl knows to do is to turn around and go back to where she came from, to smile and say "Have a nice day!" after unloading the bags into the back seat, and off she goes in a whirl, running.

Maxine stows her walker, and with the fatigue of a shipwrecked sailor washed finally ashore, eases into her car, rolls the windows down to let the dizzying heat out, and just sits there, resting, her heart sprinting again. When will that particular race ever end, and what was she thinking, to have been so ambitious? Too much, too much, and with her journey only half over.

She imagines there are old women and even old men in more or less her same predicament who are checking into rest homes for the remainder of their days, or hiring assistants, but that's irrelevant: even if she did get so worn down finally that she would accept or even seek out such a thing, she couldn't afford but a week's stay, and she might have years of exhaustion left. *What should I have done differently?* she wonders. *What could I have done differently?*

She has pushed beyond her limits, but there is a guiding hand or fate somewhere out there that gets her back to where she needs to be. In some ways it's almost like the alcoholic blackouts of long ago, from the period after she had stopped being able to record any albums—when the contracts vanished and the Browns disbanded—and before she made her uneasy peace with that new accommodation, the cessation of fame.

She's aware of honking horns, a rude screech of tires, angry drivers, sunlight and heat—but as if in a dream, she makes it back to her neighborhood, the familiar sun-and-shade patterns are flowing over her windshield, and she's so relieved to be back that she almost careens into her garage, as if into a cave, and lowers her head to the steering wheel and cries, though only for a moment—crying never helped anything—and then she sleeps, too tired to even get out of the car, much less carry the milk in to the refrigerator. *It will keep for a little while,* she thinks. *I'll just nap for a few minutes.*

She sleeps like that for a solid hour, the engine ticking quickly at first but then more slowly, and then not at all, and she dreams of her childhood.

She would sleep longer, but gradually her dreams of long ago—she is walking down a narrow road through the forest, Jim Ed and Bonnie are on either side of and slightly behind her, they have no goal or destination, are merely out walking—are intruded on by the present, the sleepy awareness of where she is now, with groceries that need putting away, and—this is what awakens her and gets her going—the phone in the kitchen, still silent but capable of ringing, capable of conveying the voice of another, inquiring about her note on the bulletin board.

Once back inside, she naps again, lies down on the couch and sleeps so hard that she doesn't awaken until dusk, and feels completely off-balance. She's slept right through Buddy's afternoon passage, and, she fears, past any phone calls that might have come in. She doesn't have an answering machine and certainly doesn't have the money to spend on one, or the space left in her mind to learn how to use one. She'll just have to hurry a little now when she goes out to check the mail each day.

There's no telling how hard she's slept. *It's probably a little too soon for anyone to have seen the ad,* she thinks, and she tells herself to keep her hopes low, not to expect anything on the first day—but still, she's excited to be putting her longing out there again, just like in the old days. She wonders if the current will pick up that hope just as it did back then, and carry her forward, with no effort at all.

I had a big life, she thinks, but the thought is hollow; it doesn't attach to anything, not pleasure or pride or even regret, and the thought floats away as if none of it ever happened. The only thing that matters is the waiting, and the possibility of the call. And it is enough.

She boils water for tea. She is too exhausted from the day to fix even a TV dinner — she'll eat tomorrow. She pulls the phone over by her bed, her cot — it has occurred to her on more than one occasion that her hip might not ever feel strong enough for her to get back up those stairs — and as she falls asleep again, she imagines her little scrap of paper up on the bulletin board in the grocery store, and the stream of people moving past it, coming and going, and stopping, often, to look at it.

Someone who knows someone, that's all it takes. The world has never abandoned her. The current was fast, and then it became slow and lazy, and finally no longer discernible. But she has put a leaf onto it now to see if it is moving, and it seems to her that it is.

She falls asleep for the night, and although she awakens the next morning in time to feed Buddy, she is still tired from the rigors of the previous day and it ends up taking her nearly the rest of the week to fully recover, to the point at which soon enough she will have to go out and do it over again. She eats sparingly, trying to make her supplies last longer.

The phone does not ring — not even Jim Ed or Bonnie call — but the silence now is a positive thing. It means only that she's moving that much closer to the point when someone *will* call — this is how it has always worked in the past — and at the end of the week, feeling the old magic begin to stir (*That's it,* she thinks, as she feels for the first time in ages the gentle hand at her back, the subtle and cunning guidance of a fate that wants something from her), she places another ad, mailing this one to an address gotten from an old issue of *Country Music Today,* stating the same particulars and a few more: "Looking for movie producer to make exciting film about country music pioneer Maxine Brown." To figure out how to pay for the one-month ad, she spends an hour scribbling on a notepad, juggling her budget. Her electricity bill is $250 a month, most of which is the air conditioning; a month without it will pay for the ad and bring her the further extravagance of hope.

Not hope; certainty. The world has never let her down before. She has been waiting, but finally it is time to go beyond waiting.

This is how it used to be. Her depression lifts slowly. She has no one to talk to, and on the outside, nothing changes. But she is merrier. *What a miracle,* one would think, noticing the change in her, if there were anyone to notice. A spirit pervades her; it is the spirit of play and hope and careless joy that was in her back in the beginning.

Where does it come from, and why is it in her? Why has it returned? She cannot change the world again; she is done with that, has already changed it. Why then would such a thing return to her now? She called for it and it has come. It did not have to come. It possessed her; she was not in possession or command of it. And yet somehow she has summoned the summons.

It means nothing. Her time is gone; her days are done. But she calls for it, and it arrives, not as if with the certitude of fate, but instead simply as if from habit, its path to and from her in some ways as worn and established as that of the little dog that is now her sole contact with intimacy, companionship, love.

CHET BROUGHT THEM their full measure of fame, in exchange for their bringing him their greatness. For three or four years he was able to nurture and develop and perfect them — but part of their greatness was the ultimate unmanageability of the sound. No accompanists could score their harmony — Chet alone came closest, and became adept, almost in jazz fashion, at not joining them with his studio instruments but following them, patiently filling in those spaces he understood, saw, and heard, and with his help their music became even more accessible, without losing its original force.

Television bands were frustrated by them, had never heard or played with anything remotely like their harmony, and stumbled badly when playing live; it was just a little thing, this diminished vigor that attended such performances — a disynchrony between the Browns and their host bands — but eventually it began to result in fewer appearances on television. They didn't care — they preferred radio anyway, and preferred the live performances of touring, playing as they always had with just the three of them.

The wobble was much slower than the ascent had been rapid. Always a harbinger of the approach of the swooping low luck, another of Floyd's restaurants burned down. After the third one had burned he had been unable to find insurance, and had nowhere to turn now but back to the mill. He was too old for such work, but it was all there was. He hired another crew on speculation, and once more he and Birdie moved into the woods — even Norma was grown now, and off at college, studying music, with her perfect voice, but unattached to the tight coil of her older siblings.

Floyd and the crew began sawing again, growling their way farther into the forest, hunting the best and straightest trees again, extending their crude muddy roads farther into the swamp. Even on a bad day it beat the restaurant business — there was less adrenaline and less money, but there was something that remotely resembled peace, even for so unsettled a spirit as Floyd's — and it brought him some satisfaction also to know of his children's improbable success. Of his own part in that success, he was able in moments of sobriety to acknowledge that although he had been a little hard on Maxine when she was growing up, neither his or even Birdie's loving support had had anything to do with eliciting or forming that greatness. It was just a freak thing: they had been in the right time at the right place. Some force had simply wanted it to happen and had instilled the talent as well as the fire in each of them. It had next to nothing to do with Birdie and Floyd, and while he would like to have claimed to have had some hand in the matter, he couldn't.

There were times when Floyd was almost cowed by the force. It had been benevolent, but still, the immensity of it could be intimidating. He had noted long ago that the people who were drawn to it were not frightened, but on the contrary, bold, even courageous. Maybe too much so. A little caution, a little restraint, wasn't always a bad thing.

The early 1960s were nowhere nearly as kind as the 1950s had been. Another of their musician friends, Ira Louvin, was killed by a drunk driver. He had been one of the most revered songwriters of the time, and during the time of his crush on Maxine (he'd been in another relationship) had written the classic "I Take the Chance/(to Be With You)" for her. Emmylou Harris would go on to cover a great number of his other songs — "If I Could Only Win Your Love" and others — and "I Take the Chance," when Emmylou Harris recorded it, spent eight weeks at number one, just as it had back when the Browns first recorded it, way back in 1956.

Where is that invisible point where any one man's or woman's power is most fully realized? In which hour does any traveler pass through that point, crossing some indefinable threshold? Do any such travelers recognize or even sense that unseen summit?

The gradient is mild, seems no different than all the accruing days that preceded. The ascension of power is for the most part all the traveler has ever known, so that the traveler has no concept of anything but further ascent; as well, the power of denial is strong, so that even if on that one day when certain threads and filaments began to grow slack, a traveler sensitive enough to notice such things would surely tell herself that the reservoir, the capital accumulated in all the days previous, was more than sufficient to carry the traveler and her youthful power beyond any momentary slack spot, any eddy, any resting place.

The traveler sensitive enough to notice the slight pause in power's ascendancy would even tell herself that she was due for a rest, had earned it, and that such a pause was actually good for her, and for the power within. Almost as if the traveler — having all her life desired greatness, and power — was beginning to grow tired of it, gradually weakened by the burden.

Most, however, step through that curtain — that one certain day, that one certain moment — with no recognition that they are passing through a veil. And the more gifted the possessor of power is, the less likely he or she is to notice anything.

And in so doing — in the blithe passage that takes the gift, like youth, for granted — perhaps the going-away, the dissolution, is hastened. Perhaps such travelers pass from young to old with no middle journey.

Most, however, circle back once they realize they are missing something and try desperately to find it again. They don't even realize the burning is gone — that it is now only the echo of the thing that stirs them. That they are no longer chosen.

She is the only one left now, has been the only one left for a long time, and it is a loneliness beyond lonely, in no way commensurate with or proportionate to the pleasure that the greatness brought her.

Bonnie got out, found a graceful way to let the greatness return to the world, as did Jim Ed — a slow, dignified release — but not a wisp of it ever left Maxine. It's simply an unsustainable venture, and there are days when she thinks she, too, will finally explode — that the top of the volcano will explode.

Floyd's ghost leg was bothering him more, not less, but what else could he do but keep on working? He gimped through the woods on his crutches, eyeing the individual trees in the forest, looking for the best and evaluating which direction he would fell them, and planning ahead of time how to get them out of the tight embrace of the forest and back to the mill.

It was when he was in the forest that the pains were deepest, as if it were there that the body most remembered how things had once been, recalling, in the echo of cellular transmission and the cooling neurology of the past, the days when Floyd had been at his strongest — the best days — though the discomfort and even pain was not entirely without recompense; for in the aching and throbbing, and the jolts of pain, it seemed that the leg was still there, so that Floyd was still able to work as he had before. His balance was off but he still felt whole, if flawed and in pain. He built a special chair that fastened to the base of whatever tree he was felling, and he would sit there in it for hours, sawing or chopping steadily.

He might fell only one or two trees all morning in this manner, while the men around him sent theirs crashing down all around him in great numbers; but he was still working, still hunting the best and biggest trees, to keep him and Birdie going, if not the rest of his family, who had grown up now and proven themselves to be capable of making a living on their own.

He wasn't the only Brown to be haunted now by how things had been. Jim Ed was having a hard time accepting the new limitations of his mill-damaged hand — of learning new chords and tempos — though strangely, people remarked that since the accident his voice had gotten even stronger, deeper and more assured. Like Floyd, however, he could feel the pain of what was no longer there, and — mercifully — the slow going-away of the unsustainable power, the gift of the maelstrom with which he had started out.

Birdie, too, moved through the days between two worlds during this time. She loved all her children, but as her own health began to falter, she found herself wondering more, not less, what Raymond, the brightest and funniest of them all, would have been like. Wondering what her days would be like were he still in her life, still in all their lives. She knew that each and all carried a bit of him forward, but it was hard traveling on in that manner. It was worse than missing part of a hand, or a leg, and though she tried to keep her spirits up, she felt herself descending, too.

Whenever the Browns went out on the road, which was often — in 1958, they toured 300 of 365 days, and not one of those days was plush — Maxine left Tommy in charge of the children, but she found out later that he was not watching them, was hiring a babysitter, who wasn't doing a good job either. One of her babies had a broken leg when Maxine got home, and another got scalded by a kettle of hot water. To complicate matters, Tommy was sleeping with the babysitter, and Maxine was no longer able to fully enjoy or concentrate on her shows, wondering if her children were safe, and usually having difficulty in reaching anyone by phone, either before or after a show. She was drinking harder still by this point, but the hits kept coming: not quite as fast as only two years earlier, and not as high — some number fives and sixes and sevens — but still, people were listening to her, people were coming to hear them play.

Floyd had another accident. A tree he was sawing began to lean, but rather than snapping off on the hinge, it pulled the whole rootwad up as it went over and took with it Floyd and his special chair, still strapped to the trunk. It launched him, as if slung from a catapult, into the branches, whereupon landing he was pinned. No other workers were nearby, and he had to cut himself free, his good leg broken badly.

He got out on his own all right, and put off going to the hospital — why spend that kind of money if he didn't have to? — and instead was laid up at home for a few days. But the leg got infected and developed gangrene. By the time the Browns got him to the hospital, it was almost too late — the poison surged, too much of it was coursing through his body, toxins everywhere, and he needed steady transfusions to keep him alive.

It turned out he had a rare type of blood, one the doctors had never seen, and the only match that could be found was his brother — the one whose cabin had burned — and so his brother gave all that he could, which kept Floyd going for a couple more days, but then his brother could give no more and no other match could be found.

The doctors began calling all over the country, and amazingly, they found a match from a donor in Illinois and had the donor flown to Little Rock to donate all the blood he could spare.

It saved Floyd's life — the Illinois man alternating now with Floyd's brother — and the fever subsided, and he came home to heal up. And within a couple of months, he was back in the woods again, logging: more cautious than before, but still, pushing farther into the forest.

Helping Floyd with his walking therapy at the hospital, Bonnie fell down the steps one day, twisting her own ankle. Floyd's kind doctor was her own age, Gene "Brownie" Ring, and he attended to her.

He was neither flamboyant nor even terribly handsome — if anything, he was as quiet and reserved as Elvis was incandescent, as self-effacing as Elvis had been self-promoting — but the moment that Brownie first touched her ankle in the preliminary exam, she felt it, the ancient electricity. There was nothing but pleasure and longing in her from that touch, so much so that for long moments she forgot she was injured, and thought he might have healed her in that first instant.

BORROWING THE OLDSMOBILE

THAT WINTER, the Browns went back out touring radio stations — playing live, one song at a time, one broadcast at a time, schmoozing one station owner after another, singing into the darkness, it seemed to them, and looking back over their shoulder now at all the new stars who were following their lead, and singing with greater and greater verve, entertainers who were not in the least bit interested in either harmony or glide, musicians such as Jerry Lee Lewis, also up from out of the swamps. The Browns, though photogenic, just didn't translate to television, weren't comfortable twisting and shouting; and here, too, they were looking back over their shoulder and telling themselves to push harder, work harder, reach deeper.

Or rather, Maxine was. Jim Ed and Bonnie were starting to slow down a little. It wasn't the workload that was getting to them; it was the pace, it was the height of the flames.

Maxine, never a people person, was beginning to get a reputation among the station owners, all of whom were powerful old men, delighted by the novelty of touring young women, and delighted, too, by the novelty of one of those attractive young women asking the station owners for assistance. It was the same with the disc jockeys, and after a drink or three, they would inevitably cross the line with Maxine, to the point where — wired tighter and tighter each time she left home, left her children and Tommy and went out on the road, and wired tighter, too, from the first hint or suspicion that her hyperbolic rate of ascent had finally crested (and never mind that no one, or almost no one, other than Elvis was above them) — Maxine became even sharper in her criticisms, pushing to have their songs on the radio more. Her reputation grew as a woman with a hard edge. An unhappy woman, a difficult woman. She would not deign to catch flies with honey.

The Browns would travel for two weeks, then come home for a day or two. She would have a fight with Tommy, a meal with children she barely knew — they were changing so quickly — then back out for another week. There was no rhythm beneath or within any of them now; the only rhythm or harmony that existed was that which they could fabricate, as if from the ether, with their voices. There was nothing else.

Elvis was starting to pull away. All three Browns had watched his trajectory with only pride — success for any one of them was success for all. And though they each had different reactions to his ascent — Maxine was excited by and approving of it, Jim Ed found it amusing, and Bonnie was discomforted by it — something different was happening now. It wasn't so much that Elvis had risen above them, but that instead he was being carried away from them, no longer just some distance above them but drifting laterally. He had lost his anchor, his connection to them. He was lost in himself, and then — just one small false step, but so easy to make amid all that clamor and energy — he got lost in who his audience wanted him to be. This was not the same thing the world wanted him to be, and for that, he was doomed.

Bonnie's unease was extraordinarily complicated by the surprising reaction she had had, meeting Brownie Ring. She hadn't ever felt such insistent hunger with Elvis. She couldn't sleep well, thinking of the young doctor, and found that almost all her waking hours were spent in dreaming schemes or fantasies about how to see him again, and how long it might be. The simplest and best thing in the world would have been to let him go, though it occurred to her that her current boyfriend, Elvis, lived essentially a thousand miles away, or farther. Elvis in Japan, Elvis in Egypt. Elvis in Australia. It wasn't just the physical distance, though. It was something else. It was the same thing Maxine had.

She took the bold step of writing Brownie a note thanking him for the kind attention he had shown her father and her. She said that he might not remember her, but that she was sure he remembered her father, who was recuperating nicely.

"I don't remember any one-legged man," he wrote back. "I do remember tending to the ankle of a beautiful young woman from Poplar Creek," he wrote back. "I remember it well."

Each of the Browns saw Elvis now in a slightly different light, or chose to observe a different part of him, like the blind man with the elephant; but as to the moment when they first realized he not only had risen above them but was beginning to detach, drifting to the point where he might not ever be able to find his way back home, they would each concur. For them, that realization was as stark and dramatic as a fixed point on a timeline.

He had just gotten back from the army, where, while certainly not absent from the public eye, he had been a little constricted, after having previously known such freedom, such whirl, such roar. He had always been handsome, but now there was something else about him that drove girls and women wild, more than even before. Some desperation, some acknowledgment of waste or loss. It wasn't the seed or flaw of rot — it was something else. The pain of the knowledge of the wrong path chosen, perhaps, or at least the suspicion.

The women were throwing their clothes at him, screaming, drowning out the sound of his music. They swooned, fell over in dead faints; mass hysteria washed through the crowds like the fast-moving shadow of a lone cloud passing over a field.

When he came back to visit the Browns, it was as if he could still recognize them, could remember who they were and what they meant to him, but otherwise, there was some internal meter, some rhythm, that was different now, and that prevented him from moving in step with them, made it difficult even to converse. In its worst moments, it was like the dreams of opening one's mouth to call out but being unable to speak: no sound coming out.

They sat around the kitchen table and tried to talk about where they had each been and where they were going next, but that was all there was.

It seemed to each of the Browns almost as if there was a little bit of meanness in him now, whereas before there had never been such a thing. It wasn't really meanness — it was more just a fear that had gotten hold of him. Having made it to the top of the world, he'd seen how far he had to fall and couldn't bear the thought of not being loved. Every day had become double or nothing.

It made no sense. The Browns were selling almost as many records. It made no sense to Maxine.

It wasn't just Elvis who was drifting, however. It seemed that way to Jim Ed and Maxine, but what they didn't see was that Bonnie's attachment had loosened as well, and that she, too, like Elvis, was moving away from them all. Unlike Elvis, however, she was moving toward happiness, more of it than she already possessed and inhabited. It was still a dream world, this idea of a life with Brownie, but she could see the steps that were required to pass from that dream world into the real one, and it did not seem an insurmountable challenge.

The incident that clarified for each of them the magnitude of Elvis's drift, if not Bonnie's, came for them that same winter. The Browns were all three back home for a week, helping out around the house and playing a little music. They were resting up from the tour.

Tommy had disappeared the day after Maxine had arrived — they simply could not abide each other any longer — and Bonnie was helping Maxine take care of the babies. They'd been home for a few days when the phone rang in the middle of the night. It was Elvis calling for Floyd. He didn't even know the Browns were back home, and neither did he ask if they were. Elvis and his band were broken down outside of Shreveport and needed a ride. They had to be in Nashville the next afternoon, so Floyd and Bonnie drove out there to get him. They each took a car. Floyd would loan Elvis his new Oldsmobile. It rained cats and dogs the whole way.

When Floyd and Bonnie got there, they beheld a sorry mess. Elvis and his band had been sitting in their broken-down car all night, drinking, and from time to time they'd gotten out and stood in the rain, trying to tinker with the car's engine, something they knew absolutely nothing about, before getting drenched and climbing back into the car and drinking some more. There were three of them: Elvis; his bass player, Bill Black; and guitarist Scotty Moore. None of them was ready yet to be driving Floyd's Oldsmobile, so Floyd and Bonnie had to drive both cars all the way back to Poplar Creek and get them showered and fed and dressed before they were sober enough to take the car on up to Nashville.

Floyd and the Browns didn't really think much about it — the band was just boys being boys — and Elvis seemed grateful enough, and a little embarrassed at having gotten them up in the middle of the night. But it was good that he had someone to turn to when he needed help and they were glad he had called, were happy to help him anytime. He said thank you and goodbye, and that he would have the car back to Floyd in a week at the most, and then they headed on up the road.

Floyd didn't see him for another six months. None of them saw Elvis during that same period, but he'd made a movie while he was gone, and the next time he came through Pine Bluff he was in a pink Cadillac, riding around with Colonel Tom Parker, wearing the white suit and the big sunglasses. He had his picture in the paper, wearing those clothes and sitting on the fender of that new Cadillac, but despite being that close to Poplar Creek, had not made it by to see them. They waited, and worried, and nursed their disappointment, trying to make it smaller — trying to keep it in a separate compartment, each of them, from all the rest of him that each of them knew and loved — but like smoke, their disappointment seeped through the cracks and began to infiltrate everything.

Floyd waited another couple of weeks, then called Elvis and asked him where his car was, and Elvis said he'd have a driver return it to him. And he did, about a week later, but it didn't look like the same car. It had dings and dents in it, and was all scratched up, as if someone had been driving it through the brush. The tread was worn off the tires, and he had put 30,000 miles on the car. It was dusty and dirty; he hadn't even bothered to have it washed.

Even then, the Browns didn't blame him. They were sad and uneasy about who he was becoming — about who he had become — but they understood better than anyone the howling forces that were buffeting him: the winds that would either snuff out his fire or fan it into something unmanageable.

They viewed his drift as more of an illness than a character flaw. "He'd just gone crazy," Bonnie said whenever she talked about him to Maxine. "It was so sad, so disappointing."

There was a part of her that tried to hold on to him in her heart, late at night when she was alone — just before sleep — but the pragmatic part of her understood he was already gone, and that the pain she was feeling wasn't so much for herself, or even for him, but instead for something that simply wasn't there anymore.

At the same level, they must have understood that it wasn't just Elvis who was being lost to them, but that they, too, were somehow vanishing.

Jim Ed sanded and buffed the car himself once they got it back. By that time, they didn't have enough money to fix it.

"If you squint your eyes, or if the car is moving, you can't really tell," he said hopefully when he was finished.

"No," Bonnie said, "you can tell."

Floyd died in his sleep that winter, while the Browns were out on one of their circuits. He had fallen ill with a cold from having been out working in the woods in the rain, but had not seemed overly sick — he had been in bed for only a couple of days, with a fever and chills and a cough, nothing more. He had a drink of moonshine that night, with the cabin warm — Birdie had been keeping the woodstove in the bedroom popping, so that his uneasy sleep would have been punctuated by the sound of burning. Fever and chills, up and down, throwing the heavy quilts off, then pulling them back over him, before finally hitting a kind of calm glide and sleeping easily.

He felt that he might have turned the corner and was possibly even anticipating work the next day — the winter rain continuing to beat down on the roof, but no matter, he was warm and dry — but then there was only silence. He simply left them, with no drama or outrage, no sentimental preparations, no turmoil; as if all of those things that had constituted their days together, in all the moments and years preceding this one, had not been how he was, but as if instead the quiet truth had finally been revealed, despite the condition of his disease: that beneath the drinking and the drama — beneath the fear of what, he never knew — he had been a hard worker and a provider. A shelter, even if a flawed one, for their greatness. And above all, a fan.

They all took it hard — Birdie, the hardest, and Maxine, she whom he had battled so fiercely, suffering the loss, the passing on, in some ways even harder, with it seeming to her that Floyd had somehow gotten the last word just as she was beginning to forgive him for the unpredictability, the chaos, with which he had imbued their childhood, and from which their gift, their ability to impose a bewitching calm, had emerged.

Now that he was gone, and without the complications of his drinking, she could see how much he had loved all of them — even her, the one who had screamed how she hated him. Now that he was gone, she could see clearly that the full weight of his ceaseless pride, like Birdie's, was the same thing as love, as elemental as love but simply unvoiced, and she was furious with him for not having been able to articulate it in other ways, and furious at herself for not having seen it or heard it back when it had existed.

Sometime that winter, and into the spring, music became work. None of them could have said where or why, only that it had changed. They still sounded the same, but the world had changed, they were in a quicker current, and something else had gone away, and the fun was wearing out.

BROWNIE DISPLACES THE KING

Can I come see you, one of the letters said. *Not at a show, but at your home. I'd like to see where you live, would like to see where you come from.*

Panic and exultation seized her simultaneously. She had suspected she wanted him in her life, but she had not known it. Terrified that if he came, he might be repulsed by the primitive conditions of her home, she nonetheless knew no other answer to give him but yes.

As she had once counseled Maxine to avoid Tommy, now Maxine came to her, advising her not to quit Elvis. It was a complicated piece of business in at least three directions. Elvis was their friend, almost like family, and to some degree he was embedded in their careers, and — now that he had gotten out ahead of them — he could do so much for them. He could reach back and help pull them through the curtain that separated fame from immortality, Maxine believed, though if he was married to Bonnie, he wouldn't even have to reach back and pull; they could just stroll on through, and be carried into that land. Could inhabit that land as if it had been no struggle at all to get there.

There was the third and least savory direction, the part that made Maxine feel not very good about herself. Her own marriage had been a failure — it had been Tommy's fault, not hers, but still, a failure — while Bonnie, as usual, was skating through life, had captured the heart of the most eligible or desirable bachelor in the world. It wasn't what nice people did, competing with their own sisters, and yet when Maxine considered a future without Elvis in their lives, and a Bonnie without that jolting radiance, the charisma that surrounded both of them when they were together, she had to admit, she felt a curious small relief, if not true pleasure.

"Go ahead and invite Brownie here, if you have to," Maxine said. "I wouldn't mind getting another look at him anyway. But you don't

Nashville Chrome

have to decide right now. You don't have to act rashly. You can think about it for a while, and decide later."

"Oh, I wouldn't do that," Bonnie said. "I wouldn't invite him if I hadn't already made up my mind."

Maxine was incredulous. It was unlike anything Bonnie had ever done; Maxine had never known her to be anything but careful and cautious.

"What instrument does he play?" Maxine asked. "Does he sing?" Meaning, *He can't possibly play or sing like Elvis.* She felt the old desperation rising in her, the ferocity of grip — *Go after what you want, get hold of it, and don't let go* — and was surprised to find how fiercely she was advocating for Elvis, how desperately she did not want him out of their lives.

"He doesn't know anything about music," Bonnie said, almost gaily. "He doesn't care anything about it at all. He's deaf in one ear," she said.

"Deaf?" Maxine said. If Bonnie had slapped her, she could not have been more offended.

"He got his medical degree on the GI Bill," she said. "He was in the navy, worked with the cannons on battleships, loading them for artillery practice. He can't hear a thing out of his left ear, and his right ear isn't real good."

"This is a joke," Maxine said. "You're teasing, right?"

"Come on," Bonnie said, taking her hand. "I have an envelope to mail to my love. Come walk with me down to the mailbox."

He came in a freak spring snowstorm, a wet, heavy snow that pulled down and then broke limbs and branches everywhere, so that all of Arkansas looked as if a tornado had blown through. The storm knocked out all the power lines, so that the entire region was without phone or electricity; people in cities and towns were reduced to gathering the runoff of snowmelt from their roofs and boiling water for coffee and tea in their fireplaces, as many of them had done before the period of new affluence had spread slowly into the region. Few if any of them were but a generation removed from such hard times, and for many of them, the storm was a welcome pause, a reminder of where they had come from and how their lives had been; a touchstone for their old identities.

On through it all, Brownie drove, marveling at the slow descent of the huge swirling flakes, the deep silence of the storm, and the world it was briefly altering, in synchrony for once with the hushed world he so often inhabited. Here, there was no variance between the shapes of things at the surface and the objects below, beneath the accruing blanket of snow.

He drove carefully, eager to see Bonnie, but paradoxically feeling there was no need to hurry, that he would get there when he needed to be there, and that all was right with the world. He would not have been conscious of the page of any history book of the world turning, but he was keenly aware of a break, a momentousness, in his own, and he was not afraid.

Usually when people looked at him, they thought he was mild, a figure of respect and authority, certainly, with the ability to heal people — but mild. He *was* reserved, it was true; he was dignified and undaring, completely averse to risks, educated as he was in statistics and probabilities — but he was a bombardier, too, had been trained to fire only the largest shells at the largest targets, so that only once was necessary.

He was mild, but he loved life fiercely. Maybe that made him not mild. Regardless, he had won her heart, had displaced a fairy-tale king, had vanquished an icon. No one would ever know his name or identity, just as they would one day soon no longer know Bonnie's or Jim Ed's or Maxine's, but his life was about to become huge, as was hers more perfect, and in its own way, more daring — and he drove on, comforted by the hush, and by the way the snow covered everything, every stilled and sleeping shape.

She had mailed him a hand-lettered map to their cabin, with cartoon representations, like a child's treasure map, of forests, dirt roads, cabins with chimney smoke, to assure him he was on the right path. It was an intricate map, not drawn at all to scale — the representations of things grew ever larger the closer he came to his destination — and he kept it spread on the passenger seat and pulled over from time to time to study it, being careful to not veer off the road and get stuck in the beautiful snow. Wanting to approach in quiet and unobtrusive style. Not wanting to have to walk miles to a stranger's cabin, where there might or might not be a phone, to call and ask for help.

All of the landmarks, it seemed, were on the map; as if Bonnie had known how the strange new landscape would appear to him, a first-time traveler. The abandoned tractor, the white bulldog that would come charging down from out of the Franklins' yard, untethered by rope or chain, a seemingly ageless dog that hated all vehicles and that for years had dictated great looping detours for any passersby on foot. Brownie was prepared for the dog, but did not see it coming at him in the snow until it was already up against the side of his car, silent and stealthy, not a barker but a killer, its claws scrabbling against the side of his car like branches in a storm, the dog's black button eyes and flared nostrils the only thing Brownie saw at first, and then the pink of the dog's gaping mouth, the slavering tongue, and finally, yellowish white amid white amid purer white, the old dog's fangs snapping and biting.

Brownie did just what Bonnie had instructed him — what local motorists had learned to do. He slowed the car further, timed the dog's leap perfectly, and then opened his door quickly, halfway, as if inviting the dog in for a ride, but instead smacked the dog midleap with the iron door wing. There was a single yelp, not so much of pain as disappointment, and then Brownie shut his door quickly and kept motoring on, slowly, deeper into the wilderness.

The hulking abandoned sawmill appeared finally, mythic in its disrepair — merely a shell now, a crumbling museum of what briefly had been — and he drove on farther, past the giant stumps, with the younger trees growing up thick around them now, and then, at the end of the road, more beautiful than he had been hoping or imagining, he saw the dark cabin with its own smoke thread rising, its own yellow squares of light in the early gloom, its own unbroken field of snow in the small yard.

Other cars were parked out front, snow shrouded — no one had traveled anywhere all day — and as he shut his lights off to approach in privacy, and turned his motor off and got out, the falling snow quickly mantling on his shoulders and his hat, he turned his good ear toward the cabin and heard faintly the tunes of enthusiastic music, balanced perfectly against all the other stillness, and he knew that if with his damaged hearing he could hear the music, it must indeed be boisterous.

In the center of one of the dull yellow windows he could see a slightly brighter portal, a hand-rubbed viewpoint of scraped-away steam and frost, and even as he stood there, he saw a hand appear, rubbing vigorously yet again, and saw Bonnie's face filling the space just behind the screen of falling snow.

At first she did not see him, motionless as he was amid the snow — but then she saw his parked car, the only unshrouded thing in the yard, and then he raised a hand to wave at her, as if he were rubbing at a similar windowpane.

Her face disappeared quickly from the window and then the door flew open and she was hurrying out to greet him. Maybe it wasn't proper, maybe she didn't know him as well as she thought she did, but maybe she knew him better, for all the words that had passed between them, with the richness of space separating their words, a week at a time — three days in the mail for a letter outgoing, three days coming back, with a day off for Sunday — and Bonnie wrapped him in a snowy hug, kissed him quickly before she could even wonder at it, and before her family came outside, unconvinced yet that her rash leap of heart was wise or even considered.

The music kept playing, though — they were midsong — and she kissed him again. Snow on both of them. He had brought flowers not just for her but for Birdie and Maxine and Norma, and he ducked back into the car to get them, three bouquets of yellow tulips and one of red, each brilliant in the snow and dim light of early evening.

The music was still winding down, and Maxine came out onto the porch in time to see Bonnie escorting Brownie up toward the steps, her arm linked in his, and looking already like a bride in white. The bouquets as brilliant as three torches, Bonnie and Brownie laughing at something, and an overwhelming wave of franticness — was it jealousy, or something even larger? — overtaking Maxine. She noted with that same feeling of terror the scufflemarks of their embrace in the snow, the space of it already being quickly covered, and she felt it again, stronger and deeper, like a third chord struck.

They came up onto the porch slowly, not caring at all that they were being covered with snow, and Bonnie introduced Maxine to Brownie, who shook her hand warmly but somehow also with the formality of his profession. "These are for you," he said, handing her one of the bouquets of yellow tulips, their cupped heads half filled with the immense flakes, and she managed a protest: "You shouldn't have, thank you, that's so sweet."

"I'm glad to get to meet you," he said, and Maxine said, "So am I." She was glad to have him out on the porch for a short while, away from the rest of her family, where she could study him more critically, but he and Bonnie were already stamping the snow from their feet and shaking it from their clothes, and then going past her, opening the door and stepping into the cabin. Maxine turned and followed.

There was an immediate outcry of welcome, a cheer for the heroism of the arrival — a greeting that far exceeded, Maxine realized, her own subdued welcoming.

The snow melted almost instantly from Brownie's and Bonnie's shoulders as they stepped into the woodstove heat of the cabin, so that for a moment they glistened as if cast into ice statues — but in a blink that sheen dissolved, steam was rising from both of them and Brownie was stepping forward, shaking hands and passing out the glistening tulips, and when he was done, he apologized to Jim Ed but said that he had something warm for him later. Brownie didn't drink much at all — there was rarely time for it with his work, and when he had any spare time, he craved and sought sleep as another might seek that whiskey — but when he did take a rare sip, he made sure that it was of good stock and not rotgut swill.

For all of the woodstove's robust heat, there were currents of cold air, frigid little pools and rivers where the outside air seeped in between certain logs or eddied beneath certain places in the loft, and the Browns knew intimately the map of these places, were arranged around the cabin in such a way as to avoid them. The cold rivers, invisible to all, flowed around each of them but touched none of them, and Bonnie took Brownie's arm and pulled him over to sit next to her on one of the islands of warmth as if pulling him to safety.

They told stories deep into the evening. Such was his hunger for their stories that they set down their guitars and for once spoke rather than sang—consolidating, over the evening, some of their greatest hits, stories Brownie needed to know about each of them. Edging close, on a couple of occasions, to a mentioning of Elvis, but veering tactfully away just in time. They spoke loudly so that he could hear, and the volume of their storytelling encouraged others to pitch in; even quiet Norma had a story. It was the best night they had had as a family since Floyd had died, and at different points of the evening each of them had the thought of how much he would have enjoyed it, even as they knew perhaps he might not have—that as always, with Floyd, things could have gone either way.

Further into the evening Brownie took out the elegant silver flask he had brought for Jim Ed and handed it to him.

"But I wanted the tulips!" Jim Ed protested. He took a too large gulp and made a small, satisfied groaning sound, then passed it around. The singers and Brownie each took a sip, while Norma and Birdie abstained. Later in the night everyone except Birdie went outside and made snow angels. The snow was still falling, the temperature right at freezing so that the flakes clumped and coalesced, some of them appearing to the upturned faces of the outstretched revelers as large as sheets of paper swirling down, while sparks from the chimney popped and spewed upward into the storm.

When they went back inside, the whole porch shook with their combined boot stamping and snow whacking, and finally—it was almost midnight—they went to bed, Brownie sleeping on a pallet in front of the fire. Norma had offered Brownie her small room, saying she could sleep with Birdie, but Brownie wouldn't hear of it. Maxine cut warning eyes at Bonnie, cautioning her against any late-night or early-morning revelry out by the fire, but she needn't have worried; desperate for sleep, Brownie had fallen as if into narcolepsy the instant everyone got up to go to their rooms, and Bonnie covered him with an extra blanket, touched his firelit cheek, and never looked back, never gave a second thought to where she was going.

He stayed for two days. He had babies due to deliver soon and was uneasy about being gone, but was having the time of his life. Everyone slept late that first morning, and then before the snow melted — it would do so quickly, in the manner of spring storms — he walked down to the mill with Jim Ed, who showed him where he had lost his fingers, and where Floyd had lost his leg. Family lore, just beneath the snow, and already the cold sun beginning to melt that shroud, with the sound of dripping starting slowly and snow-draped branches springing to life all around them. Jim Ed did not show him where Raymond had fallen — not that, yet — but Brownie understood that he was visiting a hallowed battlefield. The mill hulking there like Atlantis exposed by a gone-away ocean, and the wet snow sliding from it in sheets and slabs.

By that evening, all but a few patches of the snow was gone, and the creek was running so wild that there was no way any of them would have been able to cross. At dinner that night they told the story of Floyd and his bridge crossing, and still more stories. Brownie had noticed Birdie's difficulty in getting up and down from her seat and asked if she had had arthritis for long, asked if he could take a look at her ankles, knees, wrists, hands. The children were surprised when she said yes, and while his prescription was not revolutionary — ice for five minutes in the mornings before she got going, and again late in the afternoon — she was flattered and happy, and promised to obey his orders.

Norma had no ills, and when Brownie asked if Maxine had anything she needed tending to, she said, "You can't win me over, so don't even bother."

"What did you say?" Brownie said. "I can't hear you. Can you speak up?" But he was smiling.

The next morning he went turkey hunting with Jim Ed. All the snow was gone, and the creek, though still high, was passable again — and despite Brownie's diminished hearing, he was a good enough caller to lure a nice gobbler in for Jim Ed, who shot it, one of the largest he'd ever gotten, and their new friendship was sealed that easily.

Birdie roasted the turkey that evening—Thanksgiving in April, with baked sweet potatoes and lemon pie. Though Brownie didn't eat nearly as much as Elvis, he helped with the dishes, made an icepack for Birdie's ankles, and insisted that she stay off her feet that evening.

It was really no contest, and while an observer looking at the surface of the relationships might have expressed shock at Bonnie's cutting loose of Elvis, a more careful examiner would have remembered that there are occasionally even in the world of men and women—with mankind still so newly arrived in and not yet fully shaped to the world—certain fits so elegant and fulfilling as to seem predesigned or destined, and when Brownie left the next morning, Birdie and Jim Ed and Norma told him to be sure and come back soon.

Even after Brownie's old sedan had gone across the bridge and around the bend, back into the forest and away from them, it felt to each of the Browns as if he had not left at all, and that they could be assured, always, of his coming back. Even Maxine felt it, and though his arrival had meant a gap needed to be created elsewhere in her—the space that would have to be vacated by Elvis—she understood it was inevitable, and saw instantly how Brownie fit Bonnie's world, and precisely why there was no contest for her little sister's heart. He was not rich but he was thoughtful. He was a master at occupying the quiet spaces between spaces, and the spaces between things and events. Of course he was the thing that had been missing from Bonnie's life, maybe from all of their lives. Maxine saw that now, though still she mourned Elvis, mourned the loss of her friend, who—she understood this now—might well have been born lost.

It wasn't fair. Brownie didn't even know anything about music, and didn't care—though here, too, Maxine had to admit to the perfection of her sister's find. He would heal whatever their music couldn't reach. In barely even being able to hear her music, he would serve as a sanctuary, an oasis of downtime from that stress. A secret life: her daring little sister.

He would create a place in both their lives where—amazingly—

neither of them would have any need for music. It wasn't fair, and again Maxine felt a colossal regret and resentment that she should have to be the pioneer, going forward first and making all the mistakes, so that her younger brother and sister might then benefit from those mistakes, and those hard corrections.

In a little more than a year, Bonnie and Brownie would be married, and in nine months beyond that, their first child would be born. So much was moving now, beyond Maxine's ability to control or even change. It didn't make sense to her, how when she was young, she had had the ability to control or influence things — while at the peak of her career, every little thing seemed suddenly to be receding from her reach.

She had no proof of such a thing, it was just a suspicion, an intuition — but the more she fretted about it, the more she saw it, that her flame was burning out, the world had used her up and was done with her. She was twenty-nine.

ANOTHER BOAT RIDE

BIRDIE HAD RESURRECTED the Trio Club, was running it by herself, still working herself to death—the Browns simply couldn't keep her from working—and finally, for the first time, Birdie appeared to be capable of knowing prolonged sorrow herself, following Floyd's death. These complications the evidence that no one spirit exists bright and separate from all the others around.

Like the ghost the world had called for him to be now, Elvis had come back to see Bonnie as if trying to rescue himself: returning like a sleepwalker, an imposter of the young man he had once been, and been to her. He didn't even look quite the same; already, the edges were beginning to blur. He was a little looser, a little wilder, and though anyone who had not known him before would have described him as happy, the Browns could see that he was worse. That something larger than even his own spirit had gripped him—had captured his fear and made it large.

He and Bonnie went canoeing on Poplar Creek one last time. By that time Bonnie knew it was the last time, but Elvis did not yet. It was springtime again and they picked wildflowers to place on Floyd's grave, which was on a hill overlooking the woods where Floyd and Jim Ed had hunted, with the creek visible in patches and shining puzzle pieces. It was the breakup, but they each treated it with a calm dignity, and prepared for it no differently than they had during the courtship and love's ascendancy. They took a hamper of Birdie's cooking—a dewberry pie, fried chicken and potato salad, cornbread, hard-boiled eggs—and a blanket and their guitars. He had always had an appetite, but by that time he was insatiable; before the day was half over, he had eaten everything in the picnic basket, a whole hamper's worth.

They didn't talk much, but neither did they attempt to fill the silences with hollow chatter about touring. Instead, they just drifted down the creek. The clunk of the paddle against the gunwale as Elvis stirred the slow brown water. Bonnie sat in the bow, facing him. Smiling, but nervous. The one thing he could not bear, the idea of not being loved enough.

She had made up her mind, and knew now what she wanted, and knew how to get there, and that Elvis was in the way, that she had to go over the top of him. Sometimes her hands trembled in between paddle strokes.

The slight V of the wake as the boat moved quietly down the slow waters. They each knew what was happening but had no idea why. There were moments like this for them sometimes when they were onstage, moments when all they meant to be doing was playing, singing their hearts out, but then something happened: moments when they caught and owned the hearts of their audience, as if through some alchemy of shared emotions, some strange resonance of spirit, so much so that not only did the audience find itself inhabiting their sound, but was waiting on and wanting more, needing more — desperate to hear the next sound, the next swoop.

Sometimes the moments elicited a roar from the audience; other times, a pin-drop silence. Either way, those moments were always fraught with enormous power — a power that seemed somehow even larger for having emerged from the paradox of the performers simply having wanted to have a good time. And there on Poplar Creek, on the day of their breakup — his banishment — there was in their quiet drift that same presence of almost intolerable meaning: the power of each ticking moment both agonizing and exhilarating.

It started out all right; for a little while they were able to dance around it. Elvis in particular was gifted at such evasion, while it was more of Bonnie's nature to push ahead and give herself over to that moment of power; to give the audience more of whatever it was they had decided they wanted.

Still, in the beginning, she could tell how frightened and uneasy he was, and gave him some space to simply paddle, and fidget. It was sad, having to ride quietly and wait for that nearing moment, and she tried to concentrate on Brownie. It was as if she could see two lives, two paths — one if she chose Elvis, and one if she chose Brownie — and she could see clearly now that the distance between those two paths was exactly the measure of Elvis's hunger. Not the old Elvis, but the new one. She had to save herself, but it was more than that: she loved Brownie.

She had not told him about Brownie, and saw no need to. *I would be breaking up with him even if I had not met Brownie,* she told herself, and she believed that.

They stopped and picnicked in the same place they always had, a dazzling white sandbar at the edge of the deep green woods. There was an old driftwood spar that they leaned their backs against, and they stretched their pale legs and bare feet out and ate the fried chicken like royalty, a king and queen liberated. Birdie, who knew what was coming, had packed simple cloth napkins, and when they were done, they wiped their hands on them and then undressed and went into the creek to bathe further.

Even Elvis began to understand what was coming. After they came back out of the creek, water running off of them as if streaming from horses, they lay down and made love on the damp firm-packed sand at water's edge where there was no grit. Bonnie found herself crying and trying to hide her tears from Elvis, wanting him to know at least a few more minutes of peace, or delusion. Even a few more seconds. She was turned away from him but when some of her tears landed on his wrist, he knew they were not from the wetness of her hair. They felt as hot as melted mercury, and though he knew in that instant all that which he had already known but had been trying to keep suppressed, he still could not help but continue to pretend otherwise.

"What is it?" he said. "What?" He turned her to face him, sought desperately for clues of how he might smooth back over this disturbance. Bonnie shook her head, crying harder, and there was no going back now; things were different, and beyond them the lazy current kept spooling past, with them no longer on it. Elvis had the irrational thought that if they were still out in that current, still in their boat — if they had not come in to shore — things could still have turned out differently.

"What is it, baby?" he asked. "We can fix it," he said, betraying only now his own knowledge and understanding of all that lay below them. "We can make it right, baby," he said. "I know things have been crazy."

Such was his confidence that he never even thought to ask if there was someone else. It wasn't so much arrogance as simply nothing that fit in his reality, and further evidence of the abyss between the two paths. "Just crazy," he said, "but all that will blow over." And she felt it then, felt it like a *click* so pronounced, it seemed almost audible: the resetting of things back to how they had been, his last-gasp effort to step back and become again who he had once been.

It was dizzying; it felt to both of them as if he were crossing a fast river and had reached the middle and paused, was standing on a wobbly, slippery stone, but that for a moment — in that stepping-back — he was safe.

He was holding on to her, too, was what it felt like — holding on to how they had been — and Bonnie was seized with the desperate desire to pry his death grip loose even as her own old self remembered the pleasure — not joy, but pleasure — of that grip.

The confessions poured out of him now, from the refuge of that middle spot: how he needed her, how she was the only one he felt he could still be himself around, how he wanted to marry her, how life wouldn't be any good without her in it . . .

She had ducked her head, was crying again, but there was certainly no testimony that could be offered that would alter the vision she understood to be true — the awful distance he had traveled already and the trajectory and momentum that was taking him still farther away. There could be no negotiation on this, and to some extent, she, unlike him, had already been doing her grieving. The guilt-twined combination of grieving and exultation.

The ragged dance of such leave-taking; now it was her turn to shake her head and draw away from the density of the thing between them, while for only the first time now he sought to address it, and so much too late. She was annoyed with herself for the way the sound of his voice resurrected old hopes, old pleasures.

"Let's paddle," she said, suddenly eager to leave the beach — understanding at some level that motion would help soothe him, would begin in some way the sealing-over process of healing—and so somewhat sullenly, he got up and began gathering their picnic items, and doing the emotional math for the first time, which of the two ways he wanted go.

All his life, so many of his decisions seemed to have been made for him as if by fate, simply by following the paths of impulse or opportunity. This seemed entirely different: it seemed to require a calculation as prodigious as were the consequences risky — fame or happiness? — though even by the act of considering the two, the answer had already been reached.

So they pulled back for a while, each into a place of hurt, seeking some protection in that new distance. Elvis paddled sometimes with irritation or frustration, other times with despair — and for a while they pretended a decision had not been reached. They didn't even so much smooth it over as seal it off for a little while; and as they resumed their drift, it felt to Bonnie as if she had to paddle to catch up with a new segment of life that had flowed past during the time they had lain there on the beach, while to Elvis it seemed as if they should not have left the beach, or that something had been left there — something he had forgotten and wanted back but would not be able to find again.

At least they were not quarreling. They never had, nor would they. The closest they came was later in the afternoon, when — still trying to keep at bay the unpleasantness of the disagreement of the breakup — they pulled into an eddy and baited their cane poles with worms, feeling that since they had brought the poles, they should use them.

They fished in silence, pretending to concentrate, for nearly an hour, the heat sending slow trickles of sweat down their backs. They sat as motionless as was possible to keep from spooking any drifting-by or hanging-around fish, and Bonnie's face was partially hidden in the shadow cast by her wide straw hat, and, as ever, she was more patient. Elvis swatted at a gnat, caught it and crushed it, tossed it onto the water's surface, where no fish rose to examine it.

"Too hot for the fish to bite," he said — in his heart, thinking, *Next time we come it will be better,* a lump in his throat, a burning in his chest — and Bonnie said quietly, "Fish deeper."

"Nah," he said — be damned if he would let a girl tell him how to fish, never mind that it was her home creek — and he stilled his fidgeting, stared more intently at his red and white bobber, willing a fish to take the worm, and not just any fish, but a big one. Telling himself that he would not leave until that happened, and willing it to be a fish of such immensity that Bonnie would laugh and scream, that it would be something she'd remember always, and that the excitement of the catch would cause her to rethink things, and to change her mind.

That if the fish was large enough, they could somehow go back to where they had always been before.

Bonnie was hot and getting hotter. Her line was still in the water, and from all outward appearances she was still focusing on waiting for a fish, but in her mind she had stopped fishing, was hoping she would not catch a fish, and was already looking ahead to the business of getting on with her future — of beginning to heal up over the heartbreak and continuing on with her life, and still feeling that strange and uncomfortable sensation that she needed to catch up with something that had passed her by while she had waited there on the beach.

Elvis's bobber went under: dipped twice, then plunged deep, and he shouted, gave a yank on his pole and set the hook, and shouted again as the line sawed back and forth through the water with the unseen treasure bolting.

In that moment, he felt the old pure joy of who he had once been — who he still was, barely — rushing through him with the hope and confidence that disaster had been averted.

It wasn't a big fish, though. When he hoisted it from the water, he and Bonnie both saw that it was barely eating-size. It was right at the cusp of the size where if an angler was hungry he or she would keep the fish, though it would not make much of a meal — would not even satisfy a child's appetite — or the angler could toss the fish back, saving the trouble of having to clean it, and could feel slightly virtuous.

Elvis wanted to keep the fish — he believed that his only chance of having her remain, the only indication that she might be willing to reconsider and to remember and appreciate their love and not relinquish it, would be if she agreed to keep the middling fish, as they had done so many times before.

"Well, chum," Elvis said, speaking to the potbellied little fish as it swung at the end of his line, "we've seen bigger, but you'll do. Maybe we'll catch a few more of your friends."

"Oh, Elvis," Bonnie said, "he's too small. Let's throw him back. Let's let him live."

Elvis huffed up, looked at her as if he had never even considered such a thing and couldn't understand why she would even suggest it. "He's eating-size," he lied. "Not by much, but he'll do. I'm hungry," he lied again. His heart thrashing and darting. He was still holding the cane pole aloft, the little fish was still twisting on the line, awaiting its fate — gold-rimmed eyes wide, gills working hard in the bright air — and Elvis, in the first concession to loss, dipped the fish back down in the water just long enough to wet it, then lifted it back out. As if upon its reemergence it might somehow appear larger.

He pulled the line in then and unhooked the fish, as he had done thousands of times before. The long bronzed hook, the fragment of pale earthworm still attached, shoved up to the shank.

"Please let him go," Bonnie said. "Please throw him back." But Elvis whacked the fish hard against the side of the boat, intending to kill it, but only stunning it. The fish quivered, then recovered and resumed its thrashing.

Bonnie began to cry again, and Elvis immediately lost all heart and said, "Look, honey," and tossed the fish back into the creek — it shuddered off, inky black, back down into the deeper brown waters, where it might one day grow to be a giant, shunning all hooks and the overhead passing of boats' bellies, blocking out the sun — but it was too late: Bonnie's shoulders were shaking, and when he scooted forward in the canoe and tried to console her, she shrugged off his touch and hissed, *"Don't."*

In a way it was the kindest thing he could have done, making it easier for her. Perhaps there was even some kindness in him, some instinct, that had known that, or perhaps it was the world's instinct; whatever the reason, both of their injured hearts began the hard process of turning away and drying up, the first layer of desiccation wrinkling the surface.

They paddled on downstream in silence, both with something new in them that seemed like its own kind of fierceness, a thing that had not been in them before: a survivor's fierceness.

The afternoon was growing late; it would be almost dusk before they got to the take-out, and early dark before they got back home, and they paddled all the way to the bridge without speaking, instead concentrating only on the efficiency of their strokes so that they might get there sooner, and both furious that the beautiful thing had gone away, had been lost, let go.

There was a bonfire burning in the yard when they got back, and they came driving in slowly. They were speaking to each other now concerning only the most perfunctory of matters — who would put the picnic hamper away, did Elvis need help with the boat — and as they drew nearer they could see the figures of their family standing around the fire, could hear the music, the sound of their singing, and their hearts buckled but then grew harder, both as determined now to survive as they had been previously to love deeply. The swoop and swoon of the world, and Bonnie felt some small satisfaction that she might have caught back up with whatever had passed her by there on the beach earlier in the day, though the cloud of guilt was immense.

Elvis didn't stay the night, but left straight away, though with a hope that seemed so strange to him as to not even feel like it was quite his but coming from some further, other place. Bonnie, likewise, was plagued that night by the sound of his voice and the memory of pleasure — *I could go back,* she thought, *I could still go back* — but in the morning the sun was bright, and later that afternoon, there was another letter in the mailbox, and she moved on, further and deeper into the future.

THE MIDDLE YEARS

THERE IS A QUESTION Maxine has for herself, as she opens more boxes and vaults from that long spell when upon beholding the world beyond her she saw that the world was no longer looking at her, and in her panic at that observation, she failed to behold the world.

Her question has to do with fortune or luck — not fame, but simple luck. She and her siblings had so much of it in their early years. Did it go away, in that strange middle ground that she has trouble remembering, or was it still there, simply unnoticed by her, during that time of panic?

She thinks it went away. There had been hard times in their youth, but it seemed they got harder later in life, and that — despite what she had believed to the contrary — wealth had nothing to do with it, and neither did fame.

She expected and understood that she would one day lose Birdie, and Floyd, too; and she understood that she would miss Floyd, would even grieve him, despite or in some strange way perhaps because of his harshness and unpredictability, and his habit of pushing her hard, and of never believing that anything she ever did was quite good enough, even as he was thrilled by her, and their, fame.

The emptiness in her, after he died: it was good that was gone, but it was surprising how there was a part of her that was thrown off-balance by its absence. She had seen trees like that in the forest, a pine growing too close to an oak, each pressing against the other, so that what in some ways was initially a competition for water, light, and nutrients eventually ended up being a system of necessary support, with each of the two weakened trees helping hold up the other.

She lost Norma when Norma was only in her midfifties; the Browns' career was already long gone, with Norma never having done more than pinch-hit for Bonnie or Maxine at one show or another, on the increasingly frequent occasions when last-minute family duties had prevented Bonnie from being able to make a show, or when

Maxine's dramas with Tommy flared up, or when Maxine had simply been drinking too much and was unable to perform.

It was a different sound with Norma, and though Norma's voice was the clearest and strongest of all of them, the sound of the four of them never really took off. Their voices had never had the chance, given their age differences growing up, to become the living, supple thing — almost like a single breath — that those of Maxine and Jim Ed and Bonnie had. Norma was technically perfect, but that was almost the problem. Even to a listener not gifted with the ability to parse out the individual tones and notes, it was evident there was a difference. The sound was pleasant and accomplished but not magical. It was mistake-free but flatter for its lack of necessary corrections. It ascended and descended with a thing like caution, and lacked the restless confidence of Bonnie's and Maxine's notes together.

It was too good, Maxine thinks, *too smooth.* So good that Norma didn't need the three of them to polish her sound — but in that isolation, that position of strength, there was less magic, and a little more of what was only a cool proficiency.

Norma alone among them had gone to music school, had studied diligently, honing her perfection, and was never interested in fame, but instead only in bettering herself and her talent. She had been a teenager when the Browns were at the peak of their fame and had dreamed about it then, had longed to join in with her sisters and brother on the stage, but she insisted later in life that that yearning had gone away and that she had been utterly content with her life spent teaching middle school music — choir and band — in Indiana, at a small rural school on the outskirts of Bloomington.

Maxine had never quite believed Norma's protests of happiness or contentedness — why else had she gone to six years of music school, if not in an effort to catch up with, and join, her older, famous siblings? — and felt guilty sometimes for not having done more to help work Norma into the group, allowing her to join them in a quartet, later in life, at certain lesser venues where the standards were not as exacting, or letting Norma open for them, singing her beautiful solos.

It was just timing, just the sheer separation of years, that prevented them from all being closer, and they never really had the chance to live a life with her. They continued to think of her as the baby, long after she was no longer that, and even after she was gone, taken from them at fifty-eight by a massive heart attack, leaving a grieving husband and students in Indiana — half of her ashes scattered there, and half by the cabin at Poplar Creek — the Browns still had trouble thinking of her as anything but the baby, always waiting to join them but never able to. She left behind for her siblings a world of nieces and nephews, their photos taped to the Browns' refrigerator doors, but with the pictures increasingly a few years behind real time, until finally the children grew up, not really knowing their aunts and uncles and cousins, and the still greater distancing proceeded.

It wasn't what Birdie would have wanted, but there just wasn't time.

Why couldn't it have been different? Maxine wonders. *Why couldn't Norma have been born closer in age? Why did she have to go off to Indiana and start a whole new life — why couldn't everything have stayed the way it was?*

It simply couldn't, of course, but why did Maxine waste so much time hiding from what life had become once it turned sour? Wouldn't it have been better to experience the sour rather than walling it off and experiencing nothing at all? She wasn't there for Norma's passing, didn't write all the condolence letters she wanted to. What would Birdie, Queen of Family, say? Even Floyd would disapprove.

She wonders idly if there was some point in time at which everything began to turn inexorably and subtly from great to poor; if in the path of her life and their lives there was some precise switchplate that was activated, taking them off one path of wholeness and fullness and directing all of them down a lonely, splintering path toward failure and isolation.

What day, what event, what hour? She tries to remember the day they scattered Norma's ashes but isn't even sure she was there. The middle is so foggy; once the quick fame was gone, she lost her way entirely.

Was there one exact day when the fire went out and life changed over from wonder into a cold, long march? Where is the heat, where is the warmth, where is the recklessness they all once possessed, in a time when there was no envy or fear or longing? Is she imagining it, that she — they — had once had that, and walked away from it?

As much as she'd like to blame it on Tommy, she doesn't think that was it. She thinks the subtle flexure, the infinitesimal leave-taking — the whisper of betrayal, whisper of failure — must have come at some earlier point in her life.

There's nothing to be done about it now; no way to go so far back and fix or repair that mistake. She remembers how Chet, always concerned with their welfare, saw that in her instantly, the regret and guilt and fear that in stepping from one land to the next, she might not step forcefully enough and might fall through the cracks, ending up in neither land — abandoning home but missing great fame.

She remembers a late-night talk she and Chet had near the beginning of the middle part of her career, when she first suspected things might be changing. He would have known it long before she even suspected it, and would have been doing his level best to keep that slow creep of obscurity from happening; and he would have been working also to keep her from the terror of suspecting it.

They were recording an album — she can't remember which one — and they were staying at his home in the country. Bonnie and Jim Ed had already gone to bed after but a single nightcap, exhausted from the perfection that Chet had requested of them all day — but Maxine was still wanting to stay up and be kept company, still sipping from her shot glass and telling stories. She wanted to hear stories, too — but that evening Chet didn't want to talk about other musicians, or even the Brown trio and their sound, but instead wanted to visit about Maxine.

She remembers that he kept asking her, with real concern — with too much concern, she thought — how she was doing, how she was *really* doing. It was not his way to probe into their private lives — for all its intimacy, their relationship was about the music they shared and made together, with everything else being so secondary as to almost not even exist. But that one night he was not talking about music and kept asking her that same question — "How are you really doing?" — with a gentle insistence that told her that he cared, and that he did not want to let her off the hook this time with banter or more whiskey or stories.

She almost buckled. She almost told him. Her eyes watered, though she allowed no tears to spill over, and gradually the tears dried without falling. She didn't say she was fine — she wouldn't lie to Chet — but she wouldn't tell him the truth either. Better to keep it inside and burn it up in the slow smoldering, the incineration. She told him nothing, acknowledged no fear or weakness, and in so doing, fell ever deeper, tumbling.

She remembers how he kept pushing: the one and only time he ever attempted such ministrations. It made her eyes water again, remembering how close what he was saying was to the counsel or warning that Birdie had given her some years earlier. She had already begun to have her various illnesses by this time, but Chet wasn't so much worried about those — the hysterectomy, the appendectomy, the bleeding spleen, the bladder tumor — and instead was zeroing in on the critical thing, the way his genius (was it its own curse, like hers, or only a blessing?) allowed him to do.

"You know, Max," he said, "regret can eat you up worse than any cancer, can leave you riddled like a piece of Swiss cheese." He paused then, to ease the tension in the room — what exactly was he accusing her of? — and poured the tiniest bit of whiskey into a shot glass for himself, and gave her another splash.

He took a sip of his own, though he did not offer a toast, and she could see him pulling back, drawing inward, giving up, disappointed, even as she wanted him to ask her just one more time if everything was all right, and how she was really doing.

He was talking about music now, not about her. It was still her music he was talking about, but he wasn't speaking entirely to her. He might have been speaking to himself, or even to his God or the Muse that nurtured him yet kept him captive.

"You can hear that kind of regret in a song," he was saying. "It's one of the loneliest sounds there is. You can hear it like the wind whistling through an old board filled with holes. It's a different sound from longing or wanting. It's the loneliest sound there is, and it's not com-

fortable, listening to it. It's raw and cold and it needs adjusting, too."
He took another small sip, finishing his glass. He was becoming almost clinical now, looking at her with not so much concern or even
pity but instead just the old cool studiousness. The admiration, but
maybe not love. Maybe a protective step back from that now.

"It's a tricky business," was all he said, and they never spoke of it
again.

This is no good, she thinks, *this damned downward spiral.* Maybe
there is a reason she can't remember the middle years; maybe it's a
mercy. *All right, then,* she tells herself, *what was the best day of your
life?* When, on the other side of the switchplate, did the best day of
her life occur? Or if not the best day, then the day when she had begun to think of herself as selected or chosen, and in need of pursuing
whatever the name of it was, the thing that still, even now, lies just a
little farther on.

She's trying to remember a day without singing—a day before singing, when someone, or the world itself, might have seen her or known
her for anything other than her voice—but she can't; not even as a
child. Her identity is her voice. Was her voice. Not even her fame is
her identity, but before that, her voice. How in the world can she ever
possibly expect to get back to that? What a miracle that it ever was
once that way.

There was almost such a day. There was part of such a day. She had
been six—was already a singer, and loved it, but still possessed a freedom, was not yet owned by it but simply still in partnership with it.
She had been able to walk toward it and yet able to walk away.

It was late October, her favorite time of year. She had started school;
there was that wonder and newness to deal with, though Jim Ed and
Bonnie had not yet begun, and so there was an extra freedom, an extra
bit of the pioneering spirit she always carried. She was coming home
from school; the school bus, a marvelous adventure, more luxurious
to her then than any limousine she would ever ride in subsequently,
dropped her off every day at the end of the county road, still a mile
from home. There was certainly no gas to be wasted by having a car
meet her at the end of the road, nor was there time in either Birdie's

or Floyd's schedule for that extravagance. Birdie had met her at the top of the road the first day and had walked back with her, asking how her day had gone and making sure that Maxine remembered the way home, but after that, the journey had been all Maxine's.

It was only a thirty-minute walk—forty if she dawdled—but it was all hers, the first time in her life she had had such space and time to herself, with neither the obligation of watching after or caring for Jim Ed and Bonnie. Sometimes she would hum and sing on her walks home, other times not. The best part was always after the long bus had made its groaning big turn and headed back away from her and she was left there, standing alone, as if on a stage. It's hard for her to remember now the girl who had thought that was such a treasure, such a treat.

She would stand there in the first silence after the bus had gone away and look around at the immensity of the lane down which she would be traveling, and at the blue sky beyond the tops of those trees, and she would be seized with a happiness, a joy so fierce as to be almost frightening: a joy that was as unquestionable as it was inexplicable and unearned. She had done nothing to deserve such upwelling, she knew, and knew also that no one in the world had ever experienced such euphoria; certainly, she had never witnessed it in anyone in her family. It made her feel alien and secret, but in no way did she want to give up the secret. It was almost always there, in the silence, and in the walking.

On warm days there would be box turtles on the trail, the red and orange and brown patterns on their skulls perfectly matched to the hues and tones of the fallen leaves, so that it was impossible not to understand that the earth had made them, had breathed them up from the soil with a desire for there to be a perfect match and fittedness. The turtles moved slowly through the leaves, in that mild sunlight, as if there were so little difference and distance between the animate and the inanimate as to render any of the old rules and laws of life irrelevant, or inaccurate—as if she had stepped into a new land, new territory, where other, better laws applied.

Birds flitted in the roadside privet, birds with names she did not know, and the sound of the birds she did know: crows fussing over something in a language so familiar to her that she no longer thought of it as fussing, instead found it only a comfort, and the ax-like drumming of woodpeckers back in the swamp, the smaller flickers and the showy pileateds. Floyd had talked about seeing the Lord-God woodpeckers, the ivorybills, when he was younger and working in the woods with his father, but they were gone now, and she supposed it was no one's fault — they had simply been too rare and special, and went away.

Perhaps best of all was the dry, gentle rustling of the leaves as the breeze stirred them, and the slightly louder rustling of them as she trudged in a straight line through them, chosen for happiness.

The creek, then, with its broad gurgle as she approached it, and, gradually, the faint sounds of the mill. Every sound in the world was hers, every sound surrounded her, was made for her, poured into her, and gave her the power of her joy. She could barely stand it, and although she would soon enough become accustomed to her duties and obligations of watching over Jim Ed and Bonnie, she was not yet fully enmeshed in that identity: she was just a girl singing, other times walking, and free from everything.

The day she remembers singularly from all the other walks was little different from any other, with but one exception. It was the day the sandhill cranes went over, birds she did not recall having ever heard before, or certainly having ever seen.

She heard their cries from a long way off, and at first confused them with the much-familiar honking and braying of geese.

As the sound drew closer, however, she quickly was able to discern the difference. The cranes' callings were a rhythmic, gravelly croak, sounding both exultant, like the geese, and labored, somehow more primitive. Not imperfect, but rough; and in that roughness, there was power. In no way did they seem to fit the sky — instead, they seemed to be fighting the sky — but in that conflict, they seemed also to be imbued with tremendous power.

They came closer — she could see them through the trees now, wings rising and falling slowly, long necks outstretched, and long legs — and she had never seen anything like them. They looked like dinosaurs — as if they had come flying in from the past — and she realized with a mix of excitement and some small fear that they were coming her way. She watched them draw closer and thought about calling out to them, even trying to imitate them, but for some reason dared not. They flew low over the tops of the trees, still croaking, and instinctively she pressed tight against a tree and watched as they flared, circled, then began landing in a small field on the other side of the hedge, their long legs outstretched like those of men and women, and long wings uplifted.

Landing heavily in the field, more like paratroopers than birds, with no transition or settling-in whatsoever, they began striding and strutting, flapping their wings and bobbing their heads with their long beaks as if moving to some music only they could hear, even as the sky still held the echo of their croaking calls.

Some of them began pecking at insects in the field, crickets and grasshoppers made sluggish by the October sun, and Maxine remained motionless, watching and listening, as the birds muttered to one another.

Finally—frightened, yet rapt at witnessing this other nation, this gathering, unobserved—she made some small inadvertent movement that one of the cranes noticed. The bird's eyes widened in fear, and with a great rasping shout it took three quick steps across the field and launched itself into flight, with all the others following it immediately, unquestioning as to what had alarmed their compatriot, understanding only that they had to leave, though not knowing how or why; and at such leave-taking, Maxine felt a small, deep pleasure, a pride and power, though some shame as well.

The birds rose around her with a clapping of wings, bodies awkward at first and brushing against one another—though in seconds they had gained grace, had sorted themselves out and were in a flock once more, circling low over the field and flying away, spying her now with their keen eyes—and then they were gone and there was only their sound, as beautiful as before.

Maxine leaned against the tree moments longer, feeling weak-legged, partly wanting the birds to return but also wanting to be going before they returned, if they did decide to return. She pushed away from the tree and hurried home.

And when Birdie asked her what had taken her so long, Maxine was surprised by her evasiveness, saying only that she had gotten tired and stopped to rest.

For some reason it seemed important to her to hold on to her secret. As if it was some slight distance she could keep between herself and everyone, even her beloved family. As if that distance was something she felt she might somehow need someday, despite the way things would turn out, and the way they would be drawn together, woven into the brittleness of what lay waiting.

A MOVIE

MAXINE'S HAVING a down day — where are the up days? It's another day wrought with aches and humiliations, and she's thinking, as she has begun to do, that maybe the glory and the chase for glory just weren't worth it. She's just about to convince herself, on this bottom-most day, that her life has been a huge mistake, a huge tragedy of waste and squander, when the call comes.

The voice is small, high but strong, sounding almost like a woman's, but with some faint timbre that Maxine can somehow, despite her diminished hearing, identify as male. There are times when she can no longer trust her hearing, but that's her guess here, and though she's a little surprised — it's a young voice — it makes sense to her that the industry should be run by ever-younger executives.

The young man — somehow, she knows — is mannered, calling her Mrs. Brown. "Mrs. Brown," the high little voice says, "I saw your advertisement in the Piggly Wiggly, and I would very much appreciate the opportunity to assist with your project in any way that I might." A pause, a kind of breathlessness, which in turn gets Maxine's breathing to come faster. A leap of her fragile old heart, summoned to blind harmony with that of the hope in the voice on the other end of the line.

There's something strange about the voice, something she should be able to place or identify, but can't quite. Not the identity of the speaker, but the nature. It's a voice she's never heard before, but still it seems like one on which she should be able to get a better read.

No matter: there was no harmony she could not match, in either tone or spirit. The little voice on the line has called for her, as she knew it would — *no work is ever wasted.* So sudden is her uplift that she could be a marionette worked by the strings above, jiggling once more after fifty years of stillness, or a prisoner in shackles and manacles, the chains jerked roughly by the jailer.

In her mind, however, there is no awkwardness in the ascent, only lilting flight. She hears the young person's voice and is with him in an instant, a soul for sale, her soul for a crumb of hope.

"I don't have much experience," the voice says, "but I have a strong interest in the subject and am confident my enthusiasm and work ethic will overcome any shortcomings. I feel like I can provide a fresh perspective."

"Yes," Maxine agrees, "it can be hard to get started. But everybody's got to begin somewhere."

"Wonderful," the filmmaker says. "When would be a convenient time for us to meet? I have my calendar right in front of me."

Now, she wants to say, *come on over right now.* But she's not ready. She wants to savor it a little, though not for too long. Sometimes old people go to sleep, she knows, and just don't wake up. *Wouldn't that be a tragedy,* she thinks, *to wait all her life for a movie and then to not get to see it — to miss out on the process by a week or two, or even a few days?*

"How about in an hour?" she asks, and the executive, or the artist — she's not quite sure yet how to think of him — pauses, then asks her location.

She gives him her address — she hears a muffled exchange with someone in the room — and then he gets back on the line and says that that will be splendid.

"What is your name, if I may ask?" Maxine says, just before hanging up, and in that high small voice, not quite a girl's or a woman's voice, he says, "Jefferson," and Maxine thinks, *Aha, I was right.*

"It's a pleasure to speak with you, Jefferson," she says. "I'll see you in an hour."

"Yes, ma'am, I look forward to it. Thank you ma'am."

She hangs up and hurries to her downstairs closet and her cardboard box, and begins spreading different outfits across the couch and the backs of chairs. She's shaking so hard, she worries that indeed she might have a stroke or heart attack, and the idea that she might miss her goal by so narrow a margin causes her to begin crying.

She doesn't cry for long, however — it takes too much energy, uses resources she doesn't have to spare, and similarly, she does not try on a variety of outfits the way she would have done as a younger woman. It's too exhausting; she'll have to get it right the first time.

She chooses red — she prefers black, and has always worn black, but she feels strongly the need to try to change her luck — a red turtleneck sweater, and black and white hound's-tooth knit pants. She remembers as if it were yesterday the afternoon in 1974 when she purchased the outfit, and is surprised by the recollection, the moment illuminated suddenly in her mind as if by a column of light pouring down, cutting through the fogbank of the long slumber. Once she's got the outfit on, it takes forever to address her hair, and to apply her lipstick, and then — there are scant minutes left now — to select accompanying jewelry.

She despairs over this last choosing — *I should have worn black,* she thinks — but finally finds a wooden bead necklace that Chet had gotten for her when he went to Africa. *There's a conversation starter,* she thinks, donning it like an amulet. And though it clashes horribly, she just barely has time to slip on a silver charm bracelet that used to be Norma's. She says a quick little prayer, her first in maybe sixty or seventy years, just as the knock comes at the door, the sound striking adrenaline through her heart as would the report of a rifle.

Breathe, she tells herself, as she once used to remind herself before going out onstage those first few times, *breathe.* Amazingly, the shuddering stops, and to anyone who would behold her, she appears to be in perfect control. She glides with her walker through the darkened living room to the front door and opens it, projecting as she does so her most confident and radiant smile, and is surprised and confused to see a small boy, no older than ten or twelve, standing before her, his button-up shirt yoked with sweat as if from a long walk in the sun, and a heavy video camera case slung over one shoulder, and gripping a sturdy tripod.

With a strange mix of shyness and confidence, he reaches out his hand to introduce himself. "Jefferson Eads," he says.

So diminished are Maxine's social skills — as isolated as a detainee — that she gasps, not understanding anything. She looks beyond the boy's outstretched hand, searches the streets for the parked car where surely his mother or father, the real filmmaker, remains.

Tact has fled her; it departed a long time ago, and she's had no real reason — or any opportunity — to bring it back. She's still ignoring the boy's hand, but is looking down on him now like a hawk, mad enough to spit. The boy, who has no idea yet what he has done to summon such outrage, takes a step back, but a warrior for his cause, obsessed as perhaps only a boy of twelve can be, keeps the camera rolling, trains the blinking red eye on her, looking up at her angry, crooked, crippled advance, even as he himself wobbles in taking that step backwards down the steps.

He recovers, plants himself, squares up, and keeps shooting. He makes sure his pale hand, still outstretched, is in the forefront of the frame, and though he is connecting the dots now, understanding that he has inserted himself into something over which he has no control — he beholds the reality now before him — he also drops down simultaneously into a lower world, one where he is seeing different possibilities, different angles of attack and exploration. He is imagining himself as different characters in the narrative that he and he alone has kindled.

Is it manipulative for him to take what he's been given — her anger — and then try to adapt and make something of it — to seek to mollify it, or to show how hard it is to manage it? Absolutely. Already, he is a master of his talent.

"Please don't hurt me," he cries in his child's voice. "I only want to make a movie."

"I'm not going to hurt you, child," the elegantly dressed old woman says, pausing at the top of the steps: the edge of her kingdom. "I'm just looking for your parents. You can't make a movie by yourself, child," she says, but less angrily now — reassessing, already, the situation before her, the hand she has been dealt. "What could you possibly know about the silver screen?"

He watches her curiously, calmly, still filming. He hears and understands what those words mean to her, *the silver screen,* and knows immediately, instinctively, that herewith and henceforth, whenever he needs a little something extra from her — more anecdote, more despair, more yearning, more anything — that whenever she is down and out and can travel no further, all he will need to do is speak those three words and she will rise and push on, will follow those three words to the ends of the earth.

He pauses, situated again between two worlds. He can tell her one thing, not directly the truth, and elicit a certain response for his project, or he can tell her another thing, more nakedly the truth — that his passion is for documentaries, not drama — and he will get a different response, one that may be not as dramatic.

He wants a little drama.

He casts the words back out to her cautiously, in the manner in which fishermen who, trawling from a small boat, might toss a few flakes of dry oatmeal onto the surface, where minnows come nibble, which would in turn attract larger fish below.

"I view my project as a precursor to the silver screen," he says, and he sees that his instincts are precise and correct — that at the utterance of that phrase, all hostility leaves her and she is filled instead with a surge of gentle hope, becoming as stilled as might a previously agitated bird of prey that is hooded by the falconer, or a scrabbling lizard that is flipped over on its back so that its belly can be scratched. Jefferson is a collector and quantifier of things — lizards, turtles, snakes, stamps, old coins, anything. *Different,* in this regard, and more intense than most, living in the shadows at the edge of genius, or even all the way over into that territory, preferring animals to people — and it is from behind the lens of the camera, the other side of the camera, that he can best understand and interact with people.

She's not the same person now, and he's curious, in a scientific way, to measure how long the spoken phrase will keep her calmed. He imagines trying to show this in his documentary, maybe with a tiny stopwatch icon, the *silver screen* watch, in the lower left-hand corner of the screen; and every time the phrase is spoken, the ticking clock, with its sweep-second hand, can be reset. *Maybe.* There are so many possibilities. This is always the most exciting part of any of his ventures, any of his hobbies — the full enthusiasm of the bold beginning, when anything is possible, and his heart — his emotions — feel the equivalent of the subject.

That will fade later — the joy will seep away — and he will return to the cold familiar comfort of the chillingly technical. But here at the beginning of things, he can feel the sparks of passion, joy, and a fuller emotional engagement that, he's pretty sure, is like that of most other people's, and probably superior to theirs. A burning is what it feels like, barely able to be controlled, not even by a mind as powerful as his. Unable to be controlled, actually, which for him is a terrifying consideration, and one that requires great courage.

"Well, come on in I guess," the well-dressed dragon lady says, and turns and shuffles back into the darkness of her lair, withdrawing from the bright throw of afternoon light, which Jefferson understands intuitively is her enemy, capable of beating her down and scalding her. Whatever power she has left is concentrated in the last darkness, the seed of her isolation, and with courage and verve he follows her into her house, with the camera rolling.

Maxine thinks she has guile, believes that because she is possessed of a certain power and intelligence and hunger, she's able to control and manage all elements into successful schemes and manipulations at any level, whether grand or minute. The opposite is true, however; living alone has stripped her of all façade, and she is as transparent as the beat of an open heart before the surgeon. She has it in her mind, for instance, to be gay and charming before Jefferson's camera, and to always present to him only that which she wants him to see — but after giving him a brief little self-conscious tour around the downstairs, she is so excited to have company that she forgets about his camera, comes already to view it as simply an extension of who he is, in the way that the walker is an extension of her.

Jefferson doesn't understand it, but he's seen it before. He's filmed everything with his camera — friends, family, used car salesmen, school crossing guards, teachers, baseball coaches — and always they drop their guard after an initial period of defensiveness.

It's as if they pass through a curtain, with the burden of maintaining artifice on one side and the freedom of living for oneself, without falsity or misrepresentation, on the other.

Some of Jefferson's subjects pass through that curtain sooner than others, but they all pass through it. In a way that he does not understand, the camera helps them with this metamorphosis. Sometimes he's a little frightened by this power, and while he used to think that it resided solely in the camera, disappearing as soon as he turned the switch off and the battery's current drained to nothing, it has begun to seem to him recently that some of the power is developing in him as well, and he likes it.

Maxine's guile, and Maxine's pique, are gone within fifteen minutes. It's simply too hard to maintain such things at her age, and with her so out of the habit of manipulation. She's been honest for far too long; one day after another of avoiding the bottle has turned her, for better or worse, into an honest person.

That first day, Jefferson is able to pretty much film all that remains of her life, and in the span of only a couple of short hours. He films her watching the old movies that she pulls out to show him — she's chatty and even ebullient at first, glancing at his camera and smiling from time to time, though soon enough she passes through the veil and into a land of utter transparency, so that he is able to walk around her in that darkened room, filming from all angles and at all distances — moving in as close to her as an optometrist peering in to the optic nerve while the patient stares fixedly ahead, suspended in the darkness, lulled in a darkness that is made all the more absolute by the presence of that one beam of light and nothing else beyond.

Soon she has lapsed into brooding hypnosis, watching her old films, and Jefferson gets that on tape, and records the silent movies themselves. He captures her solemn, watchful trance, which is punctuated by small moments of laughter as if, though she's seen each tape thousands of times, the same reflexive trigger still works, time after time — and later, when she shows him the memorabilia room, he films her opening the cedar chest, and the cautious manner with which she unfolds each brittle section of newspaper, each poster, each trinket: the careful exhumations.

He films the pictures on the wall. When she is finally done in that room — she stops at the doorway, looking back at it like a surveyor staring out at some vast territory — he follows her into the kitchen and films her shaky hands struggling to tear open a teabag wrapper. "Here, let me help you with that," he says, and sets the camera down where it can keep filming as he steps around and helps her.

And though he doesn't so much feel compassion for her, or the embers of warmth that he knows should be associated with even so small an act of generosity, there is for him the tiny pleasure, tiny relief, of solving a technical problem: of smoothing over some ragged irregularity in the world, which his eyes are so adept at noticing. Maxine marvels at his youth, and the clean efficiency with which he tears open the square little colored envelope of the teabag.

He withdraws from the frame once he has the teabag open. He's a little disoriented. He's not sure how he'll fit himself into her movie, or even if he will. Maybe his job is just to roll footage.

He films her hurrying to the back door when Buddy comes trotting through on his way back home. Maxine opens the door and calls to him sweetly — Buddy lifts his head in casual acknowledgment but appears to make no move to come over and see her, is resolute in his routine of homeward bound — and Jefferson lowers his camera to ground level, films Buddy's dignified little trot. Then Buddy notices Jefferson and, as if perturbed or at least simply made curious by this variance in his world, barks once before trotting over to examine and meet the stranger.

Buddy tries to be gruff — his hackles are raised — but he can't pull it off, he sniffs Jefferson and then, strangely, rubs up against him like a cat rather than the old dog he is.

"Animals like me," Jefferson says, and for a moment his guard is down, he is just being a boy, and paying attention to Buddy so that he misses the look of complete envy and small pleasure and sharp little sorrow that passes over Maxine's face. The old jealousy, the old possessiveness. A bitter quick mix of *My dog* and *Love me*.

Will it ever come back — the feeling of being noticed, and the certainty of being the star?

Jefferson finishes one memory card on his camera and starts another. He sits at the table and interviews her, asks her questions about Elvis, and about the Beatles.

He takes her oral transcript, her testimony, with tireless patience, interjecting himself only occasionally to ask for more information, inquiring about gone-by heroes and heroines of whom he, like almost everyone else in the world now, knows nothing. *Who were Jim and Mary Reeves, what were they like, tell me more about them. What were your mother's favorite recipes, who was Chet Atkins, how did you feel when Jim Ed hurt his hand?*

He could stay all night. She could talk all night, but her energy level is flagging and he has told his parents he'll be back before dark. It's about a forty-five-minute walk, and he doesn't want them to have to come get him; he tells Maxine he likes the independence of being able to come and go on his own.

Neither of them is a particularly warm-hearted individual, but as he's leaving, she leans in to give him a small, loose hug, as if it's something she's learned to do from an instruction manual, and he turns and readjusts the camera strap on his shoulder to better allow her to do so, as if he perhaps has read the same manual, with its instructions on how to receive such a stiff and awkward embrace; though as ever, he keeps the camera rolling and is still recording even as he walks down her steps, walking slowly backwards and filming her waving goodbye.

She's so excited, he thinks. And as he has so many times before, he wishes he could feel a little more warmth — that swooning, lilting softness that he's seen inhabit others — but that particular fire is not in him right now. He waits patiently for it and thinks that someday it will be in him — but instead, his fire and attention are focused on the film he's just captured, and as he walks back home, he plays it over and over in his mind, unstacks and reassembles different sequences, and is becalmed, soothed and strengthened by this exercise of bringing precise and attractive order to the quick crumbling of her life.

And after he is gone — after Maxine has gone back inside, aflame with hope and a depth of joy she does not recall having experienced for many years, a feeling that strikes her in an odd way as being dangerously close to the highs she would sometimes experience when drinking — she goes into the kitchen and sits down and sips from a glass of water. And then, certain that she is all alone, she clears her voice and begins to sing.

THIRD CHILD

IT WASN'T EASY when she filed for the divorce; as an attorney, Tommy made sure of that. Maxine was just glad that Floyd wasn't alive to criticize her for it, and her one regret about all of it was that Birdie had to know. The shame of failure was a thing she absolutely could not abide, but neither could she carry the burden of her mistake, made so long ago, any further forward. Stubbornness alone had taken her this far, but she could not go another day. He was flaunting his affairs now, and, having finally noticed the ineffable decline of her stardust — noticing it not in the abstraction of vaguely diminished fervor among her audiences, for he never attended her shows, but instead through the steady reduction in the already modest royalty checks — Tommy began to mock her, calling her the worst thing anyone could, a has-been, telling her it was all over.

It was strange, she thought, after she had driven to the next small town, Gethsemane, and gotten help from an attorney in filling out the papers. The sheaf of them in a manila folder, resting on her bureau in the spring sunlight that afternoon, after she had gone back home to pick the children up from school. The attorney in Gethsemane had counseled her to wait a full twenty-four hours before filing and to talk to Tommy one last time. The attorney was not so concerned that the marriage was ending as instead how much harder life was about to become for Maxine financially.

After dreading it and fighting it for so long, she was surprised by the new feeling of peace, looking at the big envelope there on her dresser. It felt like the first time in a long time that she had been able to control something in her life — and while it occurred to her that this was the time of day when she sometimes liked to pour a glass of wine, she instead just sat here, in the privacy of her bedroom, listening to the shouts and cries of the children playing outside, and she watched the sunlight on the envelope, and marveled at how good it felt to be starting over.

✠ ✠ ✠

She was nervous that night when Tommy came home for dinner. There were many nights when he did not come home, and she had hoped that this would be one, but as if he existed now only to plague her, he came home before dark and spent some time in the front yard playing with the children. Maxine was jittery, wondering if he knew, but he said next to nothing, so that all seemed as it always did, detached and isolate. They ate dinner and put the children to bed and poured nightcaps and then went to bed themselves, and when Tommy moved in close to her and began to put his hands on her, she pushed them away and said, *No, not tonight.*

She felt his stillness, then felt him turning away, and once again, though in a smaller dose, she felt a whiff of that peace she had inhabited so deeply earlier in the day, and she smiled, then fell asleep, and slept all through the night, uninterrupted by even the industry of dreams.

She had a doctor's appointment the next day after dropping the children off at school, and feeling absolutely giddy—how different the world looked now that it had been returned to her, now that she had gone and gotten it back—she sat in the waiting room. Her next stop would be the courthouse.

The doctor asked if she wanted to take a pregnancy test, and she almost laughed and said it wasn't necessary, but stopped with a hitch in her heart, and the more she thought about it, the more convinced she became that she was pregnant, to the point where she didn't want to take the test.

He finished his exam, declared her fit as a fiddle—said nothing about her smoking or drinking—and she was about to leave, was about to turn her back on and move away from her fear, but then stopped and turned and went back.

"Maybe I should take that test after all," she said.

She held on to the divorce papers for another five years. She finally had them redrafted and filed when the third child, Jimmy—little Jimmy Brown, just like in the song that had first brought them fame, so long ago—was four. She took the papers back home as before, but this time did not wait the full twenty-four hours suggested, and neither did she feel the incredible peace of relief that had attended her first attempt.

Tommy moved out, but nothing really changed or got better; things were just a little harder, was all. Sometimes she would get a neighbor girl to help with the children, and other times she would take them down to Birdie's, though Birdie was aging hard now, was having trouble getting up and down from a chair—her knees and ankles were always swollen and she lost her breath easily—and there was far less money. And where previously in town there had been looks of judgment and pity from those who knew of Tommy and his ways—which was to say, everyone—there were now looks that accused her of not trying harder, or of being a bad mother, swell-headed with fame or simply a poor and unobservant judge of character for choosing Tommy in the first place. As if she had somehow deserved such misery and had set out to procure it.

⬲ LEAVING

BONNIE AND BROWNIE had bought a farm in the Ozarks. The clock was ticking now: Bonnie was renouncing the magic, was choosing a life, while Maxine chose the other thing, the heartbreak of immortality and the bitterness of pursuing it, always one full day behind it.

It was easier for Bonnie to step away from it all and choose a life on the farm with her new family, when she was still young and strong and beautiful. Bonnie would have known in some abstract fashion that she and Brownie would grow older and would eventually someday cross a threshold where forever after there was only accruing diminishment — that each day would become more and more difficult — but back then, that knowledge would have had no bite. The words *deaf* and *weak-sighted* and *stoved-up* would have had no currency in youth; the terms *feeble* and *confused* and *arthritis* were just nouns and adjectives, small foreign coins that could not be spent in the land they inhabited. It was an easier choice, back then, trading fame for Brownie.

The thing about Bonnie is that even now, with her markers coming due, she is happy, and better than happy — content — with her choice. She made the right choice. She got lucky.

All the way through, Bonnie's separation from Elvis remained amicable, and came quickly to resemble something more brotherly — as if at heart he had always been but another Brown sibling. He came to see Bonnie late one night just before her wedding, after having been out of touch with all of them for several months, and had a long heart-to-heart talk — in essence, acknowledging that she was right, that he had been gripped by something and carried away from who he was and where he had once been, acknowledging that he understood he would never be able to get back; but what he did not acknowledge was that he had taken something from her, from all of them, as he had traveled on past them.

Only the deepest, furthest part of him understood that, a place so far within him that it would be a very long time before he understood more clearly what had happened — what they had given him and the world, and what he had taken.

As it was, he stayed up near the surface, that night, with him and Bonnie sitting alone in Birdie's kitchen, crickets chirping slowly outside, and her upcoming new life about to open before her with every bit as much vigor as had all of her previous adventures. Her hard but blessed childhood. The sweet love with Elvis, and now this, a man she wanted to spend the rest of her life with: Why had life been so good to her? Why had she been chosen for such happiness?

They talked on and on, sinking a little deeper into things as the night progressed, but in no way descending all the way to the murky bottom; that in his pursuit of being loved, he had almost been like a hunter — seeking, finding, then feasting on, their magic — and that night, Bonnie did not acknowledge or understand this either, or the guilt of knowing that at some level she had been willing to shed it. To transfer it — the blessing but also the curse.

They talked above all that, never knowing, never understanding. They descended only a short distance, and talked, with great affection, about their hopes for each other. Eventually the conversation rounded a corner and came to the topic of Brownie, and here Bonnie had to ascend from even the modest depths they had been exploring, being careful and cautious now, navigating the conversation with adjusted attentiveness, a precise polish. The peacekeeper.

No one in her family could have done what he or she did without the others. They were three parts of one voice, and for a little while, they were united in the desire to spill out onto the world and to change it before realizing that they each finally had to pull away. Bonnie realizing it before anyone. Of course she needed the calm, gentle, dependable doctor with her for such a bold and essentially defiant action — spurning fate itself, and winning. In this secret way mild Bonnie was perhaps the most daring of them all.

Elvis fussed a little on the topic of Brownie, not so much in the hopes of ever getting her back — he had other business to tend to; he could see and understand that now — but hemming and hawing more out of concern for Bonnie, that she might be making a mistake, a choice that would impinge on the very thing he loved most about her, her happiness.

"But sweetie," he protested, trying to articulate it, "I don't even *know* the dude."

Her laughter, the trill of it — the pure peal — relaxed him and told him all he needed to know, that she really was in love, and that, just as important, it would last.

The knowledge of what he had left behind, and of what he had taken, would come to him slowly over the years, even as he became numbed, medicated, scarred over, detached and distanced from the brief wonder of life. Often, in recording sessions with his backup singers, the Jordanaires, an all-white chorus, he would feel that something was missing from his recording, something soulful and immense, and the older he got, the more he understood what it was.

From behind the opiates and the booze he would order another take, and then another, would call out to the producer as well as to the Jordanaires, "Give me some of that Brown sound!" — but by that time no one ever understood what he was talking about, assumed instead he was talking about James Brown, and punched their vocals up in the other direction, making it more bluesy, more rock-and-roll.

Fame still would not leave them entirely — was it gnawing on Maxine's misery, or was it attracted to Bonnie and her brilliant cheer? The year 1962 was the first in which they didn't have a number one hit, but they rebounded, had three the next year.

Perhaps the fame was drawn equally to the movements — the peace as well as the agony — of the three of them. Perhaps it could not stay away. Everything beneath them was collapsing; they had thought they were standing on stone but it turned out to be sand, and now water was lapping at their feet.

It was the same sand that had once been the tops of mountains, with not even a scar in the sky to mark where the mountains had been: sand being swept down Poplar Creek to Tishomingo Creek, where it would join with the larger Red Bluff Creek before being carried into the Mississippi — and Bonnie, with her new husband and new family, wanted out, while Maxine wanted to hold on even more fiercely, while Jim Ed didn't care one way or the other. He would be all right; all he needed was his deep voice.

Radio would soon be completely secondary to television in its ability to grip men and women's souls and hold them fixed and captive to whatever message was being delivered, and country music would soon become a distant second to rock-and-roll. One man, their friend, would see to that — he had found his path and was hurrying toward it. The Browns were growing older, too, aged by the road — Maxine was nearing thirty-two! — but most damning of all to their engagement with fame, the country was beginning to awaken from its self-willed trance, was beginning to stir to a boil. The country didn't want to sleep any longer.

Still, just before sleep went away, there was fame. They were still churning out hits: everything they put out went to gold or almost gold, and then silver, and then almost silver, and so on. They were sinking but pretended not to know it. Bonnie was as secretly delighted by the sensation of sinking as Maxine was terrified.

Always, they were just one big song away from recovery.

The record companies, which were all venturing into television now, were awash with advertising money, and were forever throwing release parties, as were the powerful radio stations, owners of the sky itself, with each independent disc jockey determining who received airtime and who didn't.

There was booze at the parties, and not only had Maxine become practiced at drinking a lot, she was becoming accustomed to tossing her drinks in other people's faces at even the slightest provocation. It was something a woman could do to a man to signify to everyone else at the party that the man had been disrespectful, boorish, even insulting, and Maxine wasn't shy about slinging the sticky liquor in anyone's face, might even by this time have been looking for opportunities to do so. Steaming receptions in little cinder-block low-wattage radio stations, attended mostly by men but also by a few women, and the scent of spilled alcohol rife in the small rooms from such tossings, and innocent bystanders sometimes catching the brunt of her rage, men's jackets and shirtfronts dashed with it, the scent of aged cigarette smoke cloaking the linings of their throats and burrowing into their lungs.

Bonnie wanted out. She had Brownie at home and two little daughters now. One of her smaller pastures was bounded by stone walls, and chickens ranged freely in the yard. Blue smoke curled from her chimney in the fall and winter, and on her drive back home each time, she would see neighbor women out in their gardens, weeding or harvesting, or out in the verdant fields of springtime, walking through the pastures with battered metal feed buckets in their hands, dairy cattle following close behind. Giant sheaf-stacked mountains of hay gleamed and glinted in the sun in the middle of such pastures, casting smooth, rounded shadows.

Maxine missed her children, too, but not like Bonnie. There is no right or wrong to greatness — there is only the forward movement of it, and those who possess the most of it are the least in control of it.

Chet Atkins avoided such parties like the plague. He didn't judge anyone who attended them, but he stayed home, guarded his time, worked in his studio, played music quietly by himself, or hung out with his family. Far down in Maxine's treasure chest, there is a photo of Chet Atkins from around the time of the Browns' incandescent ascent. He is sitting in the control room on one side of the soundproof glass, a cup of coffee at his side, and is staring across at the Browns, who are in the midst of a recording session. The three Browns are gathered around the mike, leaning in and hitting their note, their faces pure and clean and illuminated in that moment, caught perfectly in the space of what the world most wants them to do.

Atkins is back in the shadows. Countless times he had been over on the other side of that glass, playing, but in this photo he is recording, and the look on his face, which some might describe as simply attentive, is so much more than that.

It is the look of a man who has captured something he cares deeply about — there is almost guilt in his expression, at witnessing the object of his affection and admiration. It is an image of one of the rarest yet most natural things in the world, greatness attracted to greatness, greatness coming in contact with greatness.

Jim Reeves went down in a plane crash. He should have known better. Maxine is still angry about it, half a century later. He should have done the math, should have counted how many stars back then had plane crashes — a reverse kind of effluorescing, sparks rising but then tumbling.

He had gotten his pilot's license and his own little plane. Maxine was supposed to have gone up with him that day. He had been badgering her to go over to Arkansas with him to look at some property he wanted to buy for an investment. They were going to stay for the weekend. They weren't romantically involved — he was still married to Mary — he just wanted some company with one of his old touring partners. Maxine had plenty of spare time by that point; they both did. She had even found a babysitter.

She was all set to go, and then at the last second, she wouldn't: Alicia got sick. Jim Reeves tried to get her to go anyway, said to bring Alicia and they'd find a doctor up in Arkansas. He was all but summoning her, with the greatest urgency he was capable of, but in the end, she hesitated, anchored by a stronger force. It wasn't her time yet. She wanted to go, but didn't. She stayed home and took her child to the doctor.

Alicia was better the next day, and Maxine, Jim Ed, and Bonnie got in the car the day after that and headed out to Dallas, where they had gotten an increasingly rare gig to appear on *The Big D Jamboree*. They were driving through the middle of the night — it was cooler that way — and they always tried to wait to leave until after the children had fallen asleep. They were driving and listening to *The Ralph Emery Show* out of Baton Rouge when Ralph Emery came on the air between songs and said that there was sad news in the world of country music, that another great musician's plane was missing and presumed to have crashed.

They all three fell silent. Jim Ed was driving, and all they could hear was the wind coming in through the open windows. They had already completely forgotten about Jim Reeves going up to Arkansas. He just wasn't on their mind that way, but then Ralph Emery started playing a song of Jim's, "Night Rider," and they knew.

Jim Ed pulled over to the side of the road. All three of them were weeping. There wasn't any other traffic out. They got out of the car and collapsed against one another there on the shoulder of the road, gravel on their knees, the stars bright around them, moths swarming the headlights, and the crickets still chirping like nothing had happened.

The radio said they hadn't found his plane. They held out a little hope. In their hearts they knew he was gone, but they pretended he wasn't. They didn't know whether to push on or turn around and go back home. They drove through the night to Dallas, crying, while the radio played Jim's songs all night. They got almost all the way to Dallas by daylight, checked in at a little hotel just outside the city limits, and slept until about noon, then got up and went in to the coliseum to dress and rehearse.

No one had heard anything yet and everybody was asking if the plane had been found.

When Maxine remembers that time, she doesn't know why they went ahead and did the show. It was just a stupid show. There was some discussion among the three of them, and a phone call to Mary, that maybe it was what Jim would have wanted them to do. It certainly wasn't any fun, and though they sounded all right and got another standing ovation, and everyone was glad they were there to worry together, the Browns just wanted to get back home. They finished the show and drove all the way back to Nashville that same night. They got there at daylight and all went up in the hills with the volunteers who were looking for his plane.

Someone found it that day at noon. It had crashed on approach in a thunderstorm, had gone down only a mile from Jim Ed's house. That part really bothered them, wondering if he'd known where he was and was trying to bring it down close to someplace where he might be able to get help. Gone forever, at the age of forty-one. It had seemed old to them, back then.

It just got harder to keep going after that. Mary Reeves became unhinged. She cut off all contact with her friends and moved out to the desert in New Mexico, where she kept an increasing number of cats for companionship, trying to halt her slide, but there could be no halting it: they had all risen too far too fast and now had to pay the price in the falling, while the rest of the country listened to the steady, smooth crooning music and never knew a thing, never dreamed of either the ecstasy or the agony.

The life in the desert didn't heal her — the searing heat and light might have bought her some time, but it didn't heal her. She ended up needing help in an assisted living facility, a sanatorium, that tended to her basic daily needs.

It all went by pretty quick, Maxine thinks, and wonders for the ten thousandth time why she alone was left, and why she has traveled the journey unharmed and untouched. *I am unharmed,* she thinks. *I have remained untouched.*

⌒ HOLES

SHE HAS A THREE-DAY wait before Jefferson Eads returns. She's been on the phone with Bonnie and has left messages for Jim Ed, who's out on the road. Bonnie is mildly interested, though when Maxine describes the filmmaker as a nice young man, Bonnie's thinking grad school or maybe even a little older. Bonnie doesn't volunteer to come down; it's midsummer, the height of gardening season.

Jefferson Eads is all business when he returns, no chitchat — he doesn't want to sit and have any tea with her, though he does eat a couple of the cookies. Maxine's a little disappointed by how antisocial he is — how driven, almost brusque — but she quickly adapts her mood to his: *business.*

He has a little notepad on which he's sketched various scenes — places he wants her to be, things he wants her to be doing. She's not a gardener, but he wants footage of her digging a hole in the backyard, and is almost cross with her when he discovers that she doesn't even own a shovel. He won't take no for an answer, and he leaves her there in the kitchen with her tea and a plateful of cookies and hurries next door to the neighbors, whose names Maxine can't quite remember, and returns shortly with the prop he needs.

He works her hard that morning, using up all the good in her and then some, positioning her just so against the morning light, then repositioning her, and yet again: forcing her to walk back and forth, doing the same minor take over and over again, neither praising nor criticizing her, simply directing her to repeat the same thing with only the most minor of variations, and with Maxine wearing down quickly.

None of this is what I signed on for, she thinks. *Be careful what you ask for.* But time and again she answers the bell and does whatever he asks with as much energy as she can bring.

"Why would an old woman with a walker be out digging a hole?" she asks him at one point — the late-morning sun is above the trees, beating down hard, stirring the floaters in her vision — and Jefferson

Eads does not have an answer, but pushes her to do it again, though he gives her a break, lets her hobble over to the shade and sit down in a folding chair to catch her breath while he pans the camera all around the yard, filming what now looks like a battlefield for gophers.

"This was not in my life," she says, and he sighs and tells her that it's important to him, it's what the film books call metaphor, though when she asks him for what, he purses his lips and says, "We'll have to see."

"It's my life," she says, "and my movie, I deserve to know."

Jefferson Eads shrugs and tells her he can't explain it, that he works by instinct. "You're hungry," he says, "you're desperate. You're clawing at the earth. That's all I know. That's all I need to know."

Sensing that he's losing her — and he's cross about this, too — he calls it a day, tells her she can go back inside and have a glass of water.

And once inside, his demeanor changes, as if he's suddenly sated. He becomes a young boy again rather than a tyrant, and where previously he was interested in only the camera and the cold technical impassivity of light and sound, he is now interested in her life again. The camera's rolling again — the camera's always rolling — but he's not being so dictatorial; he's just a boy again, curious about the treasure of her life, and is drawn to her, like so many before him.

All she ever had to do was wait: everything came to her, always, and she had only to wish for something and it would eventually be given to her. The only flaw in the miracle was that it was never enough.

"M-O-N-E-Y"

THE DIRT-POOR hardscrabble life of chronic poverty had not been hard. Seeing her audience slip away was what was hard.

The greatness wasn't leaving her. Maybe if it had, the slipping-away of audiences would have been easier to tolerate, would have been less lonely. It would have been a bitter loss, but one that she thinks she could have managed. But what gravels her is that the greatness didn't leave.

It left Elvis. They went up and saw him once, after his peak but before his decline. It was 1970, a full decade after their own glory days.

Despite still being atop his own summit, Elvis knew something was wrong, and was quiet and somber, lonely, barely recognizable in spirit from the young man they had known only ten years earlier. He was the opposite of the Browns now: the greatness had left him, but not the audiences. If Maxine had looked more closely she would have seen that that was even lonelier than her own condition.

After years of silence, he called for them, not by phone, as he had in the past, but via the mail. He had a secretary but had not used her, had written the note himself: *Please come and visit.* He had sent it to the only address he knew, the old one, where it sat unclaimed in their mailbox for months until Jim Ed had been back home during hunting season. The young trees growing up around the sawmill now were already almost thick enough to make into lumber.

Jim Ed stayed a week, hunting by himself and camping in the old house of his childhood, sleeping on the floor next to the woodstove, lulled by the popping of the coals, and surrounded by all the old ghosts. When he arose early to make coffee, it seemed that they were all there with him, still sleeping, and each morning he walked down into the woods and into the darkness, where he sat in his tree stand quietly and watched the sun come up, and was amazed by how fast the world kept moving, whether he was in the center of it or not.

At the end of his week, feeling strong and rested, he went back to

207

Nashville Chrome

his home in Nashville, called Bonnie, who said, "Why not?" and then Maxine, who said, "Maybe he wants to do a special album with us."

Jim Ed shook his head. "I think he's just lonely, Max," he said. "He said he just wants to see us. It's not about music at all," he said, "it's just about us."

Maxine paused, absorbing the disappointment. "Well, let's go anyway," she said.

He had offered to send a car and driver — Jim Ed had winced, remembering the time Floyd had loaned his car to Elvis, and once again felt surrounded by the ghosts — and he told Elvis thanks but that they would just drive over in Jim Ed's car.

"It's a big place," Elvis said. "You can't miss it." Jim Ed laughed, thinking it was his old humor, but then was concerned when Elvis said, "What's so funny?"

Like a boy, he was waiting for them at the front gate when they drove up. His father, Vernon, was there with him, had been staying with him for about a month, and Elvis gave each of them a hug, a stage hug at first, but then it dissolved into something denser and more powerful, so that for them it felt as if they were each helping hold him up.

He spent a couple of hours showing the Browns all around: showing them this and that bedroom, bathroom, closet. Then they went back outside and walked around on the grounds for a long time. It was cold and windy, and the Browns couldn't remember ever having been to a lonelier or more unsettling place in all their lives.

They walked forever. Vernon walked with them, a skinny little old man, and at one point he took Bonnie aside and said he was sure sorry that Elvis and Bonnie didn't get married, that Elvis had told him that they were going to. Which was not the truth — she had never told him yes — but there was no need to tell Vernon that. "He's sure a sweet boy," she said instead, and Vernon said, "Yes, he is."

The Browns thought it was strange how he'd gone so long without seeing them or talking to them and then contacted them from out of the blue. At one point Maxine commented on this, trying to break the strange awkwardness that seemed to be around them, and that she thought he might have had some kind of shared album in mind, but Elvis shook his head and said he just wanted to see them was all. He said he'd been hearing them on the radio now and again and thinking about them a lot, and that he missed them. He said he was pretty sad most of the time. He wanted something from them, but they couldn't tell what.

Vernon got cold and went back inside. The rest of them sat out on the hood of one of his cars — a gold Cadillac convertible — in that cold wind, and talked about the old days. He had on a big white coat with some kind of fur around the neck, so he was warm, but the rest of them were cold, and the hood of the car was cold. They didn't mention the incident with Floyd's Oldsmobile, and Elvis didn't bring it up either. They had no reason to believe he even remembered it.

He was so lost, Maxine recalls. The car was parked out on the lawn right by the front gate, and the Browns had to be leaving soon. They had no doubt that he wanted to leave with them, wanted to go back to the way things had been. That whole day, the only time he looked even remotely happy was when he told them about one of their past hits he'd been thinking about, a single called "M-O-N-E-Y." He said he couldn't get it out of his mind. He got real animated then, told them how he'd like to hear it played — how he'd like to play it, if it was his song — and he started tapping it out right there on the hood of the car, and singing it, and for that little bit, he was like the old Elvis again, and they had to say, he was right, the song sounded pretty good the way he was doing it.

Then they went home. They each gave him another hug and went on through the gate, and none of them ever went back to Graceland while he was living. If any of them saw him three times after that, before he died in 1977, they can't remember when they would have been. He was mostly somebody else by that time, and Maxine thinks he didn't want them to see that that was how it was.

It didn't change how any of them felt about him — there was nothing that could make something like that, so deep-rooted, go away — and Maxine has to believe that even when he was lost, even after he had gone so far away that he could never get back, he still always felt the same about each of them, that nothing had changed. But that was the last time they spent with him that had even a trace of good old days to it, there when he was tapping out that song on the hood of that hideous gold brick of a car. Just for a second, and then he was sad again.

What could any of us have done? Maxine wonders. He had everything in the world, but he still needed them. Why did he call them up there? All he had to do was ask and they would have done anything for him.

He wouldn't ask. He just wanted to see them again. He called them to come up there but he could never say why he wanted to see them.

By 1962, the Browns were running out of money, and out of ambition. As bad as Maxine's agony was in beginning to suspect that their music was no longer relevant, Bonnie's was far worse, knowing that every time she went away from her home, she was trading away precious days she could have been spending with her girls, and with Brownie: days that were priceless and could never be gotten back.

Even Jim Ed was starting to feel some wear and tear; after all his hundreds of conquests, he had met a woman, Helen Cornelius, with whom he was in love. She was a singer, too. It made things a little crowded, a little complicated.

The most constant thing in the world is change. Rare and valuable are the periods in a life when it does not seem to be happening. It is always happening.

They made the decision together. Bonnie had brought it up first, but they all three soon were in agreement: the harder they worked, the more broke they became, and then had to split three ways that which was already not enough. They could never again be as poor as where they had come from, but somehow, after having briefly had a little money, it seemed worse now that it had gone away.

It made no sense to them to be trading away their time for nothing. At one point in their lives it had made sense — they had pursued that path unquestioningly — but now they each just wanted to be in three separate places, *home,* or the three places where they were attempting to build a home.

Even Maxine allowed herself to imagine days of domesticity, providing loving attention to the sustained applause of her needy children.

The Browns simply couldn't hold together anymore. "It's been a good run," Jim Ed told them, the night they committed to the breakup. "It seems like longer than ten years." His own new life opening before him.

"We have to tell Chet," Bonnie said quietly. They were all back home, checking in on Birdie, who had had a dizzy spell and fallen down the steps. She had not hurt anything, but was still dizzy. It was not yet midnight but already she had gone to bed, a thing they could never remember her doing before. They knew she had to wear down at some point, but still it caught them by surprise. They were adults now but they were still her children. Perhaps they thought that with their own strength, as strange and unvanquishable as it was unrequested by them, they could remain in control of that, too; that she would never wear all the way out—would grow old and diminish slowly, but that she would never completely vanish.

Chet never slept; he loved nothing more than to be working in his studio on either side of midnight, and further on, while most of the world was asleep, and when it was so much quieter, and sounds had more space in which to stretch and unfold, flowing around him in currents and waves that at times touched him with such intensity that it seemed he could see them, luminous in the night, and could breathe them, like smoke. He was always working, but he never called it work.

"Let's call him now," Bonnie said, "before we change our minds." She felt relief for herself, but bad for Chet, who would miss them so much.

"We won't change our minds," Jim Ed said, his voice rolling gently through the cabin, so that the words seemed to seep into the logs themselves, penetrating the wood with an authority that would render them into sacred text, with no renegotiation possible after that utterance. They were logs that their father had felled and limbed and milled, in a cabin he had built, and their mother was asleep in the other room, with those same words drifting over her as she slept—and an era was over, their work was done. The greatness was still in them, but their work was done.

Maxine was stunned, could not understand why she was agreeing: as if some larger truth was giving counsel and she was being carried along by it.

Listening to her brother and sister talk, she felt a ringing in her ears, an echo in the stillness. She felt as she did sometimes late at night when she had been drinking. *It won't let me quit but I am going to quit,* she thought, and then, a bit desperately, *I'm going to pretend I'm quitting, but I can't quit. I'll just go along with them, but they don't know what they're talking about. You can't quit something like this.*

Chet answered the phone on the first ring. The initial concern in his voice, and then the relief of hearing that everything was all right, and then the relaxation into the pleasure of having them on the line — all of it upset Bonnie. She had to hand the phone to Jim Ed, who calmly explained to Chet that the end had arrived — that they were out of money, and homesick all the time. That they wanted their lives back. That they were grateful to him for all he had done for them, and felt that they were letting him down.

Chet was silent for a moment — he had not been anticipating this — and he held his disappointment to himself, and tried to gather his thoughts, tried to remember that he only wanted what was best for them.

"How's Maxine?" he asked quietly.

Jim Ed looked over at her and paused. "Fine."

"Can I ask you one thing?" Chet said. "One favor?"

"Yes," said Jim Ed, "anything."

"There's this song I've been thinking about that I've been wanting to do," he said. "I think it's perfect, and I can't get it out of my mind. Please," he said, "I'd like to do just one more."

"All right," Jim Ed said, "we'll drive up tomorrow."

"Thank you," Chet said.

The song was called "Mommy, Please Stay Home with Me," an old sentimental Eddy Arnold ballad from the 1940s, about children who are missing their parents. The three Browns were determined to give their all for Chet in this last recording, and the song was so intense for Bonnie and Maxine that what came out was a purer, rawer sound that went all the way past sentimentality and into some further, wilder place, a keening or lamentation, so that even Chet was tearing up, behind the glass.

There was no need for a second take.

The song went to number one in the first week of its release and stayed there for nearly two months. There was just enough money to make work viable for another year. Few leave-takings of immense power are ever clean and final, and the conditions of the going-away cannot be fully controlled: the world does not want to easily release its hold on such contracts on the rare occasions when genius emerges and finds favor in and chooses an individual or individuals to carry it.

Birdie died a few months later, further into their rebound, their swooping recovery. The world loved them again, all was briefly as it had been before, and Birdie never knew of their turmoil, their plans to abandon their blessing and their curse.

They came home, buried her, broken further inside — there is no such thing as a fully balanced family, the harmonies yearned for within can only be accomplished for brief moments, which then burn bright in the remembering — and then they went back out on the road, following the same paths as before, paths they had made and which they were now trying to extend just a little more, orphans who knew in their hearts they had been loved deeply, but who wanted more.

≈ THE DIVING BELL

JEFFERSON EADS HAS been busy, viewing and cataloging the rough cuts of his film over and over. The quantification, the inventory of every external item in his world, soothes him; from order comes control, and he is no longer uneasy.

He's not always uneasy. At many points in the day he knows a great peace, sometimes earned through his work and other times descending on him like the weather, not generated through his own efforts but bestowed from afar, and unrequested, like grace.

Other times, however, it's as if a switch flips, and his agitation comes not from all the external factors he seeks to know and control, but from within. There is a disynchrony between him and the world, one that can only be calmed by numbers and their smooth, intricate, dependable precision: the way they always interlock and balance, no matter how challenging the enumeration may seem, or how difficult the equation. An equity can always be obtained, and once it is, no further changes can occur: the problem is balanced, and in that balance, the problem is controlled.

Whenever he is focused on one problem, he stays with it until it is solved, working through his agitation and unknown fear until the end; and when the problem is solved, he knows a deeper and more satisfying peace, one that cannot be gotten any other way than through his committed labor, and the feeling of control and relief is as sweet and powerful as it is brief.

Some of the other children in his school pity him his isolation and eccentricity, which seem to them to be willful, a rejection of the homogeneity toward which the others aspire and labor, and that therefore he is deserving of their ridicule and abuse — though there are not as many of these kinds of children as might be imagined.

Some, as the world begins to open before them, are beginning to realize they're a little afraid of him; not that he would alarm them, but simply afraid of what they're just beginning to understand might be an almost limitless depth, a bottomless difference — that already he knows and does things that they will never be able to. As if in his genius he has purposely chosen to distance himself from them, choosing his mind over their companionship.

He doesn't have any friends. This is not unprecedented in the other children's experience, but what is unique is that he doesn't seem to want one. He's not just pretending; he is happier when he is alone, reading up on whatever his next subject of inquiry might happen to be. Rockets, paleontology, military history, it doesn't matter; every few months, he sets up an encampment in a new land, usually one of the hard sciences, and then inhabits that territory with the commitment of a new lover.

He is happier when he is alone, or if not alone, safely distant from all others. The people he tolerates best are the ones who don't try to get too close to him. Often these are individuals who are either focused on themselves or do not want him around. It's complicated and entirely neurological, and he understands that he is different, and understands why, and accepts himself the way he is, and is grateful to have his intellect.

Later in his school career — and soon — his classmates will get over both their teasing and their fear and will accept him as he has accepted himself, and will come to take a huge pride in him, and will come in some ways to think of him as their captain. But not quite yet. Right now, they are mostly afraid, and he knows this, though it does not touch him, exists instead only at the perimeters of his consciousness. He perceives and understands that other people are concerned with what people think of them, but that simply isn't his world.

What it feels like to him sometimes is that he is in the service of another master, one whom he cannot see and about whom he knows precious little yet seeks to approach. Some master who lies far below, and whom — if only enough knowledge can be gained — can one day finally be met, and the master's power and essence more fully ascertained.

✣ ✣ ✣

It was a surprisingly long time before his parents realized more fully the nature of his gifts: his hunger for the facts, his insistence on being precise. For a long time they considered their love for him as being only their own special perspective, distanced from the world's; it was not until he was four or five that they began to understand that the indulgence of their perceptions was actually accurate, and that if anything, they had underestimated things. His recollections of all events and utterances was profound, as was his capacity to connect facts and in that manner proceed further into the depths of knowledge.

They would not have classified him as a loving child, but again, the indulgence of their own love for him made that disparity insignificant; they protected him with it, sent him out into the world with it, and though they knew the odds were long that he would change the world, they knew without a doubt that the world would not change him whatsoever, and that in that obstinate fixity, there was rarity and beauty, as there was in their own acceptance of that fact.

His mother, Louise, had been a schoolteacher for a few years before retiring; his father, Brad, managed a construction company. He, Jefferson, could have come from anywhere: he was as sudden and remarkable as their own lives had been unremarkable.

He and his mother had been shopping at the Piggly Wiggly when he had seen Maxine's note. He had been standing off by himself while she pushed her cart up the aisles. There had been nothing about the note that would have given any clue as to its provenance with greatness — no syntax or diction, or even, really, any boldness — but he had gone straight to it, had been standing there in his own reverie, looking up at the bulletin board while his mother shopped. Out of boredom, he had been mentally arranging and cataloging all the various hand-lettered postings, inventorying them by subject and their chronology, but no matter how he looked at the board, to him there had been no question. The small blue note might as well have been illuminated: somehow, he recognized it for what it was and was drawn straight toward it, with the same assurance and certainty with which he addressed all of his decisions.

The bonds of his affinity for such shared isolation, and such gift or talent, were as invisible as those of any other affinity—the call to shared companionship between two lifelong friends or the unseen but irrefutable bonds between hydrogen and oxygen, or mother and daughter, father and daughter—and he stood there for a long time beneath the note, comforted simply by being in its presence.

To have been so unremarkable in their accomplishments—and so lacking in notoriety of any sort—his parents were remarkable in other ways. They had learned to support wholeheartedly his ventures, whatever they turned out to be. They had learned to trust him and his place in the world.

Jefferson Eads returns five days later, with a clipboard, a storyboard, in hand. He informs her that her task that day is to go back to the grocery store—films her palsied efforts, successful at least one more time, to get the car backed out of the garage and onto the sunlit street, and then, like a great schooner setting out on the most intrepid of journeys, off into the heart of traffic. With some humor, amazement, fear, and grim satisfaction, he films the near misses, and the faces of the other motorists.

Everything he's filming is from the *now*, which makes Maxine uneasy; she wants to tell about the glory days. Even though it's a documentary, she wants young people to dress up and reenact the good years, though simplifying the journey—omitting the depression and alcoholism, which she has not told him about. "Couldn't you do a regular movie, too?" she asks. "Don't you know some young people you could cast as us?"

Jefferson shakes his head. "No," he says, "actually, I don't have many associates. It's just you and me. I do have some ideas, though."

She listens carefully, thrilled by his attention. All she had to do was wait; her every wish has always been delivered to her.

Totally unselfconscious, Jefferson Eads films her shopping: the slow hitch of the walker, her clumsiness with the frozen foods. The cold brick of a chicken slips from her grasp and skitters across the linoleum like a hockey puck rapped sharply across the ice. The rock-hard bird slides into a stacked display of soup cans, crumples the pyramid with the efficiency of a bowling ball striking tenpins, and the expression on Maxine's face when she looks back to see if the camera is rolling is one of guilt tinged with confusion.

How is this a movie about greatness? she wonders, and wants to quit — not just the movie, but everything.

To his credit, Jefferson Eads puts his camera down after the chaos has come to a rest, and he picks the chicken up and puts it in Maxine's cart, then begins restacking the soup cans. He holds one up and asks if she wants one.

What passes for trivia or minutiae in the lives of others — bonds so hair thin as to be irrelevant, utterly insignificant — are sometimes as strong as a bond gets, for him: as if too much electricity flows through him along some circuits and almost none at all — just a sporadic trickle — in others. For him, this is one of his bonding moments, or as close as he gets to such things: helping an old lady.

It's new territory for him; it was not his instinctive reaction. It was almost as if he had to analyze the situation, watch himself watching her, and then direct himself to offer assistance, in the manner that he would direct a character in one of his short films to block into a certain position.

He did it, though, and now he feels the faintest shimmering of electricity along those unused pathways. For him, the trickle might as well be a roar, and the two previously separate and unrelated elements are merged, the pleasure of reassembling the disorganized soup cans and his relationship with Maxine: the kindness in his heart finding some outlet. He's grateful to her for giving him that opportunity. Sometimes his coldness is a little like being in a jail.

On the way out, he stops and films her bulletin board note, which is still posted, and now it's her turn to bond a little further with him, and to give him what is her own rarest thing, trust.

"Do you want to take it down," Jefferson asks, "now that you've got a movie being made?"

Maxine hesitates, playing the odds, and with some effort, decides it's better to have his full enthusiasm than to wish for another. "Yes, you can take it down."

And again Jefferson Eads feels new warmth, electricity flowing through new places in his mind, the river current of it a little wider, and a little wilder. *This is what life is like,* he thinks. *It's enough to make you set down your camera.* It's not common, but it's fine enough to go hunting for it, and to wait, again and again, for such pleasure's return.

They make it back to her house unscathed. Maxine uses the opportunity of having Jefferson Eads along with her and stops at the gas station to fill her car. A full tank will last another six months. *What will my condition be then?* she wonders. She hands Jefferson the money and he pumps the gas.

He's so useful to have around! In a way he's far better than Buddy. She feels a warmth in her old heart that is not unlike how it was when she was drinking, but this is better. It's similar, in that it makes her want more, but it's better, in that a little is better than nothing. Which is not how it was with the bottle.

They go back into her treasure chest room and he films her unearthing more memorabilia, explaining to the camera the significance of each ancient artifact. A poster from a show with Elvis, signed by the King. A locket given to her by Johnny Cash. Jefferson Eads burns through another memory card, and at the bottom of the chest, she pulls out a nondescript cassette in a generic plastic case. The small rectangle is hand-lettered in red marker, "John Lennon — The Three Bells," and is dated December 8, 1980.

"His widow sent it to me," Maxine says. "It was the last thing he recorded. He was playing around in the studio, did this, then walked outside and got shot."

Jefferson Eads watches her face as she speaks. He's filming, is holding the camera under one arm as if it's a football, and he watches her face for a clue as to what he should be feeling.

He knows that John Lennon was a big deal, was one of the Beatles, and he senses dimly that this is a very sad event, but that part of his brain just isn't firing, isn't blossoming with the illumination, the gold light of sorrow. Still, he detects something like regret — something he can't quite identify — in Maxine's countenance, and he decides to take a chance.

"That's sad," he says carefully, and for a moment he thinks he's guessed wrong, because Maxine's expression doesn't change, her reverie remains intact.

"Yes," she says finally, "it is," though Jefferson is confused, because it seems to him she might be referring to something or someone else.

They take the tape into the front room and she plays it for him. There's not much to it — the banter, the quick confident warm-up chords, and then suddenly Lennon's into the song, rocking out, singing about Little Jimmy Brown and a valley in France — and then someone walks into the studio and interrupts him.

We were all interrupted, Maxine thinks. She is the only one who has gone the whole distance, and then beyond.

"Do you want me to dig any more holes?" she asks. She's not joking, is resigned to the gauntlet through which she must pass to regain the center of fame, and would rather get the digging out of the way sooner than later, while she still has a few shreds of energy left.

"No," Jefferson Eads says, "but I do want you to do something tonight. I've been thinking about it a lot and I want to film you walking down the street at night with a lantern," he says. "I'll probably film it from a lot of different angles. I want you to wear something white. I'll film you from a long way away," he says.

"Sure," she says, and she feels almost like she did the time she listened to Jim Ed and Bonnie discuss the breakup, and the phone call to Chet: as if she's outside of herself, listening to herself from that same distance. As if his proposal makes perfect sense.

Jefferson Eads is nothing if not a fast learner; he remembers her discomfort with his earlier prescription of hole digging and tries to explain his latest idea with a little more diplomacy. "Don't you ever want something without knowing why?" he asks. "Sometimes — a lot of times — that's how it is for me with a scene. I just *have* to see it. I feel like I already *have* seen it and need to capture it."

"I think I might know a little what that's like," Maxine says. And for a second, she really means it; there's something vaguely familiar about what he's describing, something she feels she stands at the edge of now, where once she was closer to its center.

"I have a sheet," she says. "I don't have a lantern."

"I have an old one I got in a garage sale," he says. "I'll go back home and get it and come over later this afternoon." He looks at her with mild concern, if not actually love or affection. "Do you think you should take a nap?" he asks. "It'll probably be a pretty involved shoot."

"Yes," she says, wondering if he's hypnotizing her, for now that he mentions it, she can barely stay awake, feels that she might slide from her chair and lie down right there on the carpet and sleep for hours. "I think so," she says.

Her chin drops. He is rising and saying "I'll let myself out"; she is dreaming before he reaches the door.

When she awakens it is dusk, though at first she confuses it with dawn, and then, recognizing it as evening, thinks that she has slept a day and a night, has lost her movie. She panics, and not knowing what else to do, calls the operator to ask her what day and date it is, but still that doesn't do any good, for she doesn't know what day and date it had been to begin with. She doesn't have Jefferson Eads's phone number, tries to look it up in the phone book, but can find no Eads. She just has to wait. She's slept so long that even Buddy has come and gone.

Maxine has been sitting by the front window with the curtains parted a few inches, waiting and watching, for an hour, when she sees Jefferson Eads coming down the street pulling a red wagon with all his gear in it and some self-consciousness: as if he knows or believes that he is too old for wagons.

There's still half an hour or so before true dark, but he's been placing his paper sacks with the tea candles in each one in two rows, forming a lane along the sidewalk, and as she watches, he stops and places two more, then two more, and again, working his way toward her.

How far will I have to walk? she wonders, and then with even greater worry, *Where is he leading me?* Her night vision is worse than even her dimming daylight sight—she's functionally blind at night—and her old heart thunders again, though there is no question of not stepping forward toward whatever thin opportunity might present itself.

She squints, watches his slow progress — his precision — and she dares to hope again, just as she did when she sent off the recording of Jim Ed to *The Barnyard Frolic*.

Never, not for one moment, has she had the thought that at any point along the path, or any coordinate on the timeline, has she taken a wrong turn or made a single wrong choice. There has never been a choice to make: her every gesture has been inflamed by righteousness and non-negotiability, to the point where she wants to scream, to the point where she is terrified, to the point where she realizes she has become the most imprisoned person in the world.

She rises, leaning on her walker, raps on the glass to get his attention, but her rappings are too feeble; he continues with his labors, head down, adjusting each unlit tea light just so, lost in his vision not of how the world should or could be but of how it is, if even only for a short distance around him: the distance, perhaps, of each throw of radiant light once he lights the candles, and each next step.

Why are these people drawn to Maxine? What do they take from her, what do they need from her? Must she carry their weight for them? Why do they need, much less want, her darkness?

Now Jefferson Eads is working his way up her sidewalk, and she feels overwhelmed with the success of being loved or desired; she feels as she did when she was a bride on her wedding day, back when she thought Tommy was one of the answers.

I have never made a single wrong choice, she thinks. *It has all led me to where I need to be: here, now.*

Jefferson Eads knocks at the door. He has finished; he is ready to begin. She nearly leaps to her feet and shoves her walker toward the door so quickly that she almost falls down — for a moment she is running behind the walker.

They wait for even fuller darkness, visiting quietly. Then he wraps the sheet around her like a toga or a sari, adjusting it just so.

It's been a long time since she's been touched. Her annual visits to the doctor, when the nurse takes her pulse and blood pressure. The careful, professional ministrations of the physician's assistant as he moves the stethoscope around on her bony chest, as if searching for something he's not even sure is there, or is having trouble finding.

Jefferson Eads wraps and unwraps the sheet with the care of a tailor. He's lost in the work, has no idea of the pleasure, the relief, it's bringing her. Life was amazing once and will be again.

Finally he has it just right, and steps back to be sure. It's dark enough outside now.

"Can you walk without the walker?" he asks.

"Do you need me to?"

He pauses, then says, "One sequence with, and one without." He wants everything. He will weed out almost everything in the editing, but does that make the unused parts waste?

"Start without, then come back and rest, and we'll do it again with the walker." She recognizes his obsession coming on again, the heartlessness of his ambition; he could be talking to a dog, or even an inanimate object. He is looking right at her, but the little tendrils of his connection to her have short-circuited or gone cold.

"If you get too far away and can't make it back, I can put you in the wagon and pull you home that way," he says.

Like a commando or a one-man stage lighting director, he has brought two flashlights, one with green plastic taped over the lens, and the other with red.

"I'll need to shoot from a lot of different angles," he says. "Sometimes I'll be out in the street ahead of you, sometimes behind you. Other times I'll be in the hedges, or in people's yards. Sometimes I'll be right in front of you, or walking right alongside you. When I flash the red light, I'll need you to stop while I relocate, and the green light means go. If I flash the red light several times, it means slow down, and a rapid succession of green blinks means go faster. Okay?"

No, it's not okay, she thinks. *I don't understand what you're saying.*

"All right," she says.

He's so earnest. Here they are about to set off on a grand adventure, and he's not even smiling. At best he's feeling peace, or settledness. Momentary relief.

Perhaps from that platform of relief joy might come next, but first he must reach that elusive place where he can rest for a moment, and look around.

"I'm going to go light the candles," he says.

She stands at the doorway and watches him light the first pair of luminaria, right at the doorstep, clicking a cigarette lighter, and then the next, and the next: her path, her runway, becoming illuminated before her in that manner, like a fuse being lit, showing her where to go, and again she feels like a young girl — this is how it used to be — and she wishes intensely that Jim Ed and Bonnie were here with her, as well as Floyd and Birdie, Norma, Raymond, Elvis, and all the others who have gone away. *If Jim Ed and Bonnie were here, maybe they could even sing,* she thinks. She feels like she could. She feels like she wants to.

The lights are distinct, close in, but the farther he goes, the blurrier they become and the more they converge, so that at the outer limits all she can see is one white line curling into the distance, and she is eager to start, does not want to wait for his signal.

What if I cannot see the green light, or the red light? she wonders. *What if he is signaling to me right now to begin?*

He startles her, coming back up the walk. Of course: she's forgotten about the lantern. It's an old-fashioned liquid fuel Coleman, with ashen mantles; he pumps it up with a piston until it is hissing with pressure, then opens the valve and lights it with a quick *pop!* and a bowl of light surrounds them.

"Be careful," he says, handing it to her. "Don't burn yourself."

It's heavier than she expected, but she's running on adrenaline. She swings the lantern gamely, like a railroad conductor, and Jefferson Eads smiles. In the night like this, it seems to him somehow that there is not such a gulf between him and the world, and between him and others — here in the night, on a grand cinematic adventure, it feels like he's able maybe to inhabit the full range of steady joy — not yelping, leaping spikes of joy, but a continuous rolling current of it, like that which he imagines most others experience pretty much all the time.

He feels the deep plunge of it, the bracing exhilaration, a feeling something akin to the column of light that precedes an ice cream headache, the icy wedge-shaped dagger of pleasure diving down into the skull just before the spreading arrival of the pain — the light pouring in, the stimulation just before the pain — but then, as it always does, the joy shuts off, as if a cabinet door has been closed to that compartment, or as if a switchplate has been slid closed, and he's back to all business: calm and studious and ordered and controlling.

"Try not to be quite so *merry*," he instructs her. "If you must swing the lantern at all, do so on a more circumscribed radius. Try to make it seem like you're looking for something," he says. "Like you're lost. Walk slowly. Like you're looking for something you dropped."

"All right," Maxine says. "Like this?"

"Yes," Jefferson Eads says, "that's it." He stares at her and her small surrounding dome of white light like a raptor, a hawk beholding its prey, bewitched by the improbable nearness of success. "Yes," he says, "like that." He flashes the green light and then the red light to make sure they're working. "Go to the end of the candles," he says, "then wait there for me."

He shoulders the camera and dashes off across the lawn to the first location he's already scouted, beneath a young oak tree two houses down. Some distance away, a dog begins barking, and while Jefferson Eads is thrilled with the audio quality — he flashes the green light once, to get Maxine moving — Maxine herself is terrified, and wonders what kind of dog it is, friendly or angry, and if it is unleashed. She wonders if it might attack her as she navigates the row of candles. Wonders if Jefferson Eads would set the camera down to come help her, or keep filming.

She pushes on into the darkness, one pair of candles at a time. She's terrified of falling — the throw of her lanternlight yields an intense view of each next step: she can see the tiny cracks in the sidewalk, can see each paper bag, each little candle, but nothing else — and she peers intently into the darkness where Jefferson has disappeared, watching for his signals. She trusts him as she has rarely if ever trusted anyone, and seeing neither red nor green flash, she imagines that she must be doing fine.

How many candles? Eventually she comes to the end of the lane, and like an old draft horse she stands there, waiting — she wishes she had a chair to sit down in and rest — and when he comes bustling in from out of the darkness she's almost overwhelmed to see him, having started, for some strange reason, to believe he would not be coming.

"That was good," he says, "but can you go a little quicker?"

"Yes," she says. She turns and starts toward home, the lantern banging crookedly once against her leg.

"Be careful," Jefferson Eads says, "don't catch the sheet on fire."

She can see her house ahead of her. It seems a mile away. She misses everyone she has ever known, wishes she had her life to live over again. She feels the need to at least counsel Jefferson Eads something to this effect — to caution about wrong paths, sloth, squander, and numbness, the heartlessness of ambition — but she doesn't know quite how to say it.

The house, her refuge, her last stand, draws nearer. Her legs are jelly; she doesn't know if she can make it. He's still behind her, whispering, "Good job, keep on." More dogs are barking, and a lone toad hops across the sidewalk, stops in front of her, drawn by the hope of the moths that are beginning to flit against the lantern now; and so slow is Maxine's progress that it seems the toad might hop alongside her all the rest of the way, keeping pace and feeding from time to time on whatever residue might be gleaned from the perimeter of her passage. *The toad is like something from a fairy tale,* she thinks. Was hers a real life masquerading as a fairy tale, or was it the other way around?

When she reaches her house, she calls out to Jefferson Eads to give her a hand up the steps, but he hesitates, then urges her on, tells her she can do it by herself, and that she must. She stops at the bottom step, quivering, too tired even to turn around, and starts to ask again, but knows what the answer will be. Knows that his obsession exceeds her own.

She sets the lantern down carefully, and with that last little bit of relief — her burden momentarily lessened — takes the first step, gripping the wrought-iron handrail, and then the next, and finally, the third. She leans against the door, then goes inside, leaves the door open — Jefferson Eads keeps filming — and then he follows her inside.

There is a mercy in the world. It does not exist everywhere at all times, but is present in places, and moves in tendrils and wisps. Jefferson Eads decides he doesn't want or need the footage of her with the walker — that the images he got were good enough, were more than good enough, and that the walker footage would dilute the stronger footage.

He had originally intended to show diminishment but has changed his mind. He's not sure why, because it happens so rarely; once the electricity of a thought, a desire, a goal, starts flowing through him, lighting up some circuitry but leaving other circuitry dark, he follows it through to the end.

To deviate from that one slender course would create in him the most extreme form of agitation.

And yet: that evening he knows the momentary peace of completion. He's done with her: he feels he has pretty much inhabited, in a quick ripple of something, each of her long years, that he has an artistic knowledge of them now, even if he sometimes has trouble crossing the bridges to an understanding of other people's emotions and how those emotions govern their decisions.

Sometimes when he meets a person for the first time and is trying to get to know or understand that person, it feels to him as it did the time he flew to California to visit his aunt and uncle. He flew at night, flying across the country, looking out his window down at all the darkness below. The snowcapped peaks and glacial basins glowed dully in the moonlight with a dim and terrible coldness, and the dark furze of the forest lay farther below and beyond. Still farther on, there were a few lone lights of civilization, tiny amid that darkness; and even as the plane began to draw near to its destination, with more lights becoming visible and brighter and more concentrated — individual trails and ribbons of light leading quickly now toward some central ganglia — the nexus of illumination, the fierce glow of existence, seemed infinitesimal, vulnerable, ludicrous amid all that darkness through which he had traveled; and his response was to wonder, *That's it? So much darkness to yield such a little concentrated cluster and spark of light?*

Yet like all who choose to dwell among others of their kind, in such villages — even though he does not feel or consider himself to be like others — he travels to the edge of that light and looks in at it. He throws a few sticks onto the fire, partly to stay warm but also partly to help keep that light burning, drawn to it even if he does not quite feel or experience it like most others.

He's done with Maxine. He feels completed. It's all over now except for the editing: the cutting and splicing, the compressing and attenuating; the reshaping, as if he is some little god who has decided to give her a second chance.

Even now as he sits there with her, he feels his hard-gotten empathy, the connection of the human bond like the ones he sees in so many others, fading, and he fidgets, wants to experience it a little longer.

He tries to sit very still, as if through such concentrated stillness he might summon it. He thinks this might be what people mean when they use the word *magic* — and he becomes uncomfortable again, for he does not much believe in such things, if at all.

He looks over at her and sees how exhausted she is, how brave and resolute, and he assesses from that observation that he should feel empathy, and thinks to himself, *I am going to say something empathetic* — but the fire of that quick, thin connection is leaving him, is cooling.

He tries to hold on to it a little longer. As if not through calculation or logic but instead blind instinct, he casts back, beseeching help not from the future, but from older generations who he believes were more successful in such matters, and who brought him to this place: the success of his kin, moving through the centuries.

He begins to tell Maxine a story about his great-great-grandfather, for whom he is named.

He's not quite sure of the tangle of maternal and paternal registry, the wiring that got him to this point — his mother has explained it to him, but sometimes he forgets a generation or two — but in the 1860s, the first Jefferson Eads was a hydrologic engineer, hugely gifted in the math and science of the time, who studied the Mississippi River in the years when men were first considering trying to tame it, trying to control its devastating floods, which Eads and a few others understood were also life-giving.

Not only were there plans to build dams and locks and levees along it, but bridges, too, spanning its absurd width. Most engineers merely walked up and down the muddy shores, making maps and measurements, but Jefferson Eads went into the river itself and prowled its depths in a crude diving bell apparatus of his own design, having fitted a copper shell over his head and breathing through a hundred-foot-long rubber hose attached to a float at the surface. For ballast, he clutched in both arms an immense boulder with an eyelet drilled into it, to which he would fasten himself upon reaching the bottom, so that his hands would be free to take samples and measurements.

What he found down there was different from what coursed above. There were different turbidities, different velocities. There were places where the river bottom was filled with inestimable depths of muck, and other places where the substrate was scoured to white bedrock. Giant snapping turtles tumbled through the current, spinning in cartwheels like the astronauts who would drift through space a century later, and sometimes even Eads himself would be carried downstream in similar fashion, despite the boulder to which he was attached, and despite the chains around his waist, his tether to the mother ship above, the barge from which he dived.

"It's a miracle I ever got here," Jefferson Eads tells her. Maxine is rapt, is listening as intently as she can, but is finding it hard to stay awake. All she wants, all she needs, is a little rest, but the story is too compelling; she must stay awake a little longer.

Is he casting a spell on me? she wonders, feeling herself descending toward sleep.

As she listens, it feels to her that she is fitted with a crudely hammered copper diving helmet herself, is tumbling, being swept along by a force so much greater than anyone above can know. *But you made it here,* she thinks, imagining that she is speaking to Jefferson Eads, though she is far too tired to say the words. Like an emissary, the first Jefferson Eads made it through, and this new traveler before her, his coincidental namesake, has made it. There is a line, a continuum: the journey can be completed and the connections made, no matter at what level, no matter whether at the surface or in the depths.

"There would be all these giant logs surging past," Jefferson Eads says. "None of them ever struck him or I wouldn't be here, but he'd feel them go rushing past, like battering rams. Sometimes they snaked along the bottom. He would try to grab hold of them as they swept past and ride them for a while, almost to the length of his tether. He had fashioned little numbered metal plates that he tried to tack onto them with engraved instructions, asking whoever found them to write him with their final location, hundreds or thousands of miles downstream — but he never heard from anyone. Maybe we will yet."

"Other times he would feel the logs surging past him, riding some upswell of current, some reverse vortex, which would hurl the logs straight up to the surface, propelling them into the air like rockets. Again, he passed through all these unharmed. Was he chosen, or was he lucky?"

Maxine's eyes are closing, her chin bobbing. *Am I being hypnotized,* she wonders, *or is he trying to awaken me?*

She sleeps. Jefferson Eads helps her lie down on her couch and pulls a blanket over her. He sits beside her and thinks about his great-great-grandfather. Was it true passion that sent him down into the depths, or was it only the place where he best fit the world and its destinies? A forced move in a designed space, the one lock-and-key fit where his enormous discord found brief respite.

No records or diaries, no testimonies exist, only artifacts, and the facts of his survival. His progeny, and the various histories of all their days that followed.

Jefferson Eads leaves one light on in the kitchen and gathers his gear, calls his parents to tell them he won't be staying over at the nice old lady's house after all — that he wants to come home and start working right away. It's about nine o'clock, on a weekend.

"Be careful," his mother tells him. He hears his father in the background, calling for him to be home by ten.

He loads his camera gear into the red wagon and then follows the luminaria down the sidewalk, crouching and puffing out each little candle as if kneeling in prayer, following his trail backwards toward the increasing darkness. He can imagine how others might be frightened of such darkness. He imagines that for some it is hard to learn how to wait, how to be certain that some light will always return.

LEAVING AGAIN

THE NEXT TIME they quit, Chet Atkins did not ask them for another favor. He could see what the road was doing to them, and he, better than anyone, could hear the unraveling now. He might have been able to carry them a little further, but the kindest thing was to let them go back home. He worried about Maxine, but it wasn't fair to Jim Ed, who was starting to schedule more and more concerts with Helen Cornelius, or to Bonnie, who, Chet knew, had been looking for an exit for longer than even she herself realized. The thing that had made them great — their three voices becoming one — was now the thing that would have to separate them and end it. He had seen it before — the end of a sound, and the end of fame — though never quite like this, never all in the same family, and never such a sound.

Was the sound itself going away? Sometimes he thought it might be, but even he couldn't quite be sure.

This time, the Browns made the decision over the telephone, from their own homes, rather than gathering together. It wasn't quite as hard, in that they had already done it once before, but still, it wasn't easy. Jim Ed was relieved, and Bonnie was thrilled, which was not lost on Maxine, who, after hanging up the phone, had a change of heart.

She drove up to Bonnie's farm the next day. She didn't think she could change Jim Ed's mind — he was in love, and there was nothing dumber, she knew, than a man in love — but maybe she could come to some sort of agreement with Bonnie. Perhaps they could finally turn to Norma and the three sisters could sing. Maybe they could start all over. Maybe it would be even better than before.

It was July, the height of green summer in the South, and the farther she drove, the more she came to believe she would be successful in her endeavor to reclaim Bonnie from her farm. When had she never not gotten what she wanted?

The cinderblock honky-tonks, situated at the various intersections between dry and wet counties, beckoned to her, even in the bright heat of the day, but she kept going, eager to get up into the Ozarks before too late in the afternoon. She imagined the cold gin and tonic her sister might have waiting for her, and was surprised and disappointed, when she finally pulled in at the end of the long ascending driveway — the view of the green valley sublime below her — that there was no such refreshment awaiting her, nor was there any vodka to be found in the house. She wanted to ask for a sample of the bourbon she knew Brownie must keep somewhere but didn't dare betray her weakness before so intimate a witness as family. Still, she knew it was there somewhere and could not stop thinking about it.

"How are you?" Bonnie asked, giving her a hug.

"I'm okay," Maxine said. "All things considered, I'm okay." She had told Bonnie she could stay only for a day, and Bonnie figured that Maxine just didn't want to be alone after the breakup, that she wanted to talk over old times. It was the sweetest part of the summer for Bonnie and Brownie, when so much was ready to be harvested and when the food tasted best, a time when all the hard work they had put in over the spring and early summer no longer seemed like work at all.

Bonnie and Brownie had the feeling that they were getting away with something — their happiness — and they were aware that there were people in the world who would never know the same. They marveled at this, and perhaps had their own edges moderated or sanded down a bit by this realization — but in other ways, it made their own happiness even deeper.

They didn't deserve it, and they didn't not deserve it. Fate had nothing to do with it; it was just the way things had turned out, and they never ceased to be grateful for it, particularly when Maxine came to visit, bringing with her, almost like a stranger, that massive, crackling discontent.

Midsummer, there really wasn't time for Bonnie to devote herself to a visit by Maxine, but if there wasn't time then, with the days still at their sleepy fullest, then when would there be?

Watering the garden at first light, sometimes when the crickets were still chirping, and with the garden looking bejeweled when the sun came up, and with the water already soaking down into the soil before the heat of the day could evaporate it — and watering it again at dusk, as if putting it to bed — was a feeling richer than having money in the bank, with bowls of the day's pickings resting on the kitchen table, and the certainty, or near certainty, at that time of year, that the next day would bring still more bounty, and the day after that even more.

Maxine could suck the air out of a room. Not necessarily in a bad way: her presence simply always announced itself in such a manner, with its longing and expectations, so that a bystander ended up feeling some sort of response was required. Sometimes, as at a party, that was a fun thing, though other times — such as at home, in the lazy summer, with the garden being Bonnie's focus — it could be a bit taxing.

In all these minor conflicts, however — the mild resentments, and the too narrow attentions to self — each sister would remember Birdie, and the selflessness with which she had raised them. Is the future as uncomplicated, really, as a coin flip, with one daughter assuming that such devotion and singular attention were her mother's lifelong desire, and becoming so accustomed to receiving it that she comes to depend on it, always needing more, while another, lavished with the same attention and warmth, responds instead by trying to return that kind of devotion to the world, keeping only a modest amount for herself?

"Let me show you the garden," Bonnie said. "Brownie's still at work. What would you like for dinner?" She helped Maxine with her bag. The children were down at the creek, playing with friends. Bonnie stopped in the kitchen to pour Maxine a glass of lemonade and to show her the day's harvest, and while Maxine had known for a long time that Bonnie had another life than touring, and perhaps a better life, Maxine had always managed to put that knowledge aside, or to hide it beneath the surface.

She saw it now though as if for the first time — saw it most fully — not so much in Bonnie's newly relaxed demeanor, but in the beauty of the kitchen: brighter and more modern, certainly, than Birdie's had ever been, and yet somehow harking back to those days. The afternoon sunlight illuminating the lemonade pitcher, the lemonade's translucent fibers suspended, and the stainless steel bowls of produce — redleaf lettuce, greenleaf, radishes, green beans, snap peas, and tomatoes with their pungent, summery smell — combined with the density of Bonnie's happiness lead Maxine to understand finally that which for years she had been trying to avoid seeing or knowing.

Bonnie handed her the lemonade and asked her to come down to the garden. The sun was blazing, and Bonnie tossed Maxine a straw hat.

I don't have a chance in hell, Maxine thought. *It's over.* She wondered how and when her sister had grown up and away from her; at what point had she slipped away from her control? *She doesn't care if she ever sings again,* Maxine thought. Jim Ed had left her for Helen Cornelius, was what it felt like, Norma had gone off to college, and now Bonnie had turned her back on her, just as she had on Elvis, and chosen Brownie and her new family.

Bonnie entered the waist-high garden like a woman entering surf, wading in slowly, pausing often and putting her hands down to pluck one leaf or another. The day's weeds had already been picked and lay drying in the yard, curing and withering like hay. Maxine loved a good tomato. Bonnie remembered this, sought out a small one she had passed by earlier in the day, picked it, and handed it to her. Maxine took a bite from it as if it were an apple and was surprised at the jag of envy she felt, rather than pleasure, at how delicious it was. She took a sip of the lemonade — the ice cubes rattled as she did so, and she flinched, remembering her yearning — and for a moment, there in the heat and the sun with her sister, and with the green growing odor of the garden, her head swam, and she thought, *All right, lay down your burden, step forward, and all will be all right.*

"Are you sure you're all right?" Bonnie asked, direct if not blunt, and again Maxine was surprised; she didn't remember such confidence or assurance, such fullness.

"Yes," Maxine said, wondering how she would bring up her plea. Trying to figure a way to rephrase it, repackage it. Maybe later that night. Maybe not quite yet.

"I know it can't be easy on you," Bonnie said. "I know how much it meant to you."

Maxine followed her into the garden, moving cautiously, almost as if entering a jungle.

"I don't think I can stop," Maxine said, and now the peacefulness that had been present in the garden seemed to be vanishing quickly, as if it had been only an illusion. Bonnie stopped her casual tending and turned to look at Maxine, again with that new directness. They could hear the cries and shouts and laughter of the children off in the woods, the children coming back from the creek.

"Well, you have to," Bonnie said, her tone different, and Maxine thought, *Why, she's looking at me like I'm the enemy.*

"It's just that we've worked so hard," Maxine said. "We've finally gotten free of Fabor, and we've made so many connections now. Hell," she said, "we've got Chet Atkins on our side. Do you know how many singers would kill for that?"

"No," Bonnie said, and Maxine, misunderstanding, said, "Well, plenty. Any of them would. I've been thinking," she said, "and I don't think it's right to turn your back on a gift."

"No," Bonnie said again, still in the middle of the garden but giving all of her attention to Maxine; and Maxine was about to press harder, even while knowing it to be a mistake, but the children came bursting from out of the woods, whooping and singing, then pausing at what they understood instinctively was a scene of conflict before recognizing Maxine, whom they had not seen in a long time.

They hurried over to hug her, calling out her name; softening her, in that regard, yet sharpening the ache, the terror, as she came to know further that which Bonnie had chosen and why she had chosen it.

Maxine's own children were back in West Memphis, with a babysitter. *Why,* she wondered, *had she not thought to bring them?*

They shelled peas that night, as they had when they were children. Brownie sat in the big overstuffed recliner, watching a baseball game, and Bonnie and Maxine side by side on the couch in an uneasy truce, fingers working quickly, rarely even having to look down. It seemed to Maxine that there was nothing in the world that would not remind her of music, and of their career — the Washington Senator she had dated was not playing that night but was sitting on the bench, having been demoted — but neither Bonnie nor Brownie commented on it, as if having forgotten, and they all three watched the game in contented silence while the children played board games upstairs.

The room filled steadily with the green flesh aroma of the split hulls, the fiber mushy sometimes beneath the shellers' thumbnails, and they all three worked in unified silence, lulled by the trance of the hunter-gatherer, proceeding moment by moment into the uncertain future, against which any stockpiling was always only a partial solution. The pleasure and gratification of ancient tasks.

That night there was a summer storm, and each of them awakened to the sound of limbs and branches landing on the tin roof, followed by the shooting-gallery drum of hail. Bonnie got up and went out onto the porch, worried for her garden, but there was nothing to be done; she knew she would just have to wait for morning, and hope that the broad leaves of her plants and the care with which she spaced them would be sufficient to protect the underlying vegetables. Brownie came out onto the porch with her briefly to admire the lightning, put his arm around her, and told her it would be all right.

"She wants to go back," Bonnie said, and Brownie nodded and said, "You had to know that she would." They stood there smelling the scent of fresh storm-clipped foliage — basil, tomatoes, parsley, dill — and with a tremble in her voice, Bonnie said, "I'm afraid it's going to be all ruined," but Brownie rubbed her back and said, "Nonsense, you've seen storms worse than this before. Don't worry," and then went back to bed, craving, as ever, sleep, working from a lifetime deficit he would never quite be able to catch up on.

In her room, Maxine cursed the storm's sound and pulled the pillows over her head, and worried about her drive home. The power went out sometime after midnight, but by that time she was asleep again, dreaming that she was a child at home and that none of the fame had occurred yet and none of the unhappiness; and when she next awoke, the sun was up high. It was midmorning, Brownie was long gone, off to work, and the coffee brewed in the kitchen was already too strong to drink. She poured a glass of orange juice and went out into the garden, where Bonnie, who had been working since dawn, was just finishing the cleanup.

Neat piles of leaves and limbs were stacked for burning, and Bonnie had gathered all of the shredded parts of her garden, had salvaged the vegetables that had been cut or clipped or partially bruised by the storm. There were still drifts of hail in the yard and in her garden, so that it looked as if she were working amid fields of snow, but the sun was melting those patches quickly and all the world was steaming; and despite being out in the hail, Bonnie was sweating.

There was an electricity in the storm-scrubbed air, and Maxine was ready to walk to town if necessary to secure some vodka for the orange juice. The children were still sleeping, but she had to get on the road. She would ask the question, even knowing full well what the answer would be, and then she would leave and would try to figure something else out; though how she could push on without the other two parts of her sound, she had no idea, knew only that the orange juice tasted flat and unsubstantial.

"I was thinking," she said, "what about a reduced schedule? Maybe just each spring," she said, and then, remembering the garden, "or each fall, once the children are back in school."

"Maxine," Bonnie said, with a quick flame of anger that even now she regrets, "it's over." Bonnie was clutching a handful of plants that had been cut down by the storm, and her temper, her anger, seemed to her to be coming from the new-lashed soil itself. "We had more than our fair share," she said. "Nobody can take that away, but it's gone now. You go ahead and do what you want, but I'm done. I don't want any more to do with it. I want to remember it how it was.

"Things end," Bonnie said. "You've got to stop clinging to it. You've got to find something else worthwhile in your life." She paused, knowing she had said enough, but it was like there was some kind of momentum now, in the opening-up, that wouldn't let her. "It's pathetic," she said. "Nobody wants to hear us anymore. *I* don't want to hear us anymore."

Maxine just stood there as if cast to stone. The garden was sparkling again but the steam made it look like it was burning. She stared at her sister—her little sister, whom she had saved—and for a moment wanted to say *I understand;* and for a moment, feeling the whip of Bonnie's words, and their truth, she wanted to say *I forgive you,* for she knew how much Bonnie would regret, later, having said them.

But those were not the words that came out. As if speaking in another's voice, or from another's heart, Maxine did the only thing she had ever done when hurt, which was to fight back. *"Sure,"* she said, her voice dripping with scorn now, "go ahead and say it: I fucked up. You always picked the right guy, and I always picked the wrong one. Go ahead and say it: *I told you so.*" Maxine gestured toward the garden, then up at the house. "You with your damned perfect life," she said.

"All right," Bonnie said slowly, looking straight at her, eyes glittering, and Maxine wondered, with shock, *Is she enjoying it, is she savoring it?* Even now, in the remembering, she cannot be sure.

"All right," Bonnie said again, speaking evenly now — finally getting somewhat of a grip on her temper — *"I told you so."*

There wasn't a whole lot of room left to negotiate after that. Maxine turned and hurried up to the house to pack. Bonnie wanted to apologize, wanted to follow her up to the house and explain, but she knew where that would lead, to more arguing and pleading, and that it might awaken the children.

This is the kindest thing, Bonnie told herself, and bent down and went back to work in her garden, trying, in only the course of a day, to get it back to where it had been.

~ RELENTLESS

SHE IS A FIRM believer in second chances; for her, they are an article of faith. In 1972, she flew up to New York to meet with RCA. Chet wasn't there to lobby for her anymore; she had finally outrun her guardian angels. Bonnie was retired and living on the farm with Brownie, and Jim Ed had his healthy solo career.

She was desperate both financially as well as emotionally. RCA had informed Maxine by mail and then phone that they didn't want to record or release any more of her records, or those of the Browns, that they already had plenty of backlog. That the Browns' days were over. The Swinging Sixties had come and gone and the Browns had fallen by the wayside.

Maxine was trying to adapt, had poofed her hair up into the huge gladiator helmet style and shown up in New York wearing a polka-dotted minidress and high boots — wasn't that how it was done? — but none of the RCA executives would meet with her.

She went door to door, trying to find her old publicists, and searching for the bookkeepers, accountants, secretaries, and vice presidents with whom she had corresponded in the past. They were all gone; she could gain no entrée, could not even explain who she was, who she had been. She had a folder filled with yellowing newspaper clippings about various shows the Browns had played, and photographs — she was savvy enough to know the game was no longer all about the music — of the Browns with Ed Sullivan, and with the Beatles, and of Maxine with Johnny Cash.

There were no photos in the folder of Elvis. For that, she was too proud, and something else. As if, were she to try to reach out and take back a part of that which he had claimed from them, there would be some short-circuitry, some hiss of sparks. He was off-limits.

It was too powerful to speak of. It had been something different from fame. It had been friendship.

She finally was able to intercept a junior-level executive as he came out of an office from one meeting, heading to the next. She hurried after him, her boots double-clicking to his longer strides, then caught up with him. As they both walked, briefly side by side, they passed the framed pictures of all the recording industry's luminaries, as well as those of the newly emerging RCA television industry.

The young executive hurried along, not quite yet late to his next meeting but eager to get to it.

Maxine lobbied for a touring schedule and then, unsuccessful with that, for even an audition for a contract — she who had produced more than twenty albums by that time and sold millions, in this country as well as abroad, money that had gone to Fabor and to RCA, with very little to her and her family, and with no savings.

She did everything but break into song as they hurried down the hall, running out of time. She suggested, then pleaded, for a duet with any of her friends who were still living, but the young executive shook his head tersely and quickened his pace, so much so that she had to put her hand on his arm to slow him down, at which point he threw her hand off and turned to her and said the words that would push her over the edge — this *boy*, filled with dreams of money and power, a boy who had never set foot in a logging camp or seen a man lose his arm, who had never built a fire or cleaned a deer, a boy who had never seen darkness fall over the forest while he was still in it. A boy in a hurry, but with no idea where.

"Listen, Maxine," he said — a boy who believed that compassion was weakness, and that money, his desperate god, fled weakness. "You're yesterday's news. We're done with you. You're old hat." Then he turned and walked on, having said what was necessary to separate himself from her.

Nobody had ever said it before, but it was her deepest fear — that not only had the world around her abandoned her, but the world below. That she had been forsaken. And worst of all, that if she had done things differently, it would not have turned out this way.

She went back home and drank harder. She has no real recollection of the immediate years beyond that time. It was from this humiliation, however, that she would hit rock bottom, and from that wreckage, as always, she would be saved. She eventually joined AA, stopped drinking — though it was a long time coming — and began to crawl back up out of the pit, creeping inch by inch toward the shining light above, which she perceived to be the return of fame, but which, she begins to wonder now, might have been nothing more than the next day.

JIM ED INTERVENES

ALL HIS LIFE, he had been second fiddle, third fiddle, hidden, always invisible. Heard, certainly, in every song they ever did, but taken for granted. Utilitarian, durable, pleasant, he seemed always to be a side man, on or off the stage — secondary to Jim Reeves, in the beginning, when they rambled around in those awful shows of Fabor's, and secondary to Elvis, likewise, in the beer halls and dance halls of their youth.

Certainly, it was his fate to be second shadow to Maxine and even Bonnie, and over the years, where a gradual regret and resentment might have grown — one that in no way would have served the glide or the chrome — Jim Ed had instead developed an accruing gracefulness in the way he accepted and embraced his forever background status. The tree in the forest that never pushes up through the canopy but that lives all its long life beneath the shade of larger, older trees. No one can see that tree from above, and it is rarely a tree even a traveler moving through the forest notices.

Jim Ed was fully in love now. He had known hundreds of women, so many that he knew absolutely nothing about them — had become jaded, his senses dulled, his relationships a series of automatic gestures, as if long ago choreographed, with the conclusion, postcoital departure, long ago predetermined — but one day those old habits wore away, as if through the relentlessness of erosion, and love had appeared, interfering with the comfortable predictability of his life and his career.

Helen Cornelius was ten years younger than Jim Ed, and every bit as ambitious as Maxine — an energetic showstopper of a performer with a pleasant though not necessarily extraordinary voice. Listening to her, Maxine had described her voice as accomplished but somewhat predictable — and Maxine understood, grudgingly, that there could be a value in that. Yet unlike Maxine, Helen Cornelius was relentlessly upbeat, filled with excitement, marveling and exclaiming at all that she saw. Her happiness wasn't so much the deep quiet peace of Bonnie's, but instead almost an aggressive kind. She leaned into the world with eyes bright and a smile so wide as to look almost like her teeth were bared — as if daring the resistance of negativity or unhappiness. A force for happiness, a partygoer's insistence on continual exuberance.

It might have been exhausting for others to be around, but there was something about it that Jim Ed liked, and here, too, he was secondary, and he followed, quiet and steady in the slipstream of power. Not malleable, but instead, as ever, supporting, helping out, useful, dependable. The kind of person you could send to do any chore and know, a hundred times out of a hundred, that it would get done, and done right; no surprises would occur.

He couldn't have said what it was he loved most about Helen Cornelius. Certainly, he had never intended to leave his sisters. And as with any beloved thing or person, there was no one way to describe why or what he loved most about her — what he needed, and what he gave in return. Any enumeration or listing would have sounded abstract, clichéd. Love is a rose, love is a breath of fresh air, love is a feast. He couldn't have said, but he followed it.

He felt different, singing duets with her; he knew that much. There was no tension or struggle to produce the sound, and when he sang with her, he sometimes felt what it was other audiences said they had been able to hear coming from the Browns in the old days: a stillness, and a cessation of worry. A calmness that, if not actually true peacefulness, was at least a place where everything was all right, everything was safe, and everyone was happy.

He and she had only two hits; one a duet, in their second year together — "I Don't Want to Have to Marry You," written, ironically, by Maxine — and, in the year before that, even before he and Helen Cornelius were together, a hit that was all his own, written and sung by him, performed by him, only him.

Called "Pop a Top," it became the greatest and most played jukebox hit of all time. At the time he wrote it, he was down to eight dollars in his billfold, and it was the one and only time in his life he could no longer afford to be second or third fiddle. As ever, he did what he had to do — stepped up and into the limelight — though after that one song, he quickly receded, with that one song guaranteeing him a comfortable living for the rest of his life.

"Pop a top again—I just got time for one more round." Every time the phrase "pop a top" was sung, there would be the Pavlovian sound of a poptop beer can being cracked open, thrilling a market of millions. Jim Ed pulled on all his experience, observations of his fellow troubadours and broken-down blue-collar bar-goers, confused by life if not quite beaten, or not yet realizing they were beaten. He drew on the only culture he had ever known, the legacy that Floyd and the landscape and the era had bequeathed to him—*When times get tough, start drinking harder*—and turned that misery on its head, celebrated it, made it an anthem. Made what should have been shame a source of pride. As ever, he did what he had to do, went out into the brilliance alone for once, then retreated.

As had Birdie, in her quiet and vague way, sensing possible trouble ahead for Maxine but not knowing the specificity of it, and, later, Chet, trying to warn her or even help her get back on a path that would be better for Maxine, if not necessarily for her music, Jim Ed likewise tried to give her counsel once, though only once.

He went down to see her in West Memphis by himself. He had gigs farther on, in Dardanelle and Texarkana, and came through a day early. He had told Bonnie he was going and what he was going to talk to Maxine about, but Bonnie declined to join him. Likewise, Helen Cornelius stayed home. It wasn't quite so much that she feared the wrath, but more a simple matter of emotional economics. You just about had to be blood family to be willing to sign on for that kind of duty. Such misery was definitely not something she wanted to be around, and she wisely recognized her limitations.

Once, but only once, Jim Ed left his place in the middle and went out to see her.

She had been drinking so hard then. It was 1973. She was drinking so hard that she didn't have a clue that was why he was coming out to see her.

As interventions went, it was unspectacular, and for the moment, ineffective, as Bonnie had predicted it would be. Jim Ed arrived right after the children had gone to school. His hope was to reach her before she got started, and in that he was successful, if at nothing else. She fixed him coffee — there was no food in the pantry to offer him, just a stale box of saltines, and she apologized, both of them remembering how Birdie would have received such a homecoming: the banquet that would have been prepared.

Still, it was good to see him. It wasn't what they had had as children, but it was good; it was a nice break from what the days had become. The coffee in their cups was steaming, and the crackers spilled onto his bare porcelain plate looked almost like communion. Maxine looked at the cups of coffee and was thinking how nice it would be to put a little something in the coffee, something to celebrate old times, and when she mentioned this to Jim Ed — rising before he could answer one way or the other — he said that he didn't care for that, no thank you, and that that was what he wanted to visit about with her.

She was confused, asked if he was feeling sick, imagining some dire medical procedure he might have waiting later in the day, to not be able to receive a splash. There might in that moment have been some first and dim alarm in the cunning of her subconscious, but at first she was neither offended nor suspicious, only befuddled, and concerned.

"Why the hell not?" she asked, and then as she studied the discomfort on his face she began to understand. Long accustomed to identifying the negative, spying the approach of trouble before anything else, she realized quickly, once she had gotten over the confusion of it, why he was there, and what he had come to say.

Jim Ed saw the disbelief cross her face — saw the onrush of outrage, her skin darkening in splotches, her shoulders squaring up, and he hurried to say it before she could attack.

Already she was stiffening her hands, chopping one of them in his direction like an ax. He could feel an inaudible hostility flooding from her, flowing directly toward him like a hiss of steam, and he labored to get his words out before hers, as if that might really make a difference.

"Maxine, I'm worried about you," he said, as if reading from a notecard, a rote preparation. "We all are. We —"

246

RICK BASS

She chopped at the air so savagely that she nearly upended the coffee cups. "Who is *we?*" she demanded. "Where is everybody else? Why aren't they here, if it's such a problem? There is no *we;* this is just something you've decided," she said. "I don't have a problem, and if I did, who do you think you are, to be telling me I do?"

It certainly wasn't an original defense, but Jim Ed made the mistake of pausing and trying to answer, and to defend himself. Sure, he drank — not as much as in the old days, but some — didn't everybody?

"Maxine —" he began, but she was laying into him now, terrified and yet seeming also to welcome the opportunity for a fight. What had he been thinking? He looked around at the solitude of the house — the ridiculous plate of crackers — and realized how foolish he had been.

"You're so pious!" she said. She didn't know whether to go ahead and get the rum or not — was afraid at first of conceding any scrap of territory with any small gesture, but then chose rebellion over victory and went for the rum anyway; poured two, three, four big glugs. Fire in her veins, fire in her brain. She saw Jim Ed's face go pale, saw it shut down and withdraw the way Chet's had so long ago, when he'd tried to ask her how she was doing; and as if delighted by this observation of weakness, she poured two or three more glugs into her coffee, to help aid in his retreat.

The scent of it filled the room, sweet and thick, and reminded them both of things that were not altogether unpleasant.

She was just warming up. "*You just got lucky.* You and your damned big hit, and your damned big house, and your pretty young wife, with her own damned big hit," she shouted. "You all just got lucky. You're the worst kind of hypocrite," she said, "hell, it was you and Jim Reeves who *taught* me to drink! Don't tell me to stop. Don't you *dare* tell me to stop."

She can't remember now, but she thinks she might even have taken a gulp of her coffee then, and another, and that she might even have said something along the lines that she knew how to handle her liquor. She thinks she might have said some other things but can't remember them.

It was sad, and still is sad; there was a distance in Jim Ed after that.

He argued a little with her, but never raised his voice — more of a wan disagreement — and shrugged finally and rose to leave, told her he loved her and hoped she'd think about what he'd said.

Later, after she finally did stop drinking, she would write him the requisite note, would thank him for having the courage and compassion to speak to her about it — to attempt to come to her rescue. She would thank him for his love. But even then, there was still a distance in him. As if even love, like fame, could be eroded, its moth dust finally wing-worn, wind-scoured, forgotten.

Now and again she touches the thick scar tissue of the memory, the new slight distance, the widening distance, the space that neither love nor family can quite fill. She wishes that things had been otherwise, had gone a different way, but then shrugs. That's just what happens, she tells herself, if you live that long. She remembers the boy he once was, and the girl she was, but moves on. Moves forward, into the darkness.

She did stop drinking, she tells herself. That's what matters. She survived.

ELVIS'S DEATH

WHAT SHE REMEMBERS is pretty close to the facts; what she remembers is pretty close to the truth. She doesn't recall much from those days, when she was having so many various cancers cut out of her — always, the cancers were discovered just in time — and not much memory transcends the decades-long alcoholic haze after her career went away.

Even her receipt of the news was muted. Bonnie took it hardest, but they all three had to agree, he wasn't Elvis anymore, hadn't been for a long time — but of the funeral itself, the spectacle and pageantry, her memories are piercing.

Had she been drinking that day? She can't imagine that she hadn't been, but perhaps not. She drank afterward — she knows that.

She remembers the throng as if it were a holy experience: a hundred thousand mourners, all clawing at the wrought-iron fence or prostrate in the road, in the August heat; she remembers the crowd's lamentations as the mule-drawn hearse passed by, which is what he had wanted, though the King himself was in the long white Cadillac in an open casket on ice, his insides baking, they said, decomposing faster than those of most normal people, falling apart, riven by violent internal chemistries, the simmerings of errant prescriptions and unsustainable excess.

She remembers Chet Atkins was one of the pallbearers. Things had changed between her and Chet; there was still friendship and respect, even love and affection, but there was that distance now, nearly twenty years later. She would never have guessed that.

She remembers thinking with a clarity she had not known in a long time that almost none of the people who were worshiping Elvis — neither the hundred thousand who were keening nor the millions beyond — had any clue as to who he was, or who he had been, so that despite the fame, it might almost as well have been as if he had never existed.

There were a few. Bonnie, Jim Ed, herself. Maxine remembers him as if the memory is coming up from the depths, lung-bursting, for a breath of fresh air, recalling those quick good young years when he had first entered their lives, lingered, then been drawn away.

She forgives him for what he took from them. She forgives him for his fame. She did then, there at the funeral, and she does now.

Chet had known him — had known the boy rather than the corrupted man — and certainly his daddy, Vernon, had known him, was wailing loudest that day, throwing himself onto the casket and promising that he would be joining him soon, which he did, dying of a broken heart less than two years later.

Birdie had known him, as had Bonnie, who had already said goodbye to him so long ago. There had really been no one else; no others had known him for who he really was, and no one else carried the burden of that knowledge now. No one else knew that he had had everything in the world and had traded it for nothing.

The ghouls had been there, even then — those who had been close enough to witness him cooling on those blocks of ice, or who in later days would see photos of the same; even that day at the funeral they claimed that no undertaker could have made him look that good, that young, that hale and healthy, and that it had been a ploy, a way for Elvis to evade payment of the millions of dollars he owed in back taxes. Like hounds or wolves back in the forest, they clamor even today for an exhumation: they cannot let go of the myth, they cannot say goodbye, cannot acknowledge the mortal decay of what was once great beauty.

In some ways it was dreamlike to Maxine — people in attendance all around her whose faces she knew only from the newspapers and magazines now — Sammy Davis Jr., James Brown, Caroline Kennedy, Ann-Margret, Jimmy Carter, Lisa Marie and Priscilla, the Jackson Five — and during the service, there was mention that Elvis's record sales around the world that day were nearing the four hundred million mark.

Those people didn't know anything. Hardly any of them knew anything; only she and Bonnie and Jim Ed knew the best. When she hears reports now of people continuing to claim that he still lives, she understands and forgives them, knows that they're simply not capable of letting go of their hopes and beliefs, the best parts of themselves that they imagined he could give back to them with his songs — some of that excessive beauty that they could not find in themselves except when he sang.

Who would possibly want to bid farewell to that? Who would not possibly want to hold on to that forever?

And what we had, Maxine thinks, *was even better.* We had the real beauty. The songs were just the echo of it. A fifty-year echo.

She forgives him, again and again. She would have done the same — taken his path, all the way to the end, forsaking anything else she already had — in a heartbeat.

It was not so long after the funeral — five, six years — that she stopped drinking. It was not easy, and it was made harder still by the fact that she did not relinquish her hunger for other things — but that one day, his funeral, sharp through the otherwise fog of her numbed consciousness, gave her a moment of clarity from which she could fight the enemy, which was not anonymity or obscurity, as she had once believed, but another enemy, myth and surface representations rather than any deeper truths. The enemy was herself — or who she had been, up to that point.

The hundred thousand mourners crawling all over the roads, the millions or billions beyond, had been loving someone they had never known — someone they themselves had manufactured, sleek and polished. Someone about whom they had never known the first tiny bit of sweetness or reality. They might as well have been drunk themselves, during those years.

THE DEBUT

THE DEBUT COMES only a month later. Jefferson Eads has been
working around the clock, sleeping only intermittently, as lost in his
project as his namesake was in his valiant attempts to map the unmap-
pable. He finally gets it just the way he wants it, and has it set to music — sometimes the Browns', other times Elvis's, or that of some of the
Browns' peers. He's researched on the Internet relentlessly, has pulled
up old archival photos of the Louvin Brothers, Patsy Cline, Eddy Arnold, Johnny Cash, Elvis and the Jordanaires. The cut of John Lennon
singing "The Three Bells" is in there, as is the footage of Maxine today, and the interviews. It's a good piece of work.

He shows the movie at his junior high. There won't be enough
people attending to hold it in the big auditorium, so instead it is
shown in his homeroom teacher's classroom, which is small but intimate. A couple of teachers have brought their history classes — it's extra credit — so there are forty or so squirming kids, and maybe a dozen
parents. Jefferson Eads's parents are there, prouder than proud — if
a parent could choose genius over normalcy, knowing the costs of
genius, would they still make that choice? Perhaps it is as well that
none get to make that decision — and Jefferson Eads's teachers, too,
are beaming.

Jefferson Eads seems very calm, very content. Only his parents and
teachers know how much work it has taken for him to reach this momentary plateau of calm, of peace. It is like this for some kids, some
adults, all the time, all their lives — this steady calm in the world — but
he has had to work hard to get here, and those who know this are
proud of him.

Remember this, Maxine tells herself — he escorts her in, down the
hallway with its crepe paper decorations hung only that afternoon,
past the colorful posters with children's lettering. "Welcome, Maxine
Brown!" and "Queen of Country Music!"

I should have invited Bonnie and Jim Ed, she thinks. *They would
have loved this,* and though she is beaming, in that moment she

misses her family more than she can say, and thinks, *We must get back together.*

Inside Mrs. Keys's room, there is a long table with a plastic tablecloth, on which paper plates of cheese cubes, cookies, and donuts are arranged. There's a big Igloo cooler of Kool-Aid, twin stacks of tiny Dixie cups, and Jefferson's peers, a throng of young boys, are gathered around the Igloo, drinking and refilling, and when he enters with Maxine, they greet him with a modicum of manners, formality, respect, and envy that is not customary in their relationship with him, or anyone else.

Slow this down, Maxine tells herself. She is acutely conscious of the boy's loose hold on her arm. *Why can't this last forever?* she wonders, looking around at the awe with which the children and even their parents are beholding her — and she feels the demon in her settle down in a way it has not done in a long time.

There's almost a purring going on inside her, and it's good, so good that it even feels it was worth the wait.

No work is ever wasted, she knows now; no waiting, no dreaming, is ever wasted. Soon enough Jefferson Eads is going to let go of her arm and escort her into the hard metal folding chair at the front of the room that is to be her seat of honor, soon enough he is going to stand before his class with pride and announce his project, soon enough he is going to grow up and leave her — maybe tomorrow, maybe even today — but for now, for right now, she is sixteen again and the elemental thing, the greatness within, is both contented and excited, agitated. It's the best possible combination, this elixir of sleek momentary power if not immortality, and she squeezes his hand, wanting to hold it just a little longer — these are strangers all around her, but at least they are here to see her — and then Jefferson Eads is up in front saying something, she can't quite hear all of it, and then the lights go out, and the music and the movie begin, and for the next hour, at least, she is able finally to live without regret.

Acknowledgments

I'm grateful to the Browns — Maxine, Jim Ed, and Bonnie, as well as their extremely close and extended family, past and present — for their generosity of time over the last five years — and I continue to be astounded by the living storehouse of their knowledge and experiences from the old days, and greatly appreciate their support in this venture, particularly given the novelist's mandate (as with a musician's) to occasionally temper certain highs while also adjusting or recasting certain lows; attenuating some things, creating others, and removing still others. Every novel that ever gets written carries a disclaimer of the imagination, and this one is no different. The Browns are real, and what they gave to American music, and how they did it, is real; *Nashville Chrome*, however, is a work of the imagination. For true-life details, facts, precise dates and events, see Maxine Brown's *Looking Back to See* (She and her son Tommy also maintain a web page, www.themaxinebrown.com). *Nashville Chrome* is, among other things, an attempt to portray the emotional truths of their journey and its challenges. As the writer Ron Carlson says, "I try not to confuse the facts with the truth." Lesser beings than the Browns would not have survived their journey.

From these basic truths — Maxine's heroic and indefatigable hunger, Bonnie's joy, and Jim Ed's durability — I have tempered and adjusted. They are not perfect — no more and no less than anyone else — but it might well serve a reader interested in the delineations between novelistic excess and "regular" life to view anything distasteful or negative in these pages as only an exercise of the novelist's imagination and the story's craft, rather than true-life revelation of flaws or failings in the Browns or their family.

For assistance during the writing of this novel, I'm extremely grateful to Kathi Whitley of Vector Management in Nashville and to the Browns' publicist, Norma Morris. I'm grateful to my wife, Elizabeth, for an early reading of the manuscript, and, as ever, to my agent, Bob Dattila, for his quixotic efforts to help a writer be able to keep writing. I'm grateful also to editors of the magazines in which sections of this book first appeared, in slightly different form — *Gray's Sporting Journal, Southern Cultures, The Southern Review, Whitefish Review,* and *Big Sky Journal.*

I'm grateful to all those with my publisher who have worked on this book — Alison Kerr Miller for line editing, Rachael Hoy for production assistance, David Hough for proofreading, Patrick Barry for design, Marc Burckhardt for artwork, and Taryn Roeder for publicity. In my last few years of publishing with Houghton Mifflin (now Houghton Mifflin Harcourt), I've been fortunate to work with a number of their wonderful editors — Sam Lawrence, Camille Hykes, Larry Cooper, Dorothy Henderson, Hilary Liftin, Leslie Wells, Lisa Glover, and recently the late Harry Foster, and then his assistant, Will Vincent — and when I received still another editor, Nicole Angeloro, all I could do was hope for the best, which I got. The hours and effort she put in on numerous drafts, her enthusiasm for the entire publishing process, her good cheer in helping pursue even the most mundane details, her unafraid reliance on not only her formidable intelligence but native intuition, her sense of balance and reach — all of these things remind me of what is best about publishing. The book publishing industry might lie at the edge of ruin, but what fun in the still-living.